Praise for *Degrees of Difficulty*

"Believable characters in a full, vivid world and a story both grounded and transcendent: what more could a reader of fiction ask? Style! Julie Justicz delivers."
—Abby Frucht, author of *Polly's Ghost, Life Before Death, Are You Mine? Licorice, Snap,* and *A Well Made Bed*

Degrees
of
Difficulty

Julie E. Justicz

Fomite
Burlington, Vermont

ISBN-13: 978-1-944388-74-4
Library of Congress Control Number: 2018962193
Fomite
58 Peru Street
Burlington, VT 05401

For Mary
and in memory of Clive and Robert

"But they are sailing like a pendulum between eternity and evening, diving, recovering, balancing the air."

—Deborah Digges

PART I

A SORT OF HOMECOMING

CHAPTER 1

PERRY, APRIL 1991

Perry Novotny shoved the suitcase into the back of the station wagon, while Ben piled pea gravel from the driveway onto its dull and dented hood. The early sun speckled the tiny rocks orange and pink, but did nothing to melt the fog wrapping the base of the administration building and hovering over the lake. Not much of a lake, really—barely thirty yards long, and half that across—more like a weed-wrapped silt-trap. But that hadn't stopped him from embellishing it to Caroline six months earlier, after his solo exploration of Lake Norman Residential School. What had he told his wife? *A bucolic campus. The lake nestled between two red brick buildings, a backdrop of blue-green foothills.* His words were now distant and foggy as the Appalachians. *Perfect for Ben,* he must have said, even believed, at the time. But possibly not. Making him what? Either a fool or a liar.

He slammed the hatch so the metal rim clashed against the aging car's body. Fool or liar. Lake or pond. Residential school or god-damn institution. Whatever names Perry slapped on, whatever he'd believed or just wanted to, the result was the same as every other placement: Ben had to leave. *As soon as possible*, the director said when he'd called yesterday, because of the *potential for serious harm*. Ben had shoved a specialized wheelchair into the murky waters of Lake Norman and stood clapping and laughing, knee-deep in the reeds, while mud swallowed the motor. A two-thousand-dollar piece of equipment, mechanically ruined, but empty, thank god, at the time. *But what if it hadn't been?*

What if? What now? What next? Perry always prided himself on being untroubled, but lately Caroline's questions jackhammered his brain. He stood against the car, one hand on the roof, the other covering his mouth. Despair came on like inverse motion sickness, hitting only if he stopped between tasks. *What if?* was a waste of time, like praying for what you didn't want to happen. *What now?* Well, he had to get his son home. He sucked in a deep breath of mountain air, pasted on his can-do smile. Game face on and best foot forward. *What next?* That would have to wait.

"Ready, Benno?"

The kid had organized his gravel into small piles on the hood. Perry walked over and took his forearm. Wary-eyed and furtive, Ben clasped his fists in front of his chest. He trusted Perry, of course he did, but it was still early, very early in the day. Perry had arrived before 6 a.m. and had to rouse the assistant director, Selena, by hammering on the residence hall door. Then together they'd extracted Ben from the locked single room where he'd been "safeguarded" overnight.

Perry tugged gently. "Come on, son. You can sleep in the car."

Ben's feet shuffled through the gravel as he allowed Perry to lead him to the side door, but when Perry opened it, he balked. Body rigid. Only a slight spasticity—nerves or excitement—flickered through his clenched hands. His good eye, the true-blue right, was fixated on the rocks underfoot, while the misty, wandering left looked off beyond Perry's shoulder. Under different circumstances, Perry might have asked him—*What's out there, huh, what's so interesting?*—then created a plausible response for his wordless son. Not today, though, not while navigating these all-too-familiar departures.

"Wanna go see Hugo?" Perry tried, hugging himself. "Home?" Perry repeated the gesture, the macro sign language that usually worked. "Look at me, Ben, look, okay? Home ... Hugo?"

Ben smiled as he processed the motion and understanding seeped into his brain. He nodded violently as he hugged himself in response, tight and tighter, hugged that most favored sign with two meanings, *Hugo, Home, Hugo, Home,* hugged with his fists clenched like exclamation points.

"That's right. Now, climb aboard, Captain!"

Perry had a brand-spanking-new 1990 Ford pickup parked in his driveway at home—a high-gloss, energetic blue, with silver racing stripes, a V6 engine and a top-of-the-line CD player. Most mornings before sunrise, he took the truck to one of his sites, four-wheeled it up steep, clay embankments, spitting pine straw, like so many worries, out his back tires. Later, midmorning, he'd park by the Chattahoochee River and eat a sandwich of thick salami and cheddar cheese, alone in the cab, with Springsteen blasting through the Pioneer subwoofers he'd installed as a Christmas gift to himself. *An extravagant addition,* Caroline said. But worth every penny, damn it. He loved his truck and sometimes he just needed, *yes, Caroline, needed,* to sit alone, drowning in sound. But the Buick battleship, with its shabby body and failing AC, was his preferred mode of transporting Ben, who was prone to drooling and car sickness.

At fourteen, Ben stood maybe five feet tall, all bone-juts and strange angles, still weighing only eighty or ninety pounds. Less than a sack of cement. Perry lifted him easily, set him on the back seat, then pulled in his floppy left leg.

"No foot-dragging, fella."

Time away had accentuated Ben's differences. The institutional crew cut didn't help; his mismatched ears, red and insulted, stuck out below the fresh buzz. And puberty had done him no favors: his nose had broadened and flattened; angry red pimples erupted on his chin. No breaks for kids with disabilities. Like everything else, teen gawkiness hit them harder.

Selena had already handed him a typed and signed copy of the state-mandated *Determination of Unserviceability*, said her goodbyes and good lucks, and was now, no doubt, wishing he would move things along, pull his hunk-o'-junk car and heap-o'-trouble son out of the driveway so she could head back to her room for another hour of peace before the other hundred and fifty residents—the less problematic ones—woke up and wanted breakfast. Hand on hip in the driveway, she watched Perry struggle to settle Ben in the car. Perry wanted not to dislike her. She was young—her title of Assistant Director probably a gift to make up for abysmal wages and the lonely nights on duty in the dorms. A glorified camp counselor, for god's sake. But another part of him wanted to take her by her shoulders, rattle her sleepy and selfish countenance, so she would see what this latest *Determination*, beneath its benignly bureaucratic name, meant—not for Ben (if he even understood the reason for his abrupt morning wake-up), and certainly not for Perry, who was growing used to these homecomings and mostly managed well—but for Caroline, who desperately needed to believe that some place could work out for their special son. Perry knew she did not have much reserve in her tank.

He reached the frayed lap belt across Ben and clicked him in tight. The kid reeked of the cheap, pine disinfectant sloshed around these places. Christ. Did they wash his hair with Lysol? But then again, Ben had come home from one group home last summer with a bad case of pubic lice. Perhaps a strong disinfectant scrub wasn't so bad when you considered the alternatives. Reaching over to the front seat, Perry grabbed a green and white box of doughnuts he'd bought from a gas station for the drive home. Six Krispy Kremes: three plain, three chocolate-frosted. From experience, he knew the doughnuts should get them through at least thirty minutes of the four-hour drive from central North Carolina to Atlanta; he was not oblivious to the possibility of a puke-fest on the back roads. An old beach towel covered the back seat, just in case.

Ben hugged the Krispy Kremes to his chest and offered a wickedly good smile, the cheeky, crooked one that Perry missed, even when he was relieved that Ben was away, gone for a short while or a long while, while the institutional goodwill lasted, at the latest in a long line of group homes. Gone until the next late-night phone call and the next *Determination of Unserviceability.*

So many Determinations, so little understanding, Caroline had said yesterday. But she must understand, Perry thought as he moved to the driver's seat and started the engine. After all, she'd mothered Ben fourteen eventful years, carrying the full brunt of the first few months, battling night after night for his survival, enduring the early months of hospitals and tests, chromosome smears, results and discouraging revelations; then the toddler years, the countless accidents and falls, the bruises and the stitches, as Ben learned to walk with his palsied leg and angled gait, regularly tripping into walls and doors and table tops. And she had endured the comings and goings of nannies, *au pairs*, and maids, who arrived full of fresh ideas, tried for a week or a month, but soon couldn't take it any longer. Couldn't take what as parents, Caroline and Perry had to: Ben's rampant seizures—three, four, sometimes five a week.

Early this morning (middle of the night really) when Perry had left their bed and kissed her goodbye, she murmured, "I am not sure how much longer I can do this."

As if she had a choice. As if any of them did.

"Only one doughnut now, Benno." Take one, then give me the box."

Crap. Perry had screwed up again—Ben had already torn through the lid, had a doughnut in each hand. "Guh," he said. His only sound—which had variable meanings. *Good. Yes. Go.*

When Perry first began talking a few years ago of finding Ben a permanent group home, a place he could grow to love and accept with his own special family when his own family was no longer able to give him both love and acceptance, Caroline agreed the time was right. She agreed to start the search. Could Perry help it if, after their first few mishaps and misplacements, she now seemed to have lost the will to see it through? He had warned her it wouldn't be easy; it could take a while, maybe a few disappointments and, all right, even a few damned *Determinations*, but in the end, it would work out. So, okay ... Ben's permanent placement would not be Lake Norman, North Carolina. So long, Lake Norman. So long, Selena, who couldn't even bring herself to hug Ben goodbye. Goodbye and good riddance. There would be other options. There *must* be other options for a complex kid like Ben.

Being a contractor demanded a truck-load of patience and a willingness to keep tackling problems. To puzzle them out. If it doesn't work this way, then how about like that? To manage other people, keep them upbeat and functioning, have you thought about it this way? This ability to keep moving, to see a job through, these were strengths that he brought to work, marriage, and family. Caroline could waver precisely because Perry would hold strong and steady; he wanted to give her that. Give his family that. He adjusted the rearview mirror so he could keep an eye on Ben, who'd already crammed one doughnut in his mouth and was about to tackle the second.

"Save one for me, okay?"

Perry puckered his lips for a kiss, then let the kiss morph into a long, obscene raspberry, that got Ben giggling and spraying crumbs across the seat. With his round, Czech face, high cheekbones, and a generous flap of blond hair that always fell across his eyes, Perry had been teased during his childhood in South Boston for being a pretty boy; teased so much that he gave up gymnastics without finding his natural end-point—the limit of his talents—because he was afraid of what his friends would say if he continued. The summer before his junior year of high school, he took a construction job, pouring his energy into hard labor. He continued working every summer, through high school and his college years at Boston University, until it became what he knew, as well as what he wanted to do.

Since they'd moved to Atlanta for Caroline's teaching job, he was the go-to guy for Huff Homes, largest luxury developer in northwest Atlanta. Spent his days in work boots and Wranglers, roaming several one-hundred-acre tracts of hilly land, carved out by a series of snake curves in the Chattahoochee: *River's Edge, Wesley Woods,* and *River Oaks.* Work kept him outdoors year-round, with a ruddy color in his face. He liked it when his truck wheels squealed out of the driveway at 5 a.m. and Springsteen thundered through the damp air of his domain. He liked it when he returned home at the end of the workday, pulled off his sweaty shirt to reveal the working-guy muscles. He liked that he could still backflip off the diving board he had installed a few years ago in his customized backyard pool of their Huff-built home. And he liked it when he could lighten up Caroline, the *Serious Thinker*—his one and one-half bellyflop always good for one of her throaty laughs. Only over the last couple of years did it seem that she was growing sick of Perry's antics. He saw it more often now in her gray eyes, her tight smile, the way she would look away. If she used to think him untroubled and amusing, did she now see a fool?

He pushed away this thought as the Buick's tires crunched through the gravel and Ben giggled out crumbs.

"You like that, huh?"

Ben had always been a sucker for crinkling, crackling noises. Back in Boston, when Ben was a tiny, elfin creature with mismatched ears and a recessed jaw, practically starving because of all his feeding difficulties, Perry had cocooned him in an old blanket and carried him, scuffling through piles of fallen leaves by the Charles. Ben chortled and choked; Perry quickly uncovered him, terrified. But Ben was giggling. The first time that Perry realized his son could make a sound other than the desperate, hungry wails that had lasted all night long during those early months, so he'd danced along the river bank. Danced like an idiot, an imbecile, a moron, and a fool, danced over all those outdated classifications because his beautiful baby boy—whatever his diagnosis, whatever his condition—was gonna be just fine.

Ben's laugh sounded husky this morning. Was his voice breaking? Perry did an extra crunchy loop-de-loop around the school's driveway for Ben's benefit, and honked the car horn three times long and loud to piss off Selena. Well, screw her, and screw them all—the specialists and prognosticators, the doctors and shrinks. Perry was right when he said it years ago. Ben was fine. A one of a kind specimen. Just fine, thank you very much. Heading home to Georgia.

Caroline had always called Perry her cockeyed optimist. Sometimes, when things between them were playful and good, he would amp this up, doing his *South Pacific* routine, hula-dancing naked in their bedroom, before her laughing, half-moon eyes.

A cockeyed, unflagging, and impossible optimist, she'd say and pull him to her. In the early days of their marriage, when she was finishing her thesis on the Four Humours in Renaissance literature, it had been her little joke, how opposite temperaments attract: the melancholic scholar and the sanguine laborer. Lately, she saw their differences as a liability. Because Perry kept moving, scoping out new facilities, even after a few disappointments, Caroline coined him a dreamer. *Perry on the go,* she sometimes said, *my Perry-patetic husband,* when he packed a travel bag or lifted his keys from the hook by the back door, *off on his Perry-grinations.* Yesterday, after they got the dreaded call from Lake Norman, Caroline, with her newly-graying hair and her increasingly heavy demeanor, barely bothered to look up to ask him, *What next?*

What next? Well, he'd search again until he found a home, a permanent, loving home for Ben that would allow him to reach his potential—whatever that may be—and a place that would keep him when his parents couldn't and his siblings wouldn't want to. Perry was realistic enough about that: in ten years, Ivy and Hugo would have their own lives, possibly spouses and children, too. They would not want Ben running around, tossing their toddlers' toys into toilets. So, Caroline, it's me driving him home now while you're still sleeping, and it's me who will be out pounding the pavement next week, looking into remaining options for him. He tasted his own bitterness, and did not like it. He lowered the car window and spit out onto the road. "I need *my* doughnut. How about it, Benno?"

Ben didn't catch on, so Perry kept driving. They passed through several one-light towns, each separated by miles of curving back roads, no other vehicles in sight, and no sounds from the backseat. No puking, thank god. Right before the highway, he made a stop for gas. It was 6:45 a.m.; he thought about calling Caroline from the pay phone out front of the store, but decided not to wake her up. What would he say, anyway? *We'll be home soon?* She'd need more than rest for the days to come.

Fueled up, he accelerated onto 85 South. From the entrance ramp, it was two hundred-plus miles southwest to Atlanta. Ben played with his rear control—window up, down, up, down, halfway up, halfway down, hand in, hand out, in and out, window up and down. Perry ignored it for a while, but soon he couldn't stand the phut-phutting in his ears.

"Cut it out now. Close your window, okay?"

But Ben couldn't cut it out. Or wouldn't. Perry used the master control to commandeer the rear window, raise it and lock it, stop the fooling around. Ben groaned, loud, long, mournful, to register his protest. *Sorry, Buddy.* Perry didn't relent, even when Ben screamed. Eventually settled down. Caroline and Perry had argued recently about whether Ben could control his impulses. It mattered to Perry, mattered because there might be some approach, some method out there that would work for him. Caroline carried her unbelief, her lack of trust in Perry, like another burden she had to shoulder, another needy child.

Perry had moments of despair. Of course, he did. At the outset, when the geneticist had shown him test results: twenty-three pairs of chromosomes—black xx's spread out across a white page—and pinpointed for Perry the damage to the twenty-first. Partial Monosomy 21. Yes, he'd felt devastated. What he hadn't known then was how such a little omission in the blueprint could cause so much structural damage. And how each detail would grow more complicated: the recessed jaw would lead to feeding issues, the missing kidney to frequent infections, hospitalizations, IV medications. And later, the seizures: body-wracking grand mals that daily medications could not control. So much to take in at the beginning, then so much to tackle, again and again, and still, still, still, how incomplete his sense of how Ben's life would go. Perry mostly contained his despair now to still moments in his truck. If nothing else, then surely from the doctors, the tests, the hospitals, and the homes across the many years, Perry had learned that DNA was one part of a complicated story. Love, family support, and proper care would help Ben grow into the best possible Ben he could be.

He still groaned from the back. Poor kid was exhausted, but nothing to do except continue. Perry blew some cool-ish air through the clanking AC system to keep himself awake for the rest of the drive home. He turned on the radio to 94Q and Gary McQueen, the early morning DJ, whose lazy banter and slow, throaty voice made it sound as if he had really tied one on last night.

Fifty miles outside Athens. Silence in the backseat. In the rearview mirror, Perry saw Ben's cheek pressed against the window. Sleeping off his latest expulsion? The morning music express continued: old Stones, The Who, an Aqualung flashback, and then that awesome U2 cut, *A Sort of Homecoming*. "I'll be there. I'll be there." Perry picked up speed, and sang along quietly, making good time getting back to

Atlanta with no traffic slow-downs, no more stops for gas. He exited the highway at West Paces Ferry around 10 a.m. Gary McQueen was just signing off as Perry turned onto Nancy Creek Road and cruised another mile along the high-banked, kudzu-lined streets, and into the Novotny family driveway. He coasted downhill—almost 200 yards of asphalt winding through their spring green lawn—and parked in front of the home (faux Tudor, early Huff construction specialty, circa 1980) and honked a little howdy hello to rouse Caroline from her morning haze, Ivy and Hugo from their teenage daze.

"All right, my boy. We're home, at last."

He turned off the engine, turned around to check on his quiet, sleeping son. But Ben was not sleeping. He was sitting upright, wide awake, chocolate frosting smeared all over his chin and shirt and a strange, pinched look on his face.

"We're home, buddy," Perry repeated, then signed. "Where's Hugo, huh? Where's your number one fan?"

Ben looked miserable. Car sick? Too many doughnuts? Then Perry figured it out. *Jesus Christ, who was the moron here?* Ben's left hand was sealed in the car window, trapped at the base of his fingers. For the last three homecoming hours, speeding down the interstate, no words, no scream either, and now a pained look on Ben's face, as his cloudy left eye met Perry's straight on.

"Hold on, Benno, hold on," Perry said, cranking the car engine, frantically pressing all the controls at one, "Jesus, I'm so sorry."

As he pulled his hand into the car, Ben gave that wickedly good smile again. Then slowly, carefully, he uncurled his fingers to reveal, stuck in the sweaty, cross-hatched lines of his palm, a tiny, pink pebble he had somehow managed to carry all the way back from the foothills.

CHAPTER 2

CAROLINE, MAY 1991

Mid-May, midafternoon, the sun glared through Caroline's third-floor office window fierce and unrelenting. She could sense a headache coming on. Benjamin had screamed for hours last night, before passing out next to his mattress on the floor, close to 2 a.m. Of course, this morning, when Caroline unlatched his bedroom door, she'd had to pull him from thick sleep and drag him—semi-conscious, fully belligerent—through washing, clothes, breakfast, all his meds (which he spat out three times), and finally, onto the school bus. Rush hour traffic conspired too, turning her nine-mile, cross-town commute into an hour-plus debacle. By the time she'd arrived on campus, at almost 10 a.m., she felt defeated. So much effort to get to work for a few hours, before reversing course.

Today's task: write the final exam for her *Intro to Shakespeare* course, then get it over to the department secretary for copying. Not a lot to it, honestly, but she couldn't concentrate and now she was running out of time. After several hours in front of her faithful Smith-Corona, with the last sheet of paper pinned against the platen, she needed one more section for her small group of underachieving undergraduates. A few short essay questions that would require them to probe and analyze the plays they'd read, not spew back *CliffsNotes*. But the angled afternoon light fed her headache, growing a tight root of pain between her eyes. She squeezed the skin at the bridge of her nose, willing herself to think. But how could she, when she'd been up half the night with a wailing child?

Just think. She'd covered the early comedies and put in an in-depth question on *Lear*, because the class had spent two weeks on the play, even watched the BBC production. Perhaps something on the late romances: short essays on *Pericles* or *The Winter's Tale*? Re-reading these late plays and preparing lecture notes during the semester, she found each drama strangely compelling in its disjointedness, the awkward leaps in time and place and plot line; she had an idea for an article. But priorities. She had to finish the exam and complete end-of-semester grading, of course, before turning to her own writing. And with Ben home again, it could be months. She reached under her desk and fumbled around in her tatty Kenya bag for a bottle of Excedrin, and swallowed two pills dry because she couldn't be bothered to find water. If she could finish writing the exam today, get it done, get it out to Mrs. Conroy, then she wouldn't have to return to campus—in all its brazen glory—until next week.

She hated spring here. After five years of teaching at Emory, she still found the marble buildings too bright, the coral azaleas that framed the main quad too dazzling. How could anyone work in this light, with all the fecundity, pollen dusting the sidewalks and gutters, filling eyes and sinuses, chalking the senses? Despite the university's widely-publicized investment in a first-rate humanities faculty, the brash look of this southern campus would always undermine scholarship. Not like the stolid brick buildings of Harvard, which pulled drizzle down from May's thick skies. She'd worked hard through multiple springs in Cambridge, worked as steadily as the showers. That's what university life should be: rain, the sky reflecting the brown-bloated river, while students huddled in the library for a long, hard, reading period. She had loved her time there, almost fifteen years of unapologetic work, college, masters, PhD, fellowship, and teaching, the grit of urban life, and all the hunched, gray people who refused to buoy one another with brilliant smiles and azalea greetings.

"You're a snob, Professor," Perry told her during their first year in Atlanta, "An Ivy-league snob."

"Isn't that why they hired me? To give this place some ballast?"

Emory had begun its self-improvement campaign in the mid-'80s, after receiving a record one hundred million, unrestricted, from Coca-Cola. Money used to purchase young talent for the humanities faculty—cheaper than investing in science post-docs with their laboratory needs and research mandates—and essential to taking on the Ivies. Well, maybe not taking them on ... but at least pushing Emory towards equivalence. "The Harvard of the South": that was the rallying cry of Frank Beardsley, English Department Chair, when he hired Caroline at the MLA conference in 1984.

"Coca-Cola U," Caroline told her Cambridge friends, as she prepared to move to Atlanta. She wanted to gauge her colleagues' looks: approval, jealousy, amusement? She had felt flattered by Dr. Beardsley's words, that Emory considered her an up-and-coming scholar, a worthy investment. But would a move to *any* southern institution be professional suicide? Alice Seward, her mentor, advised her to accept.

"Emory's definitely on its way up. You'll be one of the few women on faculty. Certainly, the only *real* feminist. Go, make a name for yourself. Become the big fish in the small pond. Much better than the converse."

Perry, of course, had been completely open to the new adventure. *Oh, hell yeah*, he'd said, *I love the South, y'all*. New city, new house, new job, new schools, no problem. *We're gonna be just fine*, Perry liked to say of their life—wherever they were, whatever choices they'd made, whatever was happening. A tic-like affirmation that made Caroline want to pull her hair out from the roots. He was right, of course, things were okay. They had enough money, good jobs, a nice house with a lush yard and, yes, thanks to her can-do contractor husband, even a pool out back. Ivy and Hugo were enrolled at the prestigious Westmont Academy, motivated in academics and sports, and always understanding, considerate of their special brother. It was just sometimes, and increasingly this past year, the challenges of doing it all, day by day, the job, the house, the kids, and yes, all right, the challenges of Benjamin, all his needs, well, it was getting to be ... what words could she use without splintering Perry's careful family construction? *Too much?* Perry had to feel the strain of it all, but it seemed sometimes that he didn't have the room in his life for a negative thought; he did not even have the vocabulary.

Her phone rang, a loud, piercing pain between her eyes. Should have unplugged it at the start of the day so she could work uninterrupted. But now, close to 2 p.m., what if it were Benjamin's school? Last week, he'd fallen in the cafeteria, hit the corner of a table, and needed three stitches above his eye. *What if?* Her own worries perpetuated the predictable call-and-response with Perry. *What if? Just fine.* Increasingly, they found opposing corners, whenever worries or fears loomed. It had to be as unsatisfactory for him as it was for her, but he would never say so. The phone drilled through five full cycles then stopped. The new school had an emergency number for Perry, too. He could help with crises. He was good that way.

"Riding the short bus again," Hugo had joked, when he learned Benjamin would attend Northside High, as an emergency measure for the last month of this school year. Caroline had driven Benjamin there late April, met with the principal, and together they had escorted him to meet his teacher and classmates in a highly inappropriate, cross-categorical special ed room: kids ranging in age from fourteen to eighteen, some with evident intellectual deficits, others socially maladjusted or emotionally disturbed. How long would Benjamin last here, with one teacher and sixteen other kids, half of them predator, the other half prey? In this environment, Benjamin would definitely fit in the second category. Leaving him had filled Caroline with a knowing terror. As she followed the principal down the corridor, raising her concerns about the class size, the older children, the lack of teacher's aides, the principal summarily dismissed them all.

"At this time of year, you really can't expect any more of us. We'll do an Individualized Educational Plan next fall. As required."

What else was required?

Caroline had an exam to write. Concentration was required. Block out Benjamin's needs for once and finish the exam. No time left to think up short essays, so perhaps one more comprehensive question. *The Tempest*? She closed her eyes. She should be able to write a question in her sleep. *Such stuff as dreams are made on.* But the phone again: the trill pierced to the roots of her headache. She felt nauseated. Sick from the pain, and sick with the knowledge of what the phone call would require, what it would always require. If it were the high school, calling to report Benjamin's latest violation or accident, let them track down Perry. Benjamin had a father, a more than capable father, a damn good father, who could deal with the latest situation, deal better, usually, than Caroline. She tried to breathe, to wait it out again. But the phone kept on, she counted twenty, twenty-two rings, each ring growing louder, longer, like the way Benjamin had screamed last night, softly at first, then more and more insistent, penetrating. She pushed back from her desk, stood up and yanked the telephone wire out of the wall.

If only it were so easy to cut the mental cord.

They hadn't let her hold him for the first few hours after his birth. She was still weak from the surgery. The doctors were not sure the baby would survive anyway, but she'd demanded they bring him back. A nurse carried him into her room and laid him on her chest, swaddled and helpless. She pushed his mouth against her nipple; but his jaw couldn't do what it should and he mewled softly.

"*Do you understand,*" one of the doctors said, "*If you choose to start this, we will have to continue?*"

She nodded. Of course, my baby. But had she understood? Was understanding even possible at that time? Did the doctor understand what he was asking?

Now she walked over to the window and buried a knuckle in her mouth. Outside on the grass, students gathered, some pretending to study, others flaunting their nonchalance about the impending exams. She slammed both fists against the tinny air-conditioner cover. She'd moved south, to Emory, to make a name for herself. She always knew she would have to put in her time, have the discipline to work long and late, alone, longer than the other young professors. All that was fine; all that she expected. What she hadn't planned for, what she couldn't have known back then, was the way her family would pull at her, the way her husband and children and Benjamin, with all their needs, would spill over into her office, stick with her on her head-clearing walks around campus, follow her into the library and the department meetings, insert themselves into her brain. Her own scholarship was suffering. She hadn't written a publishable piece in three years. She didn't have time. She didn't have room in her life to see anything through. Her latest idea scratched her mind: *Cymbeline, Pericles,* and *The Winter's Tale* are all temporally and tonally bifurcated, and for this strange structural "disjointedness," often dismissed by the critics as flawed, the lesser works of an aging, bored Shakespeare. But what if the lack of cohesion and unity were deliberate? Wouldn't the strength of these often-maligned romances actually be their "roominess," the way time and space afford characters the ability to grow and change? She had an idea and a killer headache. That left only the simple task of researching and writing the damn thing, with Benjamin home again for the whole damn summer. She rubbed her eyes. At the rate she'd been working lately, she would be lucky if she could finish out this semester. This exam. *Come on, Caroline. Think.*

On the quad, directly below her office, Josh Kearns, a shaggy-haired student from her *Women Wanderers* seminar, kept a hacky sack in the air with minimal movements: knee, foot, chest, foot, foot, knee, all while talking to a group of girls sitting in a semi-circle around him. He was shirtless, shamelessly performing, and obviously not sweating the final paper he still owed her. Youthful arrogance. Although he was only a second-semester sophomore, Josh had pushed his way into her graduate-level course, despite Caroline's misgivings. Given the historically low enrollment in her seminars, Caroline could hardly have said no to him, especially since, like she, Josh was a beneficiary of Coca Cola largesse:

she a Woodruff Faculty Member, he one of the acclaimed "Woodies" at the undergraduate level. Once he'd manipulated his way in, though, Josh had approached each class with a knowing smirk, an "I'm getting away with something" look. Caroline took it personally: his smugness, his cultivated nonchalance, his perpetual hacky sack, his unruly hair, and his hangers-on. If he were as smart as he thought, perhaps he should not have settled for Coke money. Perhaps he should have gone to an Ivy League. Here at Emory, every half-hearted effort got As and accolades. When she read the essay he would hand in late, no doubt, she'd be hard-pressed not to give him a C, because she knew in her heart, that he deserved it; that at Harvard, he would have been average.

She returned to her desk and searched in her bag again, found what she really needed this time. Cigarettes. She tamped down the pack of Benson & Hedges and extracted a slender menthol. Think. *The Winter's Tale.* Hermione, Queen of Sicilia, and her strange young son, Mamillius. *A sad tale's best for winter.* This fragile boy who loved to entertain his mother and her ladies-in-waiting. "Apparent to my heart," his father, King Leontes, says, meaning heir to my love. But then, a few short scenes later, the King is a raging tyrant, his Queen imprisoned, and the boy—their young Mamillius—dead from grief. Poor kid—one of the few late romance characters never to find healing or redemption. Why?

She dragged on the cigarette, and back at her window, looked out at the glorious, glaring scene beneath her. For the most part, all these plays ended with tidiness: girl finding boy, mistaken identities revealed, children once lost now found, old rivalries forgiven, death conquered, king and queen reunited. Why no happy ending for Mamillius? Shakespeare's own son, Hamnet, died at age eleven, before *The Winter's Tale* was written. Had this experience brought

Shakespeare, as playwright, or perhaps as father, to the understanding that though loss is inevitable, some sadness can never be redeemed?

If a sad tale's best for winter, what kind of tale is best for spring?

Back to her desk. She faced the typewriter. She owed poor Hermione an essay question of her own.

> Queen Hermione is, by turns, eloquent, angry, silent. Accused in Act I of adultery, she disappears in Act III, and returns only at the end of Act V. In what ways does Shakespeare use her trajectory to further his thematic concerns of loss and redemption, death and renewal?

A softball of a question. Would it do? Who was she kidding? It was a lousy question, but no time left now. She added a quick reference to Alice Seward's essay on the sacrificial feminists in the late romances and checked her wristwatch—only half an hour to drive across town and get home for Benjamin's bus. She pulled the final page out of the typewriter. She had to get it to Mrs. Conroy. "Mrs. C. for copying," was how the old woman had proudly introduced herself during Caroline's on-campus interview. Since then, she seemed to take pride in not liking Caroline.

"Only twelve copies?" Mrs. C. would no doubt ask, as if she was not already aware of Caroline's enrollment difficulties. *Yes, Mrs. C., my class is a bust.* Was that what the old biddy needed to hear? Emory's English department remained small, but Caroline's classes were particularly so. She had excuses, of course: she was a mother, with children, and not just normal children who needed her around home sometimes. After five years at Emory, she was not the academic star she had once thought she would be. As Ben's needs escalated, her own determination and energy sagged. She was growing aware that she, too, might soon be seen as average. *C is for Caroline.* Was that the point with Queen Hermione? She doesn't fight back against her husband's abuse because she has children who still need her? She was, Alice Seward famously argued in her 1972 essay, a *sacrificial feminist.* Caroline grabbed the play from her office shelves to check the final scene yet again. Act V, scene iii, Hermione revealed: a statue becoming human, a recluse returning at last to her former life. As she breathes again, moves again, walks again among the courtesans, she speaks not one word to her now-contrite husband. Instead, she turns to her sixteen-year-old daughter, her lost-and-now-found child. "Perdita," she says. "I have preserv'd myself to see the issue."

She quickly packed up her Kenya bag, and grabbed her papers. Before she left the office, she re-plugged her phone line into the wall. In the English Department office, a new flower arrangement occupied most of Mrs. Conroy's desk. Her birthday, a wedding anniversary? How many years? Caroline didn't ask, because she told herself, quite frankly, she didn't give a damn.

"Here it is." She handed Mrs. Conroy the original. "Twelve copies, please. Yes, only twelve," she added preemptively, in no mood for raised eyebrows and underlying accusations. "I'll pick them up Monday morning."

"Your husband has been calling, Caroline." Mrs. C. said with a tight, little smile. "He said he rang your office, but couldn't get through."

She stopped by the door, wanting more information, wanting to leave. Why would he have called the main office? What was Mrs. C. not saying? Mrs. C., who called all the men in the department "Professor," but had only ever used Caroline's first name. Mrs. C., who no doubt thought she should be home right now dealing with whatever calamity poor Perry was enduring. Mrs. C. who would soon give her more information about the phone call, but first wanted a little more appreciation, an act of submission, from the not-so-famous, forty-something, feminist scholar.

What could Caroline give her?

"I had my phone unplugged. I needed to get the exam finished."

Mrs. C. said nothing.

"Was there a problem at home? Did Perry say?" She took a step toward the overpowering flowers. Her son's "condition" was apparently common but unspoken knowledge around the department. Caroline could feel her heart pumping through dread and fear: *What if, what if, what if?*

"He didn't mention any problems, per se."

"Thank you," Caroline said relieved and furious, wanting to kick the old biddy in the shin, wanting to kill Perry. What was so urgent that he couldn't wait until she got home?

"Thanks," she said, again, waving her hand as she left. "I am gone for the day. Gone until next week, actually." *Watch me go, now, Mrs. C. Heading home. Where you all seem to need me to be.*

CHAPTER 3

IVY, JUNE 1991

Summer before senior year in high school and Ivy was all about extra, extra credit. Her plans definitely did not include babysitting Baby Brother Ben, thank you very much. But this June and July, for six solid weeks, she'd be gone. Her escape: a college-level science program at Emory, an "enrichment" she'd convinced Mom and Dad was essential for beefing up her high school transcript and getting into an Ivy League university. Free because of Mom's faculty position. With Ben home again—booted in April from some place in North Carolina, (*The Last Resort*, clever Hugo had said)—she knew she should offer to forgo the classes and help with his care. But she'd had her fill of Ben drama. Besides, her temporary absence would give the family a taste of things to come.

"I really need this," she justified yet again at the chaotic dinner Dad prepped the night before she left. "Especially if I plan to apply early decision to Yale." She knew the first part was true, and perhaps the second. She spooned a second serving of spaghetti on her plate and waited for some parental validation.

"Well, it's gotta be an Ivy for Ivy." Hugo said. "Swiss Miss should go get enriched. I can keep Ben busy."

"What about your diving camp?" Mom asked.

"I don't need a bunch of hot-dog divers, challenging me with their degrees of difficulty. Just me and Ben out back on the board. We'll be fine, won't we buddy?"

Ben moaned his happy moan, always glad to be back home with St. Hugo, wherever, whenever. Let them have each other. She should offer up some verbal acknowledgment of Hugo's sacrifice, but the words rooted in her throat, refusing to bloom into gratitude. He was always so damn supportive, ready to give up anything, even his sacred diving regimen, to hang out with Ben, and instead of being grateful, she felt angry, shown up for the selfish jerk she was. Honorable Hardworking Hugo. H-cubed. Mom had explained once that his name meant "Good Soul." Accurate, perhaps, but damn if that didn't make him a lousy foil for his only sister. The more he tried to bail her out with Ben duty, the more irked she became. An Irked, Irritable, Ingrate: I to the power of three. That sounded about right. When Ivy once inquired about her own name, what it meant, where it came from, her mother had said, "Imogen is the heroine of *Cymbeline*. Certainly not my favorite play, but a lovely name. Some scholars argue it's a misspelling of 'Innogen,' or 'innocent one' from the First Folio—the two n's blurring together in the transcription."

A good soul for a son, and a spelling error for a daughter. Great. Thanks a lot, Mom.

"Thanks," Ivy now forced herself to say to Hugo, through the familiar taste of resentment. Lemon rind coating her lips. "But you don't need to give up anything for me."

"Not a problem." He shrugged. "I'm staying home either way, so go or don't go. Suit yourself."

The implication being, of course, that she usually did.

Ivy was not and never would be a good and calm soul like Hugo. But if her name lacked meaning, it did demonstrate nicely the family dynamics. Mom, the Shakespearean scholar, chose prim, trim Imogen; Dad insisted on adding the middle name of Vaughan, after his own mother who loved shepherd's pie, the Blessed Virgin Mary, and Perry Como. Imogen Vaughan—daughter of a high-falutin' Harvard scholar and a working class South Boston boy. Hugo was only a toddler when he contracted the unlikely name into Ivy. The good soul's first act of family peacekeeping? Well, screw him. Screw them all. Summer school was calling.

The next morning, she swallowed a huge dose of guilt, packed up and left in the station wagon not even taking time to respond when Mom called out from the front door, "Now don't be a stranger." Accelerating up the driveway and onto Nancy Creek Road, she felt how departures could become a pattern, her choice when home spun out of control with Ben's comings and goings, his seizures, Mom's moodiness, Dad's fretting and sweating over the latest construction project, Hugo and Ben's all-day antics. Leaving—a fix she would need to repeat.

On the glistening marble campus, she registered in the Student Life building, then hauled her duffel bag and CD player a half-mile from the parking lot into her assigned single in Haygood Hall. She and fifty super nerds from high schools throughout Georgia colonized the second and third floors of the building. Each had a small beige cell, furnished with a thin mattress, a stack of white linens, and a scarred desk. Well, she wouldn't be spending much time in the dorm. According to the instructions and schedules she pulled out of a thick manila envelope, the summer program ran from eight until five each day, with lectures, labs, and research duties. Extracurriculars included Jeopardy tournaments, National Geographic movies, a trip to a nuclear reactor at Tech, as well as career counseling sessions with math and science faculty. These folks knew how to party.

Early in the session, she befriended Rowena and Elizabeth, from Americus and Albany, respectively. The three ate all their meals together in the cafeteria, studied late in the library, ordered pizza for midnight dorm parties. After lights went out on the hall, she listened through the dorm walls for the sound of Ben's wailing. When the guilt got too heavy, every third or fourth day, she duty-called home.

▲▼▲

By the end of June, time slowed under the intensity of Atlanta heat. The summer school students found relief with afternoon matinees at the Plaza Theatre. Since she'd seen all the movie offerings for the month and had two sacks of dirty clothes, she planned a visit home. A couple of hours, wash laundry, a quick dip in the backyard pool. No need to get sucked in.

When she arrived, hauling her laundry into the house, Mom sat at the kitchen counter, pulling deeply on her cigarette, as though it could answer a question she'd posed.

"Your father's in Baltimore, checking out a new place," she said. "It's been crazy here."

Ivy nodded and swallowed her anger. She was seventeen, for Christ's sake, didn't she deserve one summer away from home? She dropped her load, found a glass, and poured herself some iced mint tea.

"Where are the boys?"

Mom nodded towards the pool. "Hugo's been fantastic. I've relied on him so much the past few weeks, with Dad working long hours, traveling most weekends, and you off at camp."

Ivy tried to smile. "And what have you been doing?"

"Oh, I finally finished grading. Now I'm tackling an overdue article. But Ben's on a seizure jag. He had a big one last night. You know how that disrupts everything. I was up till three. Hugo's such a help."

"Yeah. So you said."

Ivy took a sip of tea. A mint leaf caught in her teeth and she picked it off. Mom look tired and thin—cheekbones stretched her pale skin. Ivy sipped again. A hint of Georgia soil in the brew; it didn't spoil the taste, not really, but added something peculiar and local. Was Mom jealous of her time away? Did she also want to leave sometimes? The house, Dad, the boys, Ivy, ditch them all and start over again as an unencumbered college student?

Mom wound and wound a thick strand of hair around her index finger and stared out the window.

"He doesn't have any friends, you know. Just diving and Benjamin. Diving and Benjamin. All day long they are out there. Not like you."

Not like you. Diving and Benjamin. A solitary sport and a single, untiring spectator. All Hugo seemed to want: the discipline of diving, the distraction of Ben—or was it the other way around? *The Recluse and the Retard,* Ivy dubbed them privately, adding to her internal list of abuses: *The Diver and the Dummy.* She liked reducing Hugo to tight one-word descriptions. Repressed. Controlled. Strange. She felt normal by comparison.

Mom finished her cigarette, stood up slowly and shook herself back into functioning. She poured two plastic tumblers full of the tea, added ice cubes.

"Walk these out to the boys, while I start dinner?"

Waist-deep in the shallow end of the pool, Ben ignored Ivy. His lazy eye angled off across the water to fix on the diving board at the other end where Hugo paced his approach: A light one-two-three, then the hurdle, depressing the springboard until the recoil tossed him high into the perfect takeoff. Launched over the water, Hugo pulled into a spinning ball, spinning and falling, all his power and potential contained for one tight instant in the tuck. He snapped open arrow-straight, slicing the surface.

Ben bounced in place in the shallow end, his slow brain assessing. *Where can Hugo be?* Hugo always played the moment to the max, swimming slowly, slowly, along the bottom. Ben slapped the water. *Where can Hugo be? Where can Hugo be?* His moan rose from a deep, guttural rumble into the kind of high-pitched squealing that made Ivy think for an instant that she could slap him silent. No. She was only home for a few hours. Laundry and, okay, a family dinner. But then back to Geekville. Besides, if Dad were successful with his negotiations, Ben would be departing for Baltimore and a new group home, perhaps even by mid-July or August. Mom could go back to work—teach all fall, and publish some brilliant analysis of misunderstood mothers in the tragedies. Hugo would focus on his diving season, train with the Westmont High School team, win the state title he deserved, and Ivy, well Ivy could have a *normal* senior year: friends, football games, parties, college applications. No seizures, no E.R. visits. No law against dreaming, right?

She set the drinks down on the side table, watched as Hugo circled Ben in the shallow end, waiting for him to catch on. Her brothers in their element. Through the water's distortion, Ben's usually twisted and palsied left leg looked normal.

"Where did Hugo go?" Ivy asked now. "Where is he?"

Ben pounded the pool's surface, frustrated and thrilled with the possibilities. Just when Ben was reaching fever pitch, just when Ivy thought Hugo's lungs must be ready to explode, he burst through the surface, reverse-diving to air. "Gotcha, man," he bear-hugged Ben. "You're all mine."

All mine. Is that what he really wanted? Ivy felt another surge of anger with Hugo, with her parents, for setting things up this way. Hugo could have his life as designated diver for Ben. Ivy would make her own way. She turned to leave.

"Hey, hold up," Hugo said, and squirted water at her, through his clasped hands. "Welcome home, Swiss Miss. How's the pre-med life?"

"Drinks. On the table," she said, then went inside to start her first load.

▲▼▲

At dinner, Ben was loud and messy and would not touch his lasagna.

"Try some," Hugo said, loading up his own fork and chewing big, like a friggin' caveman. "Come on, man, it's deeee-licious."

Ben took a small bite, hamstered it in his cheeks.

"Good boy, Benjamin," Mom praised, before he'd swallowed.

The food came straight out, into his milk glass. Ben laughed hysterically. Eating was his daily revenge. He put up with all the shit—the tests, needles, medicines, catheters—that fourteen years and one fragmented chromosome had dumped on him, but he ate when, where, what, and how he chose.

Hugo lifted Ben's glass, swirling its congealing contents. "Savory, man. Fix me one?" He smirked, inviting Ivy into the joke. "You're a fine dining companion. Do you know that?"

"You make me sick," Ivy said, "Do you know *that*?"

"Please," Mom said. "All of you, please."

Ben banged his spoon on the table, then started swirling his arms in the air, freestyle. Bits of food flying across the table.

"Disgusting." Ivy glared at him.

"Lighten up," Hugo said. "He's only having fun."

"Well, he needs to learn some manners. And you make things worse. How is he supposed to know what is acceptable? How's he ever going to fit in anywhere else?"

"He doesn't need to fit in anywhere else. He's fine right here. Right, buddy?"

"Enough," Mom said, and pushed back her chair. "Clean up after yourselves. And no more swimming tonight. I don't want Benjamin to have a seizure." She lingered at the counter, with her thumb and first two fingers rubbing together—longing for a cigarette. "For once, couldn't we have a quiet family meal?" It was more prayer than suggestion. "Would that be so damn hard?"

Ivy wanted to drown out the continued clanging of Ben's spoon on the table. "When's Dad getting home?"

"Tomorrow. Late in the day," Mom sighed. "Anyway, you all might as well know. Benjamin will be staying put, at least through August. Dad called before dinner. *Special Options* in Baltimore won't take him."

"So we will be a big happy family for the rest of the summer," Hugo laughed.

"Fucking Waltons," Ivy mumbled.

Mom called on the dorm phone the following Thursday with a news flash.

Ivy could hear her pull on a cigarette. Then a little inquiring cough.

Come right out and ask.

"Dad wants me to come up this weekend, see the Philly residence, and possibly tour another in Rhode Island. Services there are supposed to be top-notch. We've run out of options in the South."

So much for her plans to see *Rocky Horror* on Saturday night with a group of girls from her floor. Typical. Fucking typical.

"So you want me home? Just in case?"

"I'd be much happier if there were a driver in the house. Would you mind, darling?"

Ah, the term of endearment. Ivy wished it didn't affect her.

"Of course, not." She kicked the concrete block wall. "I'll skip fruit fly lab tomorrow afternoon, get home before he goes to bed."

"Would you believe it?" Mom said when Ivy arrived home the next evening. "Four seizures since you were last here. Hugo's calling it *The Fireworks Fiesta*." She looked worn out, grey and ashy under her eyes, dressed in a sack of a dress. Had she lost weight?

"Hugo's very gifted." Ivy put down her book bag on the kitchen counter. The ceiling shook. Shrieks from upstairs.

"The Bed Game," Mom explained, as if Ivy didn't know, didn't remember how Hugo would drive Ben into a fabulous hysteria with a series of rollicking games: *Sideways Spider. Gulliver Treatment. Where's Rabid Spot?*. The theory was that he would tire Ben out before bed, make him sleep better. The problem was now Ben expected this treatment from everyone, every night, on demand, waving his arms in his macro sign language, his gestures growing larger and his shrieks wilder, until he got his way. Which brother made her crazier? *The Retard and the Recluse* were really one and the same. She hated them almost as much as she hated her own awful thoughts. *Retard and Recluse.* Who could say such a thing? Someone who was ... *Reprehensible?* Was there a noun form of that word? An "R" word for an awful person that she could tag onto the other two? All she could come up with was *Reprobate.* A person without moral scruples. A good SAT word and, come to think of it, a damn good antonym for *good soul.*

▲▼▲

Mom left late Friday for the airport, yelling last minute instructions out of the cab window.

All day Saturday the boys stayed in the pool, cracking each other up with their pratfalls. Ivy watched them, first from the bay window in the kitchen, then later in the day, from her seat by the pool. One bouncing, one diving; one drooling, one splashing. Twenty months apart chronologically, they looked nothing alike, but they might as well be twins. *Identicals,* so mindlessly happy in their watery world. Ben, she couldn't blame, but Hugo? Why did he want this? He was clever, he was a stellar diver—everyone said—so why take this on, this role of ever-ready caregiver?

She sat on a deck chair beside the water in the late afternoon heat. Hugo asked her to time his competition dives. "All eleven, from approach to entry," he said. A strange request but she complied, clicking her Timex to get the exact splits as he executed each of his competition series, whipping his body through twists and turns, saving the two and a half tuck for last. It was a phenomenal finale when he nailed it. He came out of the water, muscled and bronze, and walked towards her, like the cover of some sports magazine.

"How'd I look?" He was one of the best ever in Georgia high school history, according to his coach, and scholarships would be coming his way—money offered if he'd commit during junior year. But Hugo always got cagey around such discussions, as if athletic scholarships were beneath him.

"Not bad," Ivy said, as earnestly as she could muster.

"Why, thanks, Swiss Miss. I have been practicing. It's been a good summer for that. Coach said I couldn't train well at home, but I get more done here than I would at any diving camp. How many seconds was that?"

"Fifty-eight-point-forty-five seconds. Why is that important?"

"It's not. I like to think about it—the ratio of practice to performance time. What you put in and what you get out: mentally, energetically, chronologically."

Wallowing in the shallow water, Ben smiled at his siblings, and turned towards the wall. His fleshy nose, heavy lips, and the remnants of his Lake Norman institutional crew cut, now bleached green-blond from all his pool time, made him a gross caricature of Hugo's good looks. When Ivy stood, the afternoon sun stretched her shadow across the deck, into a silhouette as tall and straight as her mother's. The sun could do that, just as the forgiving water blurred Ben's spastic left leg and twisted torso, until he looked like a sinewy, shaved Hugo.

"You okay?" Ivy yelled across the water. "Ben?"

He didn't turn. She dashed around the deck to the shallow end.

Ben gripped the pool ledge, his body pressed against the outlet where the fresh water poured in, his body jerking.

"Quick, Hugo. Seizure." Ivy reached the steps and squatted down, grabbed Ben by the arm and started to pull him out of the water. He let go of the ledge and slapped at her legs. His face was contorted, his eyes squeezed shut and he groaned loudly.

"What's wrong?"

"He's fine." Hugo said, across the water.

"What's he doing?"

Hugo swam the entire length underwater and popped up right next to Ben.

"His own personal vibrator," Hugo said. "Dad put those jets in to help with his muscle spasms. Little did he know."

"Jesus." Ivy pulled her hand quickly out of the water flooded, she imagined, with a fresh shipment of Ben's screwed-up sperm.

"The Great Whack-off Caper," Hugo said, squirting another handful of water at her.

"Fucking freaks. The two of you, I swear," she said as she went inside.

Despite Mom's warnings about overexerting Ben, Ivy let him swim into the evening while she sat inside at the kitchen counter and tried to work out her biology assignment. Meiosis. The diploid cell nucleus dividing into four haploid nuclei. She'd enjoyed bio class best of all until now—frogs and fetal pigs, living things—but this section was so arithmetical. One slip in the calculations and the whole assignment was shot. Like in real life. Was it that first cellular split, when Ben's fate was sealed? A single catastrophic error in nucleic division, insuring that each and every cell thereafter carried only fragments of a necessary twenty-first autosome? Next week in lab, the students would use the Denver System to cut out and arrange images of human chromosomes by size and shape and kinetochore location; they'd get both a normal and an abnormal set, and would need to describe any identified anomalies (replications, translocations, deletions), as well as the likely impact. What would her own DNA show?

The screams from the pool stabbed at Ivy and she ended up ditching the biology homework and retreating upstairs. In her parents' bathroom, she shaved her armpits, then tried on one of her mother's sleeveless blouses with a wrap-around skirt. Unlike her mother, Ivy had no waist. She stared at herself in the full-length mirror and hated her image, her straight, boyish build, her too-round face and her bushy eyebrows. Ivy stuck at home with the fucking Identicals. Why couldn't she be on campus, with her enriched cohort, playing Frisbee in Lullwater Park, or lying back on a grassy incline, with the bass from some distant R.E.M. track punctuating conversations? At least she'd have a chance at normal.

Later in the evening, Hugo biked to SportStop, supposedly, to look for a new Speedo. How urgent was that? While he was gone, Ben and Ivy watched the Raffi video three times through—Raffi in concert, followed by more Raffi tunes on the CD player. Dad had installed speakers in the den's ceiling and as Ben cranked the bass, the whole room vibrated. Songs about the earth. Songs about pollution. Ben rocking in place, stamping his foot to his all-time favorite: *BAY-bee Beluga, Oh, BAY-bee Beluga. Is the water warm? Is your mama home with you, so happy?* He grabbed his crayon box from the art table and threw it across the room, laughing loudly and bouncing, as the sixty-four wonderful colors scattered across the carpeting.

"You're going to pick those up, buddy," Ivy said turning off Raffi and spitting out the lyrics to that insipid song: *Time to tidy up, tidy up, and put your things away.* But Ben stuck the indigo crayon in his mouth as Ivy gathered the others—reds first, then yellows, deepening into greens, and aqua, calm, forgiving water. His medium. Well, his and Hugo's. But when Ivy was closing the crayon box, Ben lunged at her and knocked the whole bunch on the floor again. He laughed like a rabid hyena, crayon-speckled drool spilling off his chin.

"You little jerk," Ivy said, pulling the indigo out of his mouth and held it above his head.

He slapped at her stomach and arm, slapped again trying to get at his crayon.

"Go on then," Ivy threw the pieces across the room and pushed him after them. "Eat them. See if I care."

He sat on the floor and pulled his arms together across his chest in a hug. He rocked and moaned and hugged, *Hugo. Hugo.*

"He's gone," Ivy said, "Hugo left and I'm all you've got. How do you like that?" Two can throw a tantrum. "Oh, and look, it's time for you to go to bed." She half-dragged, half-carried him up the stairs, while he signed frantically, thumbs down, thumbs down. *Bad Ivy, bad Ivy.* "Well, I'm the only one here, dude."

In his room, Ben would not be restrained as she tried to force him into one of his adult-sized diapers. *Depends, Reliability,* or *Secure*: none held a night's worth of urine. Mom had devised a trick after Ben reached puberty. She used a newborn sized diaper cupped around his penis; then she put the adult diaper on the regular way, securing it with duct tape. But after the crayon crisis, he certainly wasn't going to let Ivy diaper him. Fine, she thought, forget the extra protection. She managed to pin him down for an instant and forced him into the large diaper.

"See what you get," she said. "See what happens when you fight me." Ben groaned, his face now confused, scared, and she saw her brutal self through his eyes.

"Jesus," she sank onto his mattress to sit beside him. "Buddy, I'm sorry. I lost it, I ... I'm sorry." Strangely, he scanned her face with his good eye, reached out and patted her thigh. In the temporary calm, she kissed him goodnight. After latching him into his room for the night, she whispered through the keyhole, "Hugo will be home soon. He'll check on you."

Downstairs, she ate three pieces of cold Kentucky Fried Chicken, straight from the bottom of a barrel she found at the back of the fridge, and plopped down in front of the TV. She flipped channels, landing on 17 in time for a *Love Boat* rerun: broken hearts, lonely hearts, desolate hearts—and not a problem on the cruise ship that couldn't be solved in sixty syrupy minutes.

Ben was quiet at first—subdued after their struggle? But then, after a commercial break, she heard him stomping around in his room. No problem, she thought, he's safe up there and not going to bother me any more tonight. She adjusted the volume, ignored the light fixture shaking overhead, and settled into the insipid plot. A divorced couple and a little girl with cancer whose dying wish was to get her parents back together. Perfect. By the next break, twenty minutes later, when Ivy went to get a bowl of ice cream, the noises from upstairs had mutated into what sounded like full body slams against the bedroom door. She cranked the TV volume even higher.

"I cannot hear a sound." Her vanilla fudge twirl so sticky and pleasing—like the impending *Love Boat* resolutions.

Hugo returned a little before 10 p.m., sweating and red-faced from his bike ride.

"What the hell's going on?" He asked. "Why's the TV so loud?"

"Have a seat," Ivy replied. "You're just in time for the happy ending. The kid's in remission and the parents are back in love. Captain Stubing has a heart of gold."

"Where's Ben?"

"Upstairs. Asleep."

A loud crash from above made Ivy a liar. Hugo looked at her accusingly, and ever the Boy Scout, rushed to find his Identical. Ivy sighed and turned down the volume a little. Fine. He could handle this. She sank back into the couch and watched the Captain dispense his final words of wisdom and shake hands with all the disembarking passengers. Let Hugo run the goddamn freak show.

Two seconds later, he yelled from upstairs, "Get a Valium. Quick."

She ran into the kitchen and found the medicine, in its usual spot under the butter-flap in the fridge, then three-stepped the stairs to find Hugo hauling their jerking brother into their parents' room.

"Here," Ivy said, holding out the vial.

"Help me get him on the bed. We need to turn him over. Quick, grab his legs."

They struggled to roll Ben's rigid, thrashing body. Then, when they flipped him face down, Hugo firmly placed his knee on the small of Ben's back.

"Pull off the diaper. Open his legs. Hold that leg still—wider. Now get out of the way."

He inserted the suppository. In an afterthought of modesty, he draped a blanket over Ben.

Now they waited. How long? Ivy counted in her head. One Mississippi, two … Ben's body still jerked furiously … eleven

Mississippi, twelve Mississippi. Hugo sat on the bed, took Ben's head in his lap and stroked his shoulders and neck.

"It's okay, buddy, it's gonna be okay."

Two minutes later, maybe it was five, Ben was still convulsing, but slower perhaps? Ivy took a quick look at his face. His lips were Crayola cornflower blue. His left hand was still jerking, thumb down, in an accusatory rhythm: *bad Ivy, bad Ivy, bad.* Why had she left him alone for so long? She had wanted, as always, to get away. She wanted to run even now, but willed herself to stay in the bedroom, to stay with the boys. She put a hand on Ben's thrashing arm, sensing the currents that controlled him. When would it stop? Would he come out of this one at home, or should they take him to the hospital for I.V. drugs? How long should they wait? How long had he been seizing while she sat stuffing her face in front of the TV? *My fault, my fault, my fault.* She should leave. But she was the oldest. The driver.

"Damn it, Ben, wake up," she heard herself say.

"Don't yell," Hugo said. He was still rubbing at the base of Ben's neck, "Get another Valium. Please."

"Hospital?" Ivy said.

"No. He'll come out of it. I can tell."

If only she were more like Hugo, taking this all on, forcing her parents to need her. Hugo, always close by, calm, steady, ready to massage Ben's scalp, talk him out of another seizure.

"It's all right, little man, Hugo's right here with you." Caressing, cajoling, "What do you say? You come out of this, and we'll go swimming. You want to push me in? You do?"

"Hospital?" Ivy said again, louder, as Ben still jerked on arhythmically. "Hugo?"

"They haven't got a clue. Please. Get another Valium."

42

She ran downstairs, opened the fridge and plucked a second Valium plug from behind the flap. By the time she had willed herself back upstairs, Hugo had dragged Ben into the bathroom and closed the door behind them. Shut her out.

"What are you doing?" There was no authority in Ivy's voice. "Open the door." But she didn't want him to; they both knew that. She retreated to her parents' bed and lay down. In the background, the bath water ran. A bath could relax the muscles—maybe it would bring Ben out of the seizing. She sank onto the mattress. She only wanted out of these situations, but Hugo, Hugo was fully submerged. The water shut off. Quiet for a minute. Then back on, a soft drip-drip over her brothers.

Dad the builder built a backyard pool, dug deeper than necessary into the sticky Georgia clay so he could add a diving board and make a diver out of Hugo. What had Ben made of all of them? She strained to hear the water ripple the bath's surface, then dropped the extra Valium suppository in a china ashtray on her mother's nightstand. There, in a simple silver frame, a photo of the boys standing, hugging, waist-deep in the shallow end: her brothers in their element, out of focus, merging. If she mustered the energy to raise her hand, hold it like a stop command in front of her eyes, it would be easy, so easy, to erase them both.

CHAPTER 4

HUGO, JULY 1991

Hugo double-knotted a thin, nylon rope around the back axle of Ben's new, adult-sized tricycle and tested the improvised controls, the strength and length of the tether, pushing the trike forward across the bottom of driveway three times, before pulling it up short of the garage.

"Okay, Houston, we're good to go."

All grin and drool, Ben shuffled his feet side to side, swiped at his mouth with the un-tucked end of his t-shirt, and checked out the trike with a confounded mix of *gotta* and *no way.*

"Hmm. You're a little nervous?" Hugo held the handlebars, stilling the trike on the lightly graded stretch of asphalt. "It's all right, Benno. Go ahead and touch it. It's like your old Big Wheel only bigger. Well, bigger *and* yellower. But that's okay, man. You know why? Because this here trike—hey, eyes right here—this is a big guy's trike." He patted the saddle, which was not yet, but soon would be, burning hot. "You can touch it. It's okay."

A quick trial run on the brutally hot side roads was what they needed to break the growing monotony of their summer pool routine. If nothing else, street-heat would create an increased—no, make that an *exponential*—demand for yet another swimming session out back later in the day. And really, who cared where or how Ben and Hugo spent the next hour, this Sunday, or the whole frigging weekend for that matter? This was their time, their show: *The Hugo and Benjamin Summer Special*. Two hopelessly handsome fellas, hangin' at home, while the parents toured Rhode Island, scoping out the next best "home" for Ben. As if he didn't have a good one, right here in Atlanta, 1237 Nancy Creek Road.

"A brand-new trike and the best brother in the world to boot. What more could you need?"

Certainly not another new group home with another nice sounding name: *Ocean Tides Residence, Newport Initiatives, Providence House*. Screw Rhode Island with its highest per capita payment rate for handicapped kids. Let them keep their tony institutions and their salt-slathered seascapes. Hugo knew how these places, with their initial promises of permanent care and sheltered workshops, worked out for Ben: down payment, followed by disruption, then discharge. Three Ds. Make that another big fat F for Ben's report card. Hugo knew, too, what these placements cost his parents, even if no one else was willing to see it. He was not stupid. Neither was Ben, for that matter, despite his "profound mental retardation." Ben did not test well, but he was smart enough to work his way back home every time.

"They always underestimate us, buddy."

And right now, folks, right now awaiting them, over the crest of the driveway, just up there, they had the whole damn road to themselves: Nancy Creek Road, miles of smoldering, curving, rolling asphalt awaited them.

"Ready?" Hugo extended a hand. "This is serious shit, son."

Ben tilted his head, angled a shy smile, uttered a "Guh." His only almost-verbalization, mostly meant *yes* and *go*, but also occasionally *help*. One sound for many reasons, a *guh* for all seasons. All about context—time, place, and temperament could change a *guh* from an ebullient *oh hell yeah* to a terrified *oh help*. And since Ben hung back, one-eying the trike with his sneakered feet still moving, but not forwards, just sliding and scuffing in place, Hugo dropped his hand and paused, a little patience to let the current meaning emerge.

Ben finally took a step forward and moved his craggy pointer finger along the chrome crossbar, then pulled back his hand. Scared.

"Don't be like that, bro! You're ready to ride. I know you are. Now lift up your leg." He tapped Ben's scrawny left thigh. "This crazy ol' leg with a mind of its own needs to go up and over that middle bar."

The leg twitched, a little palsied shake, as if trying to hop-to, trying to do the right thing.

"Yeah, leg," Hugo said, "I'm talking about you. Pull yourself together and get over that bar. Help me out, Ben."

Ben grasped a handful of Hugo's hair to balance, then stood on one leg and willed, just willed, the left up and over the cross-bar. Momentum pulled him down, fast and hard, and his scrawny butt smacked onto the comfort saddle. Another "Guh." This one all glee. And Ben was ready to go, ready to rock, ready to roll, rocking in place on the trike, his feet flailing on either side, wild as his sudden desire to get going, to get this thing moving.

"All right! You're on, one more thing."

Pedals and feet, slippery and evasive, kept missing each other, but Hugo had thought this one out. He pulled two short cuts of rope from his pockets and figure-eighted one around each ankle, shoe, pedal, tying Ben's feet in place.

"There." He straightened up. "That should do it. Look at you, man, pedal clips! We're Breaking Away."

Hugo pointed the front wheel up the hill, toward the street. "If you're really ready to ride, to ride really fast, gimme another good *guh*."

This time, it was loud and repeated: "Guh, guh, guh." A triple-G assent—Good to Go—with Ben's torso lurching backward and forward.

"Hold the handlebars. I'm gonna push you up to the top of the drive. That's right. Keep on pedaling." Hugo leaned all his weight into the rear of the seat, straining to push. "Christ. For a skinny thing, you're heavy as hell. Have you been growing on me, boy? I thought I told you to quit that shit."

The asphalt seethed black heat. Through his flimsy-soled Keds, Hugo felt heat pushing up, pushing back, it wanted to escape, but there was nowhere to go. The air was saturated and swollen, already overcome. Hugo swiped a forearm over his brow and looked up. *Great, another obstacle to contend with*: Ivy, Miss Designated Driver for the weekend, had parked the Buick diagonally across the driveway so that Hugo had to roll the tricycle off onto the lawn.

"Jesus, Ben, help me out here. Pedal, man, *pedal*."

Ivy had been on the lam at Emory most of the summer, but Mom pleaded her home for the weekend. When the parents were off, scoping out new group homes, Mom always wanted a driver in the house—just in case—with the unmentionable "case" being that Ben was known and yes, even prone, to fall into *Status Epilepticus*: a highfalutin Latin term for non-stop seizures. *Known and prone to be thrown.* Ivy, with her license and the Buick battleship at her disposal, was Ben's *just-in-case* MedEvac for the weekend. This parking job,

47

though, would be her way of saying *Yeah, I'm here, taking care of you losers again—and so very far from where I deserve to be.*

Hugo pushed the trike around to the other side of the station wagon. The door, when he brushed it with his bare leg, was hot enough to burn.

"Jesus Christ, this is definitely not biking weather."

He bore down to get Ben up the final steep narrow run of the driveway. They should give up now, head out back to the pool. Go for a swim already. But Ben was leaning forward and working hard and excited about what lay ahead.

"Keep pedaling, Ben, you're doing great."

Hugo's t-shirt was soaked, his hair, lank and wet on his head, felt like a dead thing. He straightened up at the top of the driveway, by the mailbox, to catch his breath and scout their options. The sky hung low and hazy—if you squeezed the air, it might drip. Nancy Creek Road stretched both ways, hot and empty and quiet: no cars, no pedestrians, and certainly no tricyclists. On one side of the street, several widely spaced driveways alternated with capacious flood drains. On the other side, a bank rose steep, treed and kudzu-clad. Hugo waited. Persistent cicadas whirred in the background. It was the Sabbath, and churchgoers must be sweating in their houses of worship. Only Ben and his lackey were out and about in the midday sun. Clear roads and carefree trike-ing. Either way they turned, left or right, was a steep descent on the slick asphalt. Either way they would go, they would go together.

"So which way? Everywhere you go, Hugo."

A deal they cut a long time ago.

Ben took his hands off the handlebars and hugged himself tight, smiled his broadest, breakneck smile.

48

"Yep. Hugo's here. Now lean your choice, man, a left—this way, or a right—down there." Ben sat perfectly still, trying to process the instructions, and Hugo took another blessed moment to breathe. Air moved through his lungs thick and warm as blood. The kudzu-swallowed trees added an iridescent sheen to the hazy sky. And the continued cicada sawing, a southern city's jungle-pulse. *Shickkaw, shickkaw, shickkaw.* When you didn't think about the noise, it was nowhere, but when you started to listen, it was loud enough to make you crazy. Hugo drew another deep breath; *shickkaws* ricocheted in his head. Sometimes, he thought he could live like this, live with Ben forever. Sometimes he felt that he had already drowned.

"A Ralph or a Louie. What's it gonna be?" Hugo wrapped the nylon tether around his hand, circled a little extra give around his wrist, then pushed the trike out into the middle of the street, tempting fate, waiting for gravity or Ben to decide. Ben lurched his answer, leaning hard left, and they were off.

"It's a Louieeeeee. Hold on tight now."

Hugo kept the braking rope short and taut and ran fast, keeping pace with the trike the whole way. Before full momentum built, he leaned backwards, pulling on the tether to slow the trike, gain control, and navigate them safely round the blind bottom curve.

On the second run, he let Ben pick up a little more speed. As they ran downhill, Hugo uncircled an extra foot of rope from his arm and lengthened his stride. As they neared the bottom of the hill, he managed to pull back on the rope and slow them down enough for control into the curve.

But by the third run, Ben had figured out that the rope was the enemy of speed. He wanted, of course, to break away, to experience speed as his own personal pleasure. Midway down the hill, he took his right hand off the handlebars and started batting behind him at the rope.

"Guh," he screeched. *Go on, get lost.*

"You wish, fella," Hugo said after they rounded the corner and slowed down. "You'll crash. Kaboom." He hit his own head hard with a fist. "Kaboom and a major owie!" Ben started giggling and rapped his own head. "It's not funny, man, if I let go, you'll crash. Kaboom. So look, I hold the rope and you hold the handlebars. No hitting the rope. No waving your arms. Or we have to quit."

After a few more runs, Hugo was exhausted, his shins screamed from the downhill pounding, his shirt soaked from the pushing back up. At the top of the hill, he stepped in front of the trike to get Ben's full attention. "You want to go swim?"

Ben pointed back down the street and rocked in his seat. He pointed again, jabbing his finger repeatedly. "Guh." *Go.* He wanted more. He could do this all damn day!

"All right. One last run, and we'll really let it all go this time. You and me, full speed ahead. Can you handle it? Fast!"

Ben took a moment, then nodded his head, *yes*, forcefully *yes*, putting all his weight and intention into the movement, but he didn't make a sound, as if he was aware how inadequate his only word would be to convey his desire, the full force of his conviction.

Hugo turned the front wheel downhill. "Gentlemen, start your engines. This is the weekend's final race. The crowds are anxious. The drivers are ready, the engines are revving. The Grand Finale, folks. And the favorite has to be young Ben Novotny. A fearless driver, though some would say a feckless navigator. Gentleman, take your marks." He pushed Ben forward once, then pulled him up short with the rope. "Get set," another push and back-pull. "And *Guh*."

This time, Hugo held the last few inches of the rope and offered no check, no body weight to slow the building momentum. Heisenberg's uncertainty principle said that position and momentum cannot be known exactly at the same time. The trike pulled them fast into the slope. Hugo ran alongside, but the trike quickly moved ahead. Hugo leaned forward into the hill, kicking his feet up behind him as fast as they hit the ground. Keds slapped full force against the street, minimal friction that would not cut momentum. He was building speed, and it took all his effort to keep up with the careening trike. He had become part of the momentum now, he and Ben equal products in the equation, their conjoined mass, their breakneck speed, hurtling them forward over the steaming black street. Ben loved speed, had always loved speed, and Hugo had always lived to give Ben what he loved, so he pushed hard and harder, sprinting past one, two, three wide-mouth drains that punctuated the curbside. Ben looked over his shoulder; he sensed Hugo's efforts, saw Hugo, flailing, almost falling forward with this speed, and he started to giggle. Laughter: a new wayward force, a monkey wrench in the equation. Mass and velocity and laughter, applied erratically, and the front tire, turning and skidding.

"Hold on," Hugo yelled, "you gotta hold on."

The trike swerved right, the back wheel almost tripping Hugo, who tried to stop it with a sharp tug on the tether. But the trike only bucked and Ben's arms windmilled and he laughed loud, full into the absurdity. He loved slapstick and now here he was in the middle of an absurd joke, knowing—or at least accepting—before Hugo did, what their outcome must be. Hugo tried again to pull back; this time the rope slipped through his grip. The trike careened towards a storm drain. Hugo ran, trying to catch it, but there was no way to catch and control the hurtling, senseless momentum, or the awful sickness as he watched the front wheel hit the sewer lip, and the trike somersault onto the bank. Hugo chased it, hopping the curb, leaping over the crash site. He landed face down in a shallow ditch, six feet beyond his brother. Hugo pushed up on both hands. His shoulder hurt; he slowly craned his neck to look. What had he done?

The trike on its side, front wheel spinning in the air. Ben's feet were still firmly bound to the pedals and one arm seemed to be trapped underneath the handlebars. And Hugo thought that if it were broken, or even badly sprained, then maybe Ben would stay home, at least for a few more weeks.

"Dude. That was fast. Are you all right?"

What had he done? He should have stopped it before it got crazy. But Ben loved the speed, the danger. And in that last run, they shared something, didn't they? Shared a frenzy, a crossed-wired feeling, danger and dazzle, crashing and explosion—maybe like a seizure? Maybe now he knew. Wherever I go, Hugo.

Slowly, Ben lifted his head. His cheek was smeared with drool and dirt and some kind of neon green plant juice, but he smiled broadly, thank god, smiled so big he almost choked on his *guh*, which might mean yes or more, go or help.

CHAPTER 5

CAROLINE, SEPTEMBER 1991

Curtains of long, gray-brown hair hung forward on either side of Caroline's face, cutting off, for a short while at least, the mess in the kitchen sink that she hadn't dealt with over the weekend. The mess that would be here still, after she'd finished her morning tea and pity party, got up from her stool, and made herself get on with it, get on with this day, this Monday, as she would, any minute now, when she got a grip and pulled herself together. It was still before seven—a few more minutes before the kids came down.

The shower drummed overhead: Ivy, first born and first awake, had been steaming herself for a good fifteen minutes already, preparing for her day, preparing for tests, preparing for her final year at Westmont. So young, so prepared, and so very ambitious, her daughter. This first month of her last year in high school, she was all talk of AP classes, college applications, Ivy leagues, and cross-country practice. When she was through with the shower and dressed, she'd charge into the kitchen, waving her youth and promise around like a challenge, a challenge that Caroline felt incapable of rising to meet.

Not today. Not when her own life plan seemed to be falling apart as her daughter's was getting underway. And god, not again, tears of self-pity that began as a roughness in the back of her throat filled her eyes, so that if she blinked, they would fall, they would give her away. What kind of woman envies her daughter?

Caroline knew exactly what she needed, instead of her girlish tears. On the counter, a mug of British breakfast tea steeped. She stood slowly, walked to the cabinet next to the fridge where she kept Benjamin's pharmacopeia, found the liquid Valium, unscrewed the safety cap and streamed a liberal dose into her tea. Monday was always tough: the start of a brand-new work week, a regular reminder of all she was not accomplishing, the classes she was not teaching, the articles she was not writing. Perry, already long gone at his latest site, reaped tangible rewards each day: pine-splayed lots cleared, streets paved, houses framed, then built. Ivy would leave soon for school, accumulating praise from the faculty, awards for her smarts. And Caroline would be home again all day today with Benjamin, perhaps all month, all semester. Was she wrong to find little satisfaction in that? She'd moved south with so many ideas. All the promises she'd made to herself about what she would accomplish roiled in her mind, unused and accusatory.

It was not only Mondays that magnified her failures—it was mothering. Oh, it was fine when the kids were young, wheeling babies around Cambridge in a stroller, showing off her Czech-cheeked toddlers at grad student parties. Even the first few years, when she and Perry were adjusting to Benjamin's complexities, she'd hung on, willing herself to search for solutions to the multiple medical problems. But now, fourteen years later, Benjamin was home, with no care plan in place, no respite available—and she, Caroline Clissold, once-promising scholar, stuck with the daily caretaking—feeding, clothing, washing, doling out medications that worked and then didn't work at all, handling all the seizures that you expected but never predicted, the endless diapers at night and accidents in the day with no end in sight. This was not what she signed on for, not what she could sustain.

Benjamin's wake-up screech cut through the shower's steady overhead thrumming. His adolescent call was gull-like, slightly menacing. He'd been home all summer and would stay home a good while longer, until they, until Perry, figured out the next move. *What next?* She tried not to ask too often. Just as they'd divided chores with the house—she did the kitchen, Perry did the yard work, so, too, had they separated Benjamin duties. Caroline did all the hands-on care: baths, diapers, clothes, food and meds, while Perry managed the big issues—hiring nannies, long-term placement, finding respite workers. Perry always willing, of course, to help with baths and bedtime, but was she wrong to feel resentful that each day she checked off all her tasks, and the next day the list was the same? If Perry failed at his job, if the next great housing hope did not pan out for Benjamin, that meant all the daily caregiving tasks were still waiting for Caroline.

"We're a team," Perry liked to say, but she was the one doing the heavy lifting. The one too tired this morning to lift anything more than a medicine bottle.

"If we can't find another placement for him, Perry, let's at least admit that," she had reasoned with him over the Labor Day weekend. "We have tried and tried. Let's acknowledge, at least, that perpetually *trying*, the build-up and the inevitable let-down, is exhausting for everyone. Good for no one. Not even Ben."

"For god's sake, Caroline. We've talked about this: Ben needs to have his own life. A community of his own. Have a little patience," Perry jolted himself with his gruffness. He added more gently, "Just trust me."

She wanted to trust him, wanted to believe that things would get better, but then he added his usual hollow summation: "It's all going to be just fine." And she knew it wasn't. Not anymore.

When he'd left this morning, it was still dark out, the dawn chorus beginning and his truck tires squealing at the top of the driveway, as if sounding Perry's relief at getting away.

Ivy's lengthy morning shower had stopped. Caroline could hear the screeches from Benjamin, locked under hook-and-eye in his upstairs bedroom. She swept her hair aside, looked at the clock on the stove. *Five more minutes of alone time?* She let her hair fall again.

Last month, she had taken an emergency leave from Emory. She had awakened each morning flat, empty, even as her brain kicked into its usual anxious overdrive. She expected any day now to hear from Dr. Beardsley, telling her she would have to be replaced come New Year if things didn't change.

She took a sip of tea. Then another. With each swallow, a bitter, but healing steam filled her throat, promising calmer thoughts. Five more minutes until she felt its full effect and was able to get off of the stool—was that too much to ask? *Too much to ask.* Could a child ever ask too much of his parents? And if he did, what should a parent ask in return? That the child go away? Wasn't that essentially what Perry and Caroline had asked of Benjamin? Go, please, for a while. But Ben didn't understand the message: he had gone and come back, gone and come back, gone and come back. Each time they started to believe, maybe this time, maybe we have found the right place, a new crisis brought an end to the temporary calm.

Her mug was the only one left from a set of four that she and

Perry received as a wedding gift from her mentor, Alice Seward. It was ceramic, over-sized, with dark green bull-rushes glazed onto a rough, speckled gray-blue background. She ran her thumb up a long glossy leaf. Caroline had always loved these mugs, not just because they came from *Admir'd Alice*; she loved the way the handle wrapped across the back of her hand, how the clay transmitted the perfect amount of warmth through her palm. Alice had been disappointed when Caroline married so young; she never said so, but Caroline felt the pull-back, the withdrawal of some investment Alice had made in her protégé. Almost nineteen years now, she and Perry had been married: six years for each of the three broken wedding mugs. If the law of averages held true, this final mug should carry her another six years, through 1997. Ivy and Hugo would have left home by then. Finished college, too. They'd be off on their own somewhere—medical school, graduate work? Maybe Caroline's book on the Late Romances would be finally finished. And, yes, well received!

Ha and another bitter *ha*.

And where would Benjamin be? According to Perry's fantasy recipe book, Benjamin would find himself housed, stable and secure, in some loving group home, where Caroline and Perry could visit him regularly and bring him home for holidays. That was the script that Perry had written and was still doggedly pursuing.

Tonight, Perry would leave for another "scouting" trip in the Midwest to convince some nuns—the Sisters of Mercy—to take Benjamin into their expensive, but highly regarded program. *Please take him,* Caroline allowed herself to pray into her empty tea cup, despite all she knew, *take our son and help him, please.*

It was not likely that the Sisters would have him. The options were drying up, as Benjamin's list of discharges grew. Their last attempt at a residential placement at the end of the summer had not panned out. Ben's disability was simply "too much," the administrator had said, during the two-day on-campus evaluation.

"Too profound for Philly," Perry had said.

"Then he's surely too ill for Illinois," Hugo had quipped only last night, when Perry spoke of the latest possibility and his impending scouting trip. "Why can't he stay here with me?"

"Shut up," Perry had snapped at poor Hugo. "You know he can't survive at Northside. And he can't stay home, either. Don't make this any harder on Mom than it has to be."

Before he left for Illinois tomorrow morning, Perry would prepare some ever-lasting casserole to carry Caroline and the kids through the weekend. Then he would kiss her gently on the lips and say, "I feel good about this place, Carrie." So consistently upbeat. And she should be thankful in return. Thankful for his plans and positive predictions, when so many husbands opted out.

She had seen the women most husbands left behind; she'd seen them during the family nights at the special schools, at the Support Systems meetings, when she used to go to such things, as well as in the public parks and shopping malls, where they sought company or a break from routine. *He couldn't take it. He was a weak man.* Caroline listened without hearing, stood slightly apart, not wanting to become a *special needs parent.* It was Perry who introduced himself to the other mothers, showed them he was not like their exes, the departed dads. Perry who determinedly included all their children, even the fully-grown ones, in his crazy games. He found something everyone could play. Her Perry.

Your husband is marvelous, they would say, if Caroline stayed close. *You are lucky to have him.*

58

"Mom," Ivy yelled from upstairs. "Mother?"

Come to me, Caroline thought. *Come down the stairs to speak to me.*

"In case you haven't noticed, Ben is awake."

"I'll get him," Hugo yelled from the top of the stairs.

She should force herself off the stool, move her leaden legs upstairs and take over, tell Hugo, *It's not your job to dress your brother, it's not your job to care for him,* but she let the impulse pass. If Hugo wanted to help her out now, before school, just a little, what was the harm? Five more minutes; time for a second cup of tea. Hugo could handle this part so well, he always did.

She walked to the kettle, and poured more hot water over her tea bag, opened the oak cabinet and added a second slug of Ben's Valium, then put it back with the other bottles and jars before the kids descended. Ben had never liked the taste of the liquid diazepam. He managed much better now with the crushed-up Dilantin on a spoonful of yogurt, but Caroline kept re-filling the liquid prescription. She could taste its bitterness beneath the tea, and it left a strange coating on her teeth.

Ivy clomped down the stairs, stood across from Caroline and dropped a stack of text books on the countertop. Caroline sat back down, not rising to the bait. "Do you want breakfast? Toast or something?"

"I have a chemistry test."

"You have time to eat." Caroline swept her hair back from her face and tried to energize herself.

"Where's Hugo? I told him we have to leave early." Ivy opened the fridge and filled a plastic cup with orange juice. "I've got to study." She sipped her juice and looked around the kitchen, with disgust. "Someplace where I can think."

"You need to eat something. Hugo's helping Benjamin get dressed."

"Isn't that your job?"

Caroline's cheeks flushed. "You know what? I don't need it. I really don't need it."

"I just asked if ... "

"You did not just *ask*. You accused, and I don't appreciate it. If you don't want to help with Ben, that's fine. But please, please. I am barely hanging on here."

"Jesus," Ivy muttered, and placed her cup on the pile in the sink, too. "It's not as if I don't help out. I spent my entire summer ..."

"Shut up." Caroline slammed her mug on the counter; the handle broke off in her hand, and half the tea spilled out. "Please ... shut up." Her heart pounded in her ear. "I'm at my wits' end." She already regretted her outburst, wanted to suck it back in, reverse the perverse cartoon. She reached for a dishtowel and patted the counter. And now the pounding, anger, regret, anger, regret, a pulsatile tinnitus that would stay with her all day. *Oh god.* How did she get to this place already? On a Monday morning. She held the sopping towel out, towards Ivy, like a limp peace offering. "Look, I'm sorry. It's been a very long semester."

"It's not even October," Ivy tossed her head as she walked to the base of the stairs. "Hugo. I'm leaving. Now."

She could afford to be young, dismissive, and hurtful. She was seventeen, on her way up and out, off to college in less than a year, and no doubt she would flee somewhere far away, far away from her family, from Benjamin. Could Caroline blame her? No. Ivy was ambitious, bright, competitive. Like her mother had once been. Well, she would have years to find herself, settle down, before she would circle back to her family, and then she, too, would no doubt come to know the same steady pulse of anger turned to regret. Anger shifting to melancholia. What age brings.

Hugo called down from the top of the stairs, "One minute."

"I told you I have to go." Ivy walked out.

"Ivy!" She won't drive off. She wouldn't dare. Through the curtain, Caroline watched her approach the car, clutching her books to her chest, in her jerky strut, concertedly not looking behind her. She got in the station wagon and started the engine. Revved it. Revved it again and beeped the horn.

Hugo came running downstairs with Benjamin riding on his back. Wearing red cowboy boots and a yellow bandana, Benjamin was kicking wildly at Hugo's thighs, rodeo glee all over his face.

"One cowboy rarin' for breakfast," said Hugo, depositing him on the floor, and picking up his backpack and gym bag instead. He ran out the front door to catch Ivy who had started up the driveway; he turned and waved back at them through the kitchen window.

Caroline raised her hand to wave back. She took a final long draught from the dregs still left in her mug, watched Ivy crest the driveway and peel off up Nancy Creek Road, while Hugo, ever the peace-maker, ran after the car. She'd pull over, after half a block. After making her point. Little bitch.

Caroline turned to Benjamin as he poured half the box of Cap'n Crunch cereal onto the floor and gleefully held up a green plastic whistle.

"Okay," she said as gamely as she could. "It looks like you found your toy surprise."

She walked towards him and took the cellophane-wrapped whistle out of his hand. "Now, get up, sit at the table, and eat your cereal while I do some dishes? You can have the whistle after breakfast. After medicine."

Benjamin shrieked as she tried to seat him, slapped the tabletop, demanding the toy.

"After your medicine. You can have it after breakfast and medicine." He shrieked again, and she relented, handed over the toy, and turned to the sink, turned the water on. Too early to do battle with him. Water cascaded over the pile of mismatched plates that Perry had not rinsed off. The dishes in front of her, and now Benjamin and his cereal mess. Her domain.

What was it Perry had said, years ago, after her first leave of absence? *Give it a chance, you might even enjoy the time at home, more than you know.* Did he at any level believe it? What about when he said, last week, *We'll have it sorted out by Thanksgiving.* Perry Novotny, the relentless optimist. Optimist, a nice word for liar. Benjamin started grinding crunch-berries into the table top. Soon he would stomp them on the kitchen floor, relishing the happy, crinkly sound of so many Cap'n Crunch under his red boots. Kids off at school and where was Perry at this moment? Off at his job. Tomorrow Illinois. The water ran hot over her hands. The Valium was making her eyelids heavy. She turned the water off and sat back down at her stool. Eighteen years, they'd been married. Eight more hours until Perry got home, prepped a casserole, cast a furtive, angry eye on the pile of dishes she would not have washed, and headed upstairs to pack his travel bag.

Chapter 6

Perry, October 1991

As they left the men's dorm and Sister Colleen talked on about employment opportunities, the cafeteria food (that she claimed to eat every day), and the handmade quilts on all the residents' beds, Perry reminded himself to breathe in deeply. Smell was crucial. By the end of the tour of any potential group home, beneath the pseudo-pine or lemon disinfectant slathered on the floors, Perry would have isolated the true nature of the institution. Sometimes sickness, sweet and sticky in the air. More often, though, it was fear: body odor, cut with a hint of blood. What hit him today, after they had crunched down a long gravel path and entered the sprawling on-site workshop, was neither fear nor sickness. It was longing, packed in a smell so familiar to him—linseed oil on freshly sanded cedar—that he half-expected to see his papa, Jan Karel Novotny, dead now for over twenty years, at work in this place, varnishing one of his sculling boats.

Papa had left Prague in '38, before the war, left all his family, left an apartment building that he and his brother owned in the city center, as well as his own successful boat-making business, to arrive jobless, penniless in Boston. He never talked of his reasons for leaving, only ever offered up the tiniest details about his past, though he carried the Old World in his looks, accent, and workmanship. In 1948, he met a much-younger Mary Catherine Vaughan, herself a fresh immigrant from Ireland, and married her. Jan must have aged quickly into the dour man with thick, gray hair, heavy, curling eyebrows, and an unpredictable temper that Perry remembered. His mother sometimes spoke privately about a tender side, but Perry never saw it. Perhaps because his father's craft demanded tremendous patience, months of sanding and shaping the sculling boats he produced one by one, mostly for rich Ivy League alumni, he had little of it left for Perry. All that calm and precision passed through his hands into each shell that proudly carried the *Novotny* name in maroon italics, where the bow tapered to a thin line. When the boats were finished, they were sleek as racehorses, frail as bird skeletons. They frightened Perry, somehow: the work, the trapped desire, as if the shells held all he would never understand about his father.

Now, under the tin roof of the Providentia Workshop, fifteen adult men pieced together Christmas ornaments. At the first of several long wooden tables, three or four sanded chunks of pine into ovals. Further along, another small group painted the shapes black and white with tiny brushes and thick paints, transforming the nondescript ovals into penguins. On a side table, drying on racks, a flock of penguins. What was the correct collective noun? A pack of penguins? No. He would have to ask Hugo when he got home.

"Hello, hello, hello," one of the sanders, a short, chubby man with an oversized green baseball cap, yelled in a loud monotone. "Hello, Sister Colleen. We're very busy here. Please don't disturb."

"You *look* busy, George," said Sister Colleen, nodding approvingly.

"That your brother?" George asked. "He look like your brother."

"No, George. This is Mr. Novotny. He's visiting us today."

"I have a brother, but he didn't visit me last year because he throwed up."

"We know that story, George," his neighbor interrupted. He looked at Perry and shrugged as he explained, "It's a boring story."

"He throwed up so much he could not visit me for Christmas. He throwed up so bad he went to the hospital in Ohio. He throwed up so bad he almost dived," George continued, staring at Perry for acknowledgement. "He almost dived," he repeated.

"I'm sorry," Perry said. "I hope he's much better now." He walked over to the table and picked up an unpainted bird body, rolled it in his palm, the soothing feel of sanded wood. "You guys are doing a great job here."

"Please don't touch the merchandise." George said. "You have a brother?"

Perry put the smooth oval back down the table. "No. Not a brother, but I do have a son. Benjamin, Ben. He would like to come here and help out. He's a good hard worker."

Would Ben ever be capable of this? Sitting in a workshop, sanding wood, painting, passing hours with the guys, admonishing visitors? Ben would never talk, of course; Perry had learned that years ago, after many doctors ran their tests and concluded that the first and only sound Ben had ever uttered—a hard "g"—would be the full extent of his oral communication. But would he be able to work—in his own way—to participate? When visitors like Perry passed through the workshop, would Ben be able to take pride in his job?

Papa had died, a heart attack at age sixty, alone in his woodshop, well before any of his grandchildren were born. Perry's mother was felled by a massive brain aneurysm a few years later, when she was still a young woman in her fifties, and when Ivy was a baby. Perry grieved for both his parents, but he had a wife, a new baby, so he didn't dwell on loss. Only times like now, with the smell of the linseed oil, he'd miss them so sharply it took his breath. He'd think how it might have been if they'd all stayed in Boston, if his parents had lived longer, lived long enough to help out with their grandkids, lived long enough to see Perry as a father of three, making a living, trying his best, game face on and best foot forward. They would have helped. His mother would have delivered a few meals each week to their apartment: her famous shepherd's pie, perhaps, or the occasional roast beef. And Papa, he might have taken a special interest in Hugo. Yes, he would have admitted the quiet, serious, middle child into his workshop and shown him a thing or two about his craft. Maybe even talked to him about his youth in Prague, his family's apartment building in the city, the ancient boat house on the banks of the Vltava, where he first began his life's work. Things that, for some reason, he'd never been willing to share with Perry.

How would his parents have understood Benjamin? People—people you didn't even know or even those you thought you knew well—would surprise you with the things they would say. *Perhaps he will die young.* People would offer all kinds of unsolicited advice. *You have to think about the other kids.* Then, once in a while, someone unexpected with such understanding—the little girl at McDonald's last week who played with Ben on the slide for an hour, then cried when he had to leave.

At the back table by the emergency exit, two men with identical pudding bowl haircuts and oversized Chicago Bears sweatshirts put the finishing touches on the painted penguin bodies, attaching felt feet and beaks, little knit stocking caps and scarves, as well as silver hooks and sparkling string.

"Go Chicago Bears," said Perry.

"The Bears are going all the way," one of the men said.

"All the way, Sister Colleen," echoed the second.

"My brother doesn't like the Bears," yelled George from the other end of the shop. "He likes the Cleveland Browns."

"Browns stink," said one of the Bears fans.

"Yeah. Browns stink," concurred the other. They gave each other an uncoordinated high five, then got back to work.

Dozens of finished ornaments, well-clad, smiling penguins, hung on a large metal display tree.

"See you all later," Sister Colleen said to the men, with a broad, queenly wave. "Keep up the good work." And to Perry, as they headed back to the administrative building, she added, "Those guys are our A-team. Eric and Steven, the twins by the exit, they've been with us since they were infants. They practically run the place. Die-hard Bears fans, as if you couldn't tell. And George, he came to us when an awful state hospital in Ohio was closed down, maybe five years ago. He had no job training, no social skills, barely spoke when he arrived. He has really blossomed here."

"He seems happy," Perry said, wondering if this was true. "Does his brother actually visit him?" Before she could answer, he continued with the question he always reminded himself to pose of program directors. "What is your policy—Providentia's policy, that is, on family visits, by the way? Can we stop by anytime?"

Usually, this query was met with a cough, a sideways glance followed by a lengthy explanation of how visiting was not encouraged, tended to upset routines, resulted in prolonged separation problems.

Instead, Sister Colleen stopped walking, pausing on the path to turn and look directly at Perry. The red brick building stood behind her, an emphatic and enduring backdrop for her small, birdlike frame. She peered into his face, as if she were the one with the questions to ask, an evaluation to complete. "Regular visits won't be feasible for you, I assume, coming all the way from Georgia?" She hesitated a second, pushed her oversized glasses back up her nose before continuing. "But if you're asking if we value family involvement, let me assure you, we do. We encourage it. Some of our residents have weekly visits from family. That's great. If I had my druthers, I would *require* visits. Everyone wants to belong to a family, their family of origin—even as they make a new different kind of family here. Of course, I can't mandate that relatives come here and visit. Families are, well, complicated, as I am sure you know."

Golden and burnt-red leaves scattered across the lawn like Perry's thoughts. *Complicated.* Certainly, families were that. You tried your best and still things turned out all wrong. Other times, moments of tenderness caught you unawares—when you least expected and most needed it: A kind word from your daughter who'd been acting like a stranger lately. A quick, unsolicited kiss from Caroline whose distrust was growing each month. The softness that took over the house every time after a major seizure—Ben sleeping deeply, heavily medicated, and childlike—and everyone tired and relieved, because, with this one past, the next grand mal episode was perhaps days or even a week away. Perry liked Sister Colleen and already felt he could trust her. Trust, like optimism, came easily to Perry. *Much too easily,* Caroline said. *You never seem to remember that trust is something people are supposed to earn.* So he reminded himself now to stay grounded, not get swept away in flimsy possibilities—like one of the falling leaves. Yes, the Providentia campus was beautiful, obviously well-endowed by private money as well as the diocese. Yes, the programs and staffing and volunteer involvement he had seen were exemplary. Yes, Sister Colleen's answers were right on; she was smart, direct, and obviously dedicated. But be careful, he told himself. Ask questions, get answers. In writing, if possible. A "revocable trust"—wasn't that what his lawyer in Atlanta had advised setting up for Ben—a trust that would help with residential placements and program eligibility? Don't get carried away with possibilities. *Hold trust in trust.*

"Do all the residents here work?" Perry asked. "I am not sure if Ben could do the woodshop ..."

"No—no, not at all. The guys in the shed are, as I said, our A-team. They are older, more experienced, and, as you probably guessed, they are all mildly to moderately retarded. Some of our more *profound* residents, they can't work, not even in the most structured settings, not even with all our supports. We have art classes, equine therapy. But for those who can—like George and the twins—the job program is very rewarding. Those guys in the workshop put out about two thousand ornaments between now and Christmas. I'll show you the gift shop later, where we sell them. Perhaps you can buy a holiday penguin for Mrs. Novotny?" She laughed lightly, "A whole family of penguins, if you want."

Her short gray hair was fine and feathery around her face, her smile quick and darting as she held the heavy front door of the main building open for Perry.

"After you," she said. She could be forty or sixty; it was hard to tell—in her blue suit, she seemed ageless, as well as sexless. Or maybe that was some latent prejudice on Perry's part that made him view all nuns as asexual and otherworldly. What did you call a group of nuns? Another question for Hugo. Or maybe he could ask Sister Colleen, if she knew—if things continued to go well and they were pals by the end of this visit. Did nuns joke about themselves? *Say sister, what do you call a group of nuns?*

"I'd love to see the gift shop." Perry said. "And yes, I will buy my wife a gift. She'd love that." Though Perry doubted very much that she would. The ornaments were not the kind of thing that appealed to Caroline. So *group-homey,* she might say. She had never been the kind to show off any of the children's artwork. Ben's productions— the noodle trees and leaf stencils—usually went directly from his backpack to the trash. Once when Perry asked her about it—why she never hung any of his work on the refrigerator—she replied, "You don't *really* believe Benjamin made them, do you?"

"Let's head back to my office, first," Sister Colleen said. "We can take a look at all the paperwork and I can answer any other questions you might have. I want to get all the important stuff out of the way before you have to head to the airport. We'll leave time for you to stop in at the gift shop on your way out, while you wait for your taxi."

Perry had arranged to do this visit all in two days, because Caroline had Ben at home alone. With Ivy and Hugo back in school, Caroline was bearing the brunt of it. And showing the stress. She snapped at the kids, she walked around the house in a funk, letting the sink overflow, the laundry mildew. When Perry had mentioned his plan to visit this place, Caroline had been quickly dismissive.

"It's a waste of time," she had said. "Why do you think some nuns in Chicago would take him when the Southeast, the entire east coast, as a matter of fact, has already blackballed him?"

Perry was determined to bring back good news. If not a firm commitment, then at least, not a no. Not a definitive no. The last time he counted, six residential facilities had booted Ben: Elmfield, Woodlands, Milledgeville State School, Gracewood Residential Center, Sunlands, and Lake Norman. Spring Hill in the summer with the aborted trial period was too short to count, if anyone, besides Perry was counting. Each place with a name like so much wishful thinking. Bucolic pastures, sheltering trees, fresh starts. With each new beginning, Perry had high hopes for his son, for his family. High hopes had become false hopes, each time. Well, at least Providentia had a name that sounded more lugubrious and weighty than some of the others. Latin, no less. Maybe that would give Caroline something to relate to—or maybe would she laugh and say, *Providentia: well, then, this must be part of God's plan.*

Sister Colleen's office was a large room in the front corner of the main building. She had done nothing with it, obviously not focused on her own material comforts. Or was that another stereotype Perry had about nuns? Two solid oak filing cabinets covered most of one wall; a floral couch with faded green cushions obfuscated the room's best feature, a bay window that looked out over the driveway. Two visitors chairs sat directly across from Sister Colleen's huge desk. When she sat down behind the desk, in her own oversized leather chair, she looked like a child playing lawyer.

"Have a seat, please. Let's talk about Ben." She patted a file on her desk.

Perry sat on the edge of the armchair.

"You and your wife have had quite a hard row to hoe, Mr. Novotny." She smiled, "I am a gardener, can you tell? Anyway, after reading through this, I know that it hasn't been easy." She tilted her bird-like head a little and met his eyes, held them for a second before continuing. "Ben's garnered quite a rap sheet." She smiled at her little colloquialism.

Perry nodded. "Some of the places were dumps. He's not easy, I am aware of that, of course, but ..."

"To be honest, when I first got his records, I was not convinced that Providentia—that our housing and services—could work for Benjamin."

Perry paused. "He has a lot of challenges, his seizures ..."

She raised a hand. "Please. I wouldn't have had you fly up here to meet with me, to tour the premises, to go through the preliminary paperwork if I didn't think it was worth a try." She pulled a document out of the folder and offered it to Perry, across the expanse of her desk. "That's the psych evaluation that was done down in Georgia—at a place called Gracewood, dated... It should say there on the cover?"

"November 1989." Perry's neck tensed as he remembered. "Those idiots." He said, then blushed, "Sorry. It's just, that place looked so good from the outside, but turns out it was really ... medieval. They discharged him because he supposedly bit another student. But we found bruises up and down his back—he was the one who had been abused. If he bit someone, it must have been because he was provoked. I know how that sounds. But we did file reports with the Department of Children and Family Services and other agencies."

Sister Colleen nodded. "Yes. I saw the Determination. *A danger to other residents.* That's certainly a catch-all, isn't it? But let's not revisit Gracewood. What I want to draw your attention to is *this* particular evaluation. It's a consultative psych—that means it was done by an independent contractor, not by Gracewood staff. And, well, I see it as a very optimistic report."

Perry turned to the first page of the document. *Benjamin Karel Novotny. DOB: 4/9/77; age at evaluation, 12 years, 7 months. Examiner: Janet Griswold, Psy.D. AXIS II diagnosis: Severe Mental Retardation; AXIS III diagnosis: Seizure Disorder*

Sister Colleen kept talking while he read. "This Dr. Griswold spent two whole days observing Benjamin. That's quite unusual. Especially at a state residential center. She completed a battery of tests—sometimes it's hard to administer them for a child with Ben's limitations—but she seems to have made appropriate adjustments. She credits him with a Full Scale IQ of 32. Performance and verbal scores a little lower—let's see, 29 and 28; which puts him in the severe range of mental retardation. And, of course, she noted significant limitations in his adaptive functioning."

"That's about where he always comes out," Perry said.

"However," Sister Colleen continued, "if you look at the summation on the first page, you will find Dr. Griswold lists *no* Axis I diagnosis." She paused, looked intently at Perry. "Only Axis II mental retardation. Do you get what I am saying?"

"No," Perry looked down at the report again. "No, sorry, I don't really. I'm a moron. That's *my* diagnosis."

This time she smiled back, then all business again. "Well, based on Benjamin's history of aggression, multiple discharges, seizure disorder, behavior issues, I was sure there would be a dual diagnosis. And Dr. Griswold apparently looked hard for one. She took her time with him, got to know him, but what she concluded was that Benjamin is angry and frustrated. No separate mental health diagnosis. When he can't convey his needs, he gets mad. When people don't understand him, he gets frustrated. So mad he cannot talk. So mad that other people don't get his gestures. So mad that he might kick, hit, or even bite." She placed her hands on the desk. When she met Perry's eyes, her gaze was firm, unsmiling but not unkind. No, not unkind. "Of course, this strategy has backfired on him."

"God, that is so true," said Perry. "The poor kid wants to participate, he really does. I tell my wife that all the time."

"At Providentia, we do not serve the dually diagnosed. The test results from Dr. Griswold were crucial to me, because our bailiwick is mental retardation—from moderate all the way to profound. But no dually diagnosed kids. Children or adults who have both mental retardation *and* another independent *mental* illness, like schizophrenia, bipolar disorder, something like that, they won't be placed here. What I am saying—what I am taking my time getting to, is that we are willing to give Benjamin a try. Based on what we know and what we have talked about today, we are willing to have him come up here for a trial visit."

Perry stared at Sister Colleen and his eyes prickled. He wanted to jump over the desk and kiss her. When he spoke, his voice cracked.

"Wow," he said. "Wow. I mean, it's been a long haul. Especially lately." He let out a huge choking gasp. "Sorry. I am so sorry. It's only that I have been trying to tell people. I have been trying so long to tell so many people this. Exactly this." He held the report out, then put his forehead in his other hand. "I was ... to be honest with you, Sister, I was starting to give up hope."

Sister Colleen walked around from behind her desk and put a hand on his shoulder. "It can certainly be overwhelming. For families. Truly all resources, especially emotional resources, get spent."

"None of those places worked out—they all said it was Benjamin's fault. Not his disability, but his fault. My family, my wife. We can't do it anymore."

Sister Colleen handed him a box of tissues and he began to weep. She patted his back softly. "Hopefully, we can help him learn some new strategies to cope with all his feelings. And we are good with seizures, too. We have an excellent consulting neurologist from Northwestern. Unfortunately, services for kids like Benjamin have tended to be one size fits all. We are just becoming aware that services should meet the individual's needs—not vice versa. At some point, I will want to talk to you about the homes we plan to build—out in the community. Still way in the future, but Providentia envisions community independent living for some of our residents. We need money, and public will, but it's not out of reach. For today, though, what I am saying, is we will give Benjamin a chance." She walked back to her side of the desk. "After the initial on-site assessment, if that goes to plan, all our residents come in for a standard ninety-day probationary period. We have to see how they adjust to us, to the surroundings, to the other residents and staff. Do you understand?"

She sat back down and waited quietly a minute as Perry blew his nose.

"I know you are pressed for time, but we should talk finances," she said. "Since you are not Illinois residents, you will be private payers, of course. At least until Benjamin reaches age eighteen, when he can seek residency here in Illinois and apply for a Medicaid waiver as an adult."

Perry nodded. "I understand," he said.

"We're not cheap," she said. "You already know that from our phone talks."

"Yes. Shall I—can I give you a deposit today?"

"No, no," she said. "Go home, talk it over with your wife and family. Weigh all your options. You can let me know in a couple of weeks. If you decide to come, if you want Benjamin to try, we could have him start out with an assessment in November. You could come up before Thanksgiving. If all goes well, he could start then, too."

Weigh the other options? Sister Colleen must know as well as Perry did there weren't any. Like most out-of-staters who found their way up here, the Novotnys had tried it all. Beginning with day cares, private schools, public schools, centers for exceptional children. In town, out of town. Then old ladies who wanted to earn a little-extra cash, fat redneck girls who claimed Ben was spoiled rotten, and poor black women from southeast Atlanta, maids-cum-child care workers, who kept Benjamin spruced up and polished. Illegal immigrants from Central America on at least two occasions. *Must have driver's license. Must have patience. Degrees not necessary. English not required.* Residential day programs, weekly boarding, in-state, out of state, state hospitals, state residential centers. It had been one long and desperate road to Providentia.

CHAPTER 7

IVY, NOVEMBER 1991

They all flew up to Chicago with Ben the day before Thanksgiving. Ivy wasn't sure why Dad was making such a big deal about this particular placement. Prior ones had been quick, private affairs, with Dad doing the drop off. Maybe he felt that bringing everyone along, letting the whole family see Ben's new home, would generate *buy-in*. Was that the right term? Collective guilt, more like. Or maybe Dad couldn't stand the thought of doing the deed over a holiday—one supposedly focused on family and gratitude. Some families stayed home at Thanksgiving, ate too much turkey and pumpkin pie, and then stuffed themselves into sweatshirts to play ball in their backyards, Kennedy-family, Hyannisport-style. Not the Novotnys, who favored upheaval and institutionalization over food and football.

"It was Rose Kennedy, right?" Ivy asked Hugo, towards the end of the two-hour flight. Row 22 and Ben crashed out between them. "The kid they institutionalized?"

"Rose*mary*," Hugo whispered over Ben's head. "JFK's big sis."

He needn't worry about waking Ben. The jet hummed white noise and Ben was done in by the full dose of whatever Mom gave him before takeoff. His head rested on Hugo's shoulder with his feet tangled up in Ivy's floor space. Occasionally, his arm jerked, a bad dream, or perhaps a subconscious sense of what was going down. Yet again. In the Midwest, this time. Placement number seven, by Ivy's count.

"Where is she now? Rosemary?"

Hugo leaned toward her. "Wisconsin, I think, or maybe Iowa. They gave her a lobotomy, you know." He scanned her face, waiting for reaction.

"Yeah?" Ivy said, refusing to be fazed.

Hugo whispered, "Well, if Ben doesn't like this place, I won't let him stay. It's only a trial visit. If he doesn't like it, I'll drive right up and bring him back home."

Like you'll have any say," she said. "Like you'll even know if he's unhappy."

"Oh, I'll know."

"How?" Ivy asked. "Smoke signals? Some *special* communication shared only by you two?"

"I always know with Ben." He turned away to look out the window, as the plane slowed for the final approach.

▲▼▲

The merciful sister who met them after lunch in the large administration building at Providentia wore a practical, stretchy blue pantsuit. Like one of the gym teachers at Westmont. She approached the Novotnys with a purposeful stride—seventies-style Hush Puppies on her feet—and extended a firm, bony hand, first to Mom. She was about Mom's age, perhaps even younger, with ruddy skin, crow's feet, and a prominent vertical crease down the middle of her brow. It deepened when she smiled.

"Hello, Mrs. Novotny. I am Sister Colleen." She wrapped Mom's right hand in both of hers and held on until Mom pulled away.

"Call me Caroline," Mom said.

The good sister gave Dad a quick hug. Were nuns supposed to touch men?

"It's good to see you again, Sister Colleen," Dad said. He flushed with his special greeting. "We're all excited to look around, to show Ben where he's going to be staying."

"It's wonderful that the whole family could come to help Ben settle in." She took both of Ben's hands in hers, then held his gaze for a long moment. "I have heard a lot about you, young man." He was still dopey from his plane meds, or she would never have got him to stay still for the greeting.

"And you must be Hugo. Your father has told me all about you— your special bond with your brother." She winked as if Hugo were five, as if she might hand him a lollipop.

She didn't single out Ivy for any special mention, just said, "Hi there."

"We have a full afternoon scheduled. Sister Theresa—our program director—will show you the grounds first. Then Ben's going to have a quick intake and assessment with some of our staff. When he's all finished with that, he can meet his dormitory counselor and you all can go and see his room. We close to visitors at 4 p.m. today, since we're getting ready for our big Thanksgiving feast tomorrow."

Dad practically bounced in place. "Kids, I can't wait for you to see everything: the dorms, the grounds—the vegetable garden is amazing. Hugo, you and Ben are going to *love* the indoor pool. They keep it incredibly warm for swimming lessons and hydrotherapy."

"Jesus," Ivy muttered to Hugo, as they fell in step behind their parents. "Mike Brady tours the asylum."

"Dad's being upbeat."

"Precisely my point," she replied.

On the tour though, Ivy had to agree that this place did look half-decent. With its large, red brick buildings and thick green lawn, Providentia could have been a small college campus or a wealthy private school. Not that different from Westmont Academy, where she and Hugo attended on academic scholarships with a cohort of super-rich Atlanta kids. Several flowerbeds in front of the buildings cradled bountiful displays of orange, red, and yellow chrysanthemums. The nuns, too, seemed better than okay—kind, patient.

Up front, Dad was testing the patience of Sister Theresa, with stories about his construction work, waxing poetic about irrigation and drainage. He always talked too much when he got happy or nervous, and he must have been both, believing perhaps that he had finally found the right place for Ben, hopeful that maybe, maybe this time it would last. Making promises that he probably meant to keep, about helping out in the spring with construction of a new patio.

"Dad's such a schmoozer," Ivy said, loud enough for Mom to hear, stop, and turn around.

"Please don't criticize," she replied, in a rare show of parental solidarity. "He's being friendly, trying to earn a little extra tolerance for Ben. God knows, we'll need that before too long."

She, too, must be holding out hope for this place, this new placement, against her better judgment.

Between the administration building and the workshop, they passed a group of residents: some raking, some jumping on leaf piles, undoing the work. A couple of supervisors stood off to one side, smoking, but no one bossed or yelled. A good sign, Ivy thought.

For the first fifteen minutes of the tour, Ben and Hugo walked together holding hands. Ben seemed groggy and unsure of what was going on, but with the brisk fall air, and the airplane sedation wearing off, he grew livelier. And sure enough, the escape artist within him started seeing possibilities: a wide lawn, perfect for a chase; the tall wrought iron fence in the distance. Ben jerked away from Hugo.

"Not now, buddy," Hugo said, and grabbed his forearm.

But as always, Ben had already fixated: *Escape.* The best part of any attempt for him was the chase and the best chaser was always Hugo. He jerked his arm free and made a break.

Hugo jogged after him, his voice calm. "Not now, fella. Hey, Ben, get back here."

Mom whispered, "Quick. We don't want a scene."

But Ben was lurching forward, picking up speed, in his fastest, gravity-defying lean. He glanced back over his shoulder, flashed his best grin at Hugo. And Hugo, of course, joined the game, slowing down to let Ben get away. As always, Hugo had to play along—pretending to try to catch him, chasing and letting up, racing and slowing down. Wasn't this their life? Wasn't their life one hell of a game? When Hugo caught up to him, Ben collapsed onto the turf and laughed hysterically. Hugo stood him up and marched him back towards the family, "Hut two, three, four."

Mom put a stop to it.

"Enough," she said. "I mean it."

They finished the grand rounds and headed back to the administration building for hot cider and caramel apples made by the residents. Sister Theresa told them to wait in the spacious lobby—a huge fireplace, a grand piano!—for a few minutes, while she found another staff member. This time it was Ben's aide-to-be who came to meet them. She was a broad-shouldered Jamaican woman named Pearl, with a close-cropped afro and a cherry pink tracksuit. Nikes on her feet, which she'd definitely need with Ben. Pearl stood close to six feet tall, the muscle of the institution, no doubt. She told Mom and Dad that she'd be on Ben's dorm floor every night, and with him at each meal. She called herself his Q, which was short for something—a qualified provider for the mentally retarded? *Ha.* Hugo should get an honorary certificate. Ben took an immediate liking to Pearl, her heft, her hue, or her throaty laugh. He often had an embarrassing attraction to people of color, but Pearl didn't seem to mind. Maybe she was used to being prodded and poked. She explained that she would work with the whole treatment team to plan Ben's daily activities, classes, work, and social programs. She assured Mom and Dad that she was trained in CPR, had finished a special course on epilepsy, and knew how to handle seizures. Her last client had them frequently. But right now, she wanted to take Ben for a quick assessment with the rest of his daily activities team—get a sense of where he would fit in best with learning, recreation and chores. While Mom and Dad would go meet with Sister Colleen to fill out paperwork, Hugo and Ivy could hang out in the lobby or the coffee shop, wait until Ben was done, then they'd all head back to the hotel for the night.

▲▼▲

Ivy and the brothers spent all Friday morning in the hotel pool. Hugo was trying to explain to Ben what was coming that afternoon: The Nuns. Pearl. Providentia. But Ben wasn't interested. He was splash-happy in the water, then later delighted with Elmo on TV. He had all

82

he needed in life—water, television, Hugo. Big bonus: a hotel bed to bounce on.

After lunch, they checked out and drove the rental back over to Providentia, through the wrought iron gates, along the long gravel driveway. While the parents met again with Sister Colleen, Ivy and Hugo took Ben to his dorm to check in with Pearl and to begin to unpack. Pearl went to get sheets for the bed. Hugo tacked his favorite diving poster over Ben's headboard. Full-frontal Greg Louganis captured and held mid-flight, his legs extending to the sky, each muscle on his torso rippling and striving; his arms at ninety degrees on either side of his body.

"Isn't that kind of mean?" Ivy asked, "Pinning up such physical perfection in a place where so many are struggling?"

But Ben was intrigued; he stood on his mattress besides Hugo and stared at the poster. "Guh," he said.

"Go ahead," Hugo said to Ben, "You can touch it. I am like the diver. Flying high. I'm gonna have my eye on you, boy. Yes, I am. I'll be tuning in."

Ivy shook her head and started to sort out Ben's belongings. She divided them among three empty dresser drawers: underwear, socks and a stack of bandana bibs on top; t-shirts and sweat shirts in the middle, pants on the bottom drawer. Sneakers and winter boots in the closet. Hats, scarves, mittens, stored for the coming cold. Two swimsuits and a towel on a hook. She put a photo of Ben with Hugo on top of the dresser. Pearl returned with linens and helped Ivy make the bed. When they were finished, Ivy placed Ben's Teddy Ruxpin sing-along bear on his pillow.

At 3 p.m., Charlie, the new roomie, returned from his workshop job, escorted by his very own Q, a blond-haired white guy with a straggly goatee. Charlie had black paint on his hands and under his fingernails as he shook hands with everyone and looked around, slightly bewildered by the Novotny influx. Charlie had tousled brown hair, a pale face with a swath of freckles across his nose and cheeks. He was shorter than Ben—around five feet, two—and beefier. Down syndrome's telltale almond eyes. He seemed slightly older, too—Twenty? Twenty-three? Hard to tell—but definitely not a kid anymore. Ivy guessed that placid Charlie was supposed to balance out Ben's frenetic energy. After his Q left, Charlie sat on his own bed and licked his lips. Hugo tried to draw him out a little, talking, asking about his day, his work, but he remained silent. At least until Ben began bouncing on his bed.

"He's silly," Charlie said, and laughed. "Silly boy."

Charlie's laughter only spurred Ben on. He bounced up and down again, whooping with glee, up and down, up and down, while Charlie said, "Silly, silly boy."

Hugo said. "It will be all right. Ben's having some fun. He'll settle down soon."

"You're right," Ivy said. "Ben is a bit silly; but if we ignore him, he'll stop soon." She sat down on the bed next to Charlie, tried to distract him. "So how long have you been here?"

He didn't reply at first, but as she continued talking, he looked at Ben and said, "That your brother?"

"Yes," she said. "That's right. Ben's going to be your new roommate."

"That your Dad?" Charlie asked, pointing at Hugo.

"No, he's my brother, too. I have two brothers."

"You their sister?"

"That's right. My name is Ivy."

Ben kept bouncing, but Ivy had Charlie distracted now. She picked up a picture from Charlie's side table. An image of him in winter garb, ski hat, gloves, dark green parka, looking intently, into the camera. In the background a hill and a ski lift. "Do you like to ski?"

Charlie laughed. "I don't do skiing," he says. "You a silly sister."

"Yes, I am." Ivy laughed.

"You are so silly." Charlie repeated. "I got more photos." He reached under his pillow and pulled out a small vinyl album.

Ivy sat next to Charlie on his bed and looked at his photos. Ben bounced across from them on his own twin bed. Up and down, down and up, down and reverse down. What one was missing genetically, the other overdid. Charlie's book held a series of 4 x 6 photos, all solo shots of him, taken in a formal yearbook pose. In most of them, he looked serious—never cracking a smile or showing a tooth. Years of his life—sixteen, eighteen, maybe more—marked off by another institutional photo day. Shirts changed from blue to green to red, hair was longer or shorter, and Charlie aged a little with each page turn. How long had he been here? How many roommates had this nice respectable, rule-bound boy been through? How many Qs? Did he even have a family? Did they visit?

Ivy had to stand up and walk around. Two beds, two side tables, a closet and some photos. Two Qs for the two roomies. Would Ben have a chance here? Charlie may fit in, but Ben? Was it better to follow the rules and get to stay in one place forever—to build a sense of stability and permanence, even if it could be measured only by annual photos—or to be like Ben, loving his family, but being shuffled back and forth between home and homes, coming and going, loved but not really wanted, and not belonging anywhere?

Ben was still bouncing when Mom and Dad returned together and said it was time for goodbyes. Planes to catch, places to go, lives to lead. Without Ben, at least for a while. Ivy patted him on the arm and said, "Be good, buddy." But he bounced through her advice, then through his parents' hugs and kisses. Mom wept as she tried to pull him to her for a last embrace, but he batted her away, *killjoy, fun-blocker. Don't stop my bouncing.* Dad said, "Maybe it's better this way—not to make a big deal—not to draw this out. Hug him quick, Hugo, and let's get going."

As Ivy and her family walked away down the dormitory hall, the bed creaked, and Pearl closed the bedroom door. How long would she tolerate the bouncing? How patient could any Q be?

▲▼▲

Later that afternoon, at O'Hare, a thunderstorm moved through, stopping all air traffic for two hours. Finally, they boarded. Ivy watched as Mom and Dad argued quietly while the plane taxied. When they reached cruising altitude, and the seatbelt sign shut off, Dad fell asleep, with his right temple pressed against the little oval window, his blond hair flapping down over his eye. *Mission accomplished?* Mom leaned over to tuck a strand behind his exposed ear. If he felt this gesture as a sign of affection, or perhaps conciliation, he did not let her know. Mom pulled out an article from her over-stuffed Kenya bag and started to read. Something for her never-ending project on sacrificial feminists? How could she already turn her attention to her work? A few hours removed from Ben, was she feeling a sweet, small seed of relief? Ivy listened to her music, wanting to tune her family out. Beside her, though, Hugo did not read or sleep or listen to his Walkman. He studied the tray table. Focused on the plastic latch. What was he thinking? Was his mind on Ben?

Was it yesterday—it felt like such a long time ago—that after a

86

huge Thanksgiving buffet, they took Ben to the hotel's indoor pool and teamed up to create a crazy new game? Ben in the water, Hugo and Ivy pushing one another on the deck above him, yelling back and forth: "You go first," "No, Hugo." "Hugo first," "No, you go." On and on, tugging and pushing, until one or both of them ended up splashing in the pool, next to a squealing and delighted Ben.

Thirty thousand feet high, and the four of them heading home. Dad, Mom, Hugo, and Ivy. A perfect nuclear family. The airplane's hum worked through the seat and into Ivy's legs and back and brain. She closed her eyes. Ben. By now, he would have finished his first dinner in the bright fluorescent lighting of the Providentia cafeteria. Would he charge the fence on the walk back to his dorm? Would Pearl play along like Hugo always did? Would she let him bed bounce tonight? *Just tonight, one more night.* Maybe Ivy should have tried to talk to Pearl a bit more; she should have explained how bouncing had always, always seemed to soothe him. *Please, let him bounce. Please be more patient with him than I sometimes have been.* If Dad had wanted all the family along on this trip to see the new place and to make him feel better about leaving Ben again, it hadn't worked. Now, images, smells, and names flooded Ivy's brain: freckle-faced and somber Charlie and caramel-colored Pearl. The goateed Q who dropped off Charlie. The nasty stench of the cafeteria food, the neatly manicured campus. Nuns in habits, skimming across the wooden floors. Maybe this was precisely why Dad had brought the family along—so the rest of the family would carry this weight. A shared burden. Ivy wanted to give it all back—the faces, the smells, the sounds. But now the pictures came fast and powerful: Ben flat out on his bed, getting diapered for the night. Pearl pinning him down, pulling on his PJs. Teddy Ruxpin beginning to sing: *come dream with me tonight.* Pearl turning off the light, saying good night, closing the door and walking slowly down the hall. Oh god, let him sleep. Teddy spinning through his saccharine lullaby repertoire. *We'll go to far off places.* Ben under his quilt, his thoughts bouncing up and down, but landing finally on Hugo. Ben figuring it out, in the dark and the quiet. *Hugo?* Soon, soon, the groaning would begin, deep in his belly, then louder and longer, across the city sky and melding into the airplane's roar.

CHAPTER 8

HUGO, FEBRUARY 1992

The last dive, a forward two-and-a-half somersault, tuck position, was Hugo's favorite. Not because the degree of difficulty at 2.4 ranked highest of his eleven competition dives, and if he nailed it tonight, he would win. He loved the dive for its purity. Distilled to its essence, it was launch and commit. At practice after practice, through the fall and winter, Billy Joe had deconstructed it into many more phases—the approach, the hurdle, the flight, the grab, the spin, the spot, the kick-out and the entry—so that Hugo sometimes spent an entire two-hour session on one such element. But despite his coach's dissection and instruction, he still loved the dive, loved what it demanded: launch the body high above the board, then commit to the tight, fierce vortex of the spin.

In three years of diving for Westmont Academy, he had witnessed much more launching than committing. Muscular wrestlers who had come to the first diving practice, only to quit after a few face-smacks. Big football types who balked on their first attempt off the three-meter board, then bad-mouthed diving as a sissy-sport. Lean-limbed, arty boys who thought their sense of style would transfer from dry land to diving, only to find themselves scattered like a pile of sticks across the pool's hard surface.

"There is a reason the swim team has fifty members trying out today, the diving team only ten," Billy Joe had told his divers, back in September, after their first grueling practice of the season. He paced across the deck-tile, barely raising his voice above a conspiratorial whisper while the boys shivered on a long, wooden bench, nursing bruised egos and bodies. "Every one of you here today could be a diver. Even if you lack talent, strength, a certain body type. I don't require those things. Diving does not require those things." He waited until he felt them relax a little, begin to think themselves capable, then he turned in a squinty-eyed inquisition, his finger poking at the air. "But do you have the will? I bet half of you have no idea why you are here. Well, I *demand* will. I *demand* persistence. I *demand* courage." His tongue slid across his thin top lip, as if tasting the demands. "If you can give me those things, come back tomorrow. If you can give me those things, then you can call yourself a diver."

The ones who returned the next day and the next and through the weeks and months that followed, learned that to call yourself a diver, you had to be both strange and driven. Hugo had first understood it late one summer afternoon when he was eleven years old, fooling around in the water, trying desperately to entertain Ben. He leapt and spun and twisted off the crappy aluminum board Dad had added to the backyard pool, all afternoon shamelessly working that board, splashing cannonballs, crashing jack-knifes, arcing swallow dives ending with a belly-flop, while Ben, the easiest of audiences, his most loyal fan, laughed and slapped the surface. Then, as dusk was settling, Hugo stood on the board, gathered himself, and paced forward three steps, hurdled into his first one and a half somersault dive. The height, the spin, and the rip of the entry in his ears. The name settled onto him as he swam underwater to the pool's edge. *Diver.* A name he could use to channel chaos, to turn all his feelings into a tight and disciplined practice, beginning at home with Ben, and later at Westmont. He would master mechanics under Billy Joe's gaze, always pushing beyond what he thought he could do, more spinning, more practice, and more pain, punishing his body for the brilliant things it learned how to do.

Tonight was the payoff. A group of forty-two state qualifiers started the competition in the early morning, completing five preliminary dives. They were all respectable—hard workers. They had to be to complete the required dives in all five groups—forward, backward, inward, reverse, and twisting; they had to be to earn the minimum state qualifying score. After the scores were tallied, the top sixteen divers went through to the afternoon semifinals and completed three more dives. More tallying, more elimination until eight competitors remained for the finals. All Hugo's training and preparation would come down to these few seconds of performance, capped by his final, and yes, favorite, forward two-and-a-half tuck.

He sat on the finalists' bench, waiting his turn.

Divers got used to playing sloppy seconds to swimmers, but not here at UGA's Kreidler complex. This was the big time, boys. Three concrete platforms and four springboards, as well as a trampoline, and dry board off in a separate section. The names of All-American divers were scripted on large red flags hanging high in the humid air. All day, divers were the star attraction; they owned the natatorium, marked it with their backpacks and towels, their rituals and their compulsions, wiping down with chamois towels, stretching on the deck, pacing their practice-approaches, closing their eyes, and visualizing their flips and rips. At night, only diving royalty remained for the last round. And Hugo would be king.

A small crowd waited in the bleachers—the obligated teammates and, of course, the families of the finalists. All waiting. Watching. Hugo's own misfit family showed up late in the day and spread out across the natatorium's benches in a visual manifestation of their usual disconnection. Mom, hollow-cheeked and wild-haired, gray sacks under both her eyes, sat in the rarefied air of the top row, while Dad, restless, leaned over the balcony that scarcely railed in his enthusiasm. Dad's face always had a feverish glow and his body a pumped-up vigor that Hugo found embarrassing—made him want to put a hand on his shoulder and say patiently, "relax." Ivy anchored the mid-section of the bleachers with a heavy textbook open on her lap; she perused it, while occasionally casting a martyrish eye on bouncy Ben, beside her.

Ben ... back home again. Booted from his Chicago group home after only two months. He had pushed his roommate into the pool. A joke. Hugo knew that Ben had intended it as a joke. How many times—thousands—a hundred thousand, perhaps, had Ben pushed Hugo into their backyard pool, day after summer day? How many times had Ivy and Hugo pushed each other into the pool for Ben's amusement? Even at the hotel last Thanksgiving in Chicago, on the night before they left him they'd played the same game: *Hugo first, no, you go.* Shoving each other into the pool, pushing and falling and splashing and all for Ben's amusement. What idiots they had been—teaching Ben dangerous tricks and wrapping them up in good feelings. Ben only wanted to share *his* good feelings with Charlie, an intimacy, a brotherly love. This is what brothers do. Thing is, idiot-love almost killed poor Charlie. Ambulances, EMTs, CPR. How the two boys had gotten over to the pool in another building unsupervised was a question no one seemed to want to discuss. Ben—Ben was the one who pulled the fire alarm at the last minute. And that alarm had saved Charlie's life. Did Ben know what he was doing? Making all that noise? Or was that more fun? Splash, Screams, Sirens! And where was the Qualified Mental Retardation Professional who should have known the two boys had left the dorm? The nuns were sorry, they said, terribly sorry to see Ben go. He'd been doing great in his new home. But Charlie's father was some big-wig banker on the Providentia Board of Trustees, and insisted on expulsion. *For the safety of all the residents.* The QMRPs—poor Pearl who wasn't watching and some other guy— also got the sack.

With his new driver's license, Hugo had helped Dad drive to Chicago: twenty-four hours up and back in one weekend, to bring Hugo's number one fan back home, back to the State of Georgia, and woo-hoo, in time for the state diving competition. Could Ben possibly have known *that*? Known what he needed to do to get home?

Sorry, Charlie, was the name Hugo had come up with for this latest incident.

Hugo felt now that he was the one who owed Charlie an apology. *It was all my fault for teaching Ben how to push people in.* Someday Hugo would find Charlie and tell him to his face. Or, at least, write his family a letter. *I know you are angry with my brother, but blame me; I taught him a very dangerous game.*

Ben started jumping up and down in the stands and waving at Hugo. Ivy offered him a lollipop, trying to pull him back to sitting. With his family here as fans, who needed competition? But Hugo had plenty of it tonight. The top divers from throughout the state. Even Michael Hickey, a senior on his own team who'd put on a surprisingly strong performance in the prelims and made it through to the final round, would love nothing better than to dethrone Hugo, the target for all the other divers for the past two years. And the rest of the Westmont team would be behind Michael's coup attempt. Hugo could almost feel them as Michael began his chase in the prelims, feel them willing Hugo to fail, wanting him to misstep, misjudge, miss. They wanted to punish him for his hard work, because he was too aloof with the other divers, because he skipped summer camps and trained on his own, because he worked silently at practice, even when coach's demands seemed outlandish, verging on the abusive. Billy Joe punching him in the stomach to show him how to tighten; Billy Joe making him hold a handstand for thirty minutes straight. No matter, he could take it. And his teammate's dislike was respect, if you thought about it—respect that Hugo had earned for his commitment, for his hard work. Thank you, he wanted to tell them, as they willed him to smack hard against the surface, thank you for the tribute of your jealousy.

After the semis—eight dives—Hugo was a close second behind Randy Schmidt of Lovett School. As Hugo stood and shook out in preparation for his final three, he caught Billy Joe watching him from the coaches' bench. It could have been the angle of his gaze across the pool, or the enhanced night lighting of the natatorium, but Hugo realized Billy Joe's eyes were the same dappled blue as the water; not even the tone so much as the way the color never rested. The movement of color. He felt an impulse to run over and tell him. But Billy Joe had already turned away and was looking back down at his clipboard—playing with his slide rule, not offering Hugo his full attention. Hugo felt a new surge—impatience with his coach. He leaned into the wall to stretch out his left calf, pressing his heel into the concrete deck. Screw him. He could ignore his coach right back. Then again, he felt it: Billy Joe's watery eyes finding him, observing his movements, locking in on his back, cool, controlling. That's better, Hugo thought. Focus on me, now. I am your hope. For all your efforts at appearing unbiased, working with the other divers, admit that I am your real interest. I feel it when your hands correct my form. I sense it now in your gaze. Keep looking at me. Show me how good I am, tell me what I am worth.

On the tenth dive, Hugo over-rotated his reverse one and one-half pike and splashed high and loud on his entry. Stupid mistake on a familiar dive. Ben loved it, though, and screeched out his approval, even as the judges marked it down. Now Hugo would have to perform his final dive flawlessly. Billy Joe started to tap his pencil in agitation. All season, they'd argued about the placement of the two-and-a-half tuck. Hugo always wanted to save the big dive for last—the big finale, loaded with difficulty. Billy Joe disagreed, *You don't want to have to perform the hardest dive under the heaviest pressure.* He wanted a lineup that put Hugo's strengths up front, got the tricky optional dives out of the way early, so he could enter the last round with a commanding lead and a psychological advantage over his opponents.

As he waited for the final round to begin, Hugo knew he was right. *I do want it*—the heaviest pressure to perform. He wanted to be in that hole and dig his way out. *I want the dive, the audience, the last moment to be my own, no one else's preparations or demands coming into play.* What he loved, had always loved about this sport, this art, since he first front-flipped off that crappy, backyard board was that he alone took control. Diving required the ultimate harnessing and capture of forces normally out of control: The pull of gravity opposes, but you marshal your body—not to beat gravity, a futile endeavor—but to shape it, turn the flailing into a controlled work of beauty. Control it and hold it, just a second, even if only for a fleeting moment of harmony. Eleven dives. Eleven moments.

Last summer in the backyard pool, he had asked Ivy to sit with her watch and actually time each second he was in the air during a series of competition dives. Each second, each micro-second between launch and entry. She did it reluctantly, but accurately, she said, from the pacing through the entry on each of his dives. The tally was under a minute. Each moment that he would spend suspended before the judge's gaze—how to score those segments of hurtling, controlled energy? A minor balk or a slight misstep ended the performance. Not like in swimming, where you got two false starts before elimination, a 200 IM where a slow butterfly leg could be recovered in the breaststroke, or even running track, where a miler could stumble, recover, and then go on to win. Diving was all or nothing, control or lack of it. Launch and commit. Succeed or fail.

On his final, eleventh dive, Michael Hickey's inward one-and-a-half brought him perilously close to the board; he fell to seventh place in the standings—*where he belongs*, Hugo thought. Competitors five, four, and three held their places. Hugo wrung out his chamois, gave his shoulders a final wipe down, and walked quickly toward the waiting area. He let himself glance briefly up at the spectator's gallery. His family was trying to sit and spectate, to be, for once, a normal family. His parents had, remarkably, found space together in the middle row, and pinned Ben between them, given him another lollipop to keep him quiet. Ivy was gone—who knows where—leaving her massive textbook stranded on the bench—but what else was new? He was better off without her agitation stirring the air.

Billy Joe waved Hugo over for a final check-in, annoyed no doubt that Hugo had dared to look up to find his family, annoyed more certainly that the family brought Ben along. He wanted Hugo focused only on the dive and not thinking about the spectators, his family, his loony-tune brother who could undo years of preparation with one of his fits. He made that clear throughout the season, throughout the week prior to state—focus on your rituals, no distractions, you and your dive. But this moment right before the dive was Hugo's. *It's my moment, Coach.* And instead of stopping for last minute advice, he pretended not to see Billy Joe, walked right past him to wave instead at Ben in the stands. Hail the King of Loonies. For this was Ben's moment, too. He'd been there with Hugo, training since the beginning. Each summer, every day. *Tonight, we will both be kings.*

And Hugo waited at the steps of the one-meter board. The announcer calls out: *Hugo Novotny.* The attributes of his dive. *Forward two-and-one-half somersault. Tuck position. Degree of difficulty, two point four.* Billy Joe, Hugo's parents, and he sensed, even Ben, held their breath. He climbed one-two up the sandpaper steps, then stopped, waited. He heard a single loud cough from the gallery, then caught the head judge's nod to proceed, before pulling into himself for his final count.

One, two, three, hurdle. Launch and commit.

▲▼▲

Deep beneath the surface, for the instant between the expectation of the intended dive and the dissection of the actual dive, there was nothing to prove, nothing to improve, just a few seconds without scrutiny.

Light and shadows danced together in the water at the bottom of the well, silent motion, moving silence. Nothing left to do. Sometimes during diving practice, Hugo lingered in this moment, drawing it out, letting the water caress him outside of real time, deferring the inevitable critique that would come with surfacing. If only life were like this, the water wrapping him, softening him, protecting him. But today he burst back into the thick echoing air so fast that his ears popped and he stroked rapidly to the wall, shaking out his hair, eager to take his rewards, eager to live in the emerging moment. And yes, already, the buzz—the small, distinct truth of Hugo's dive—from the first step of the approach through the hand-over-hand rip through the surface— was filtered and processed by the seven judges. He pushed out of the water, stood on the deck, found his chamois and swabbed at his chest and thighs, before looking at the scoreboard. And the crowd's buzz exploded into a roar. His marks captured, as close to perfect as had been awarded in Georgia high school diving history. And even before the final competitor, Randy Schmidt, completed his very respectable two-and-a-half pike, Hugo knew; the crowds knew. Hugo would hold first place by more than twenty points.

Billy Joe ran over, thumped him on the shoulder and pulled him into a bear hug, then quickly pushed him back to arms' length and mouthed through the cheers of the crowd. "Didn't I tell you we could do it?"

Ben loped across the pool deck, his arms in a big bear hug around his own torso, moaning his happy moan as he closed in.

"Hey, little man," Hugo held up his index finger. "First place. You and me. First place." Ben charged and Hugo bent and lifted him into a long, wet hug. Hugo lifted him up high and spun him around and around on the deck, his feet swinging out and over the diving well.

"I am so proud of you," Dad said, when they stopped spinning. "All that practicing out back... Your hard work really paid off." He pulled Hugo and Ben into a three-way hug.

Mom, too, waited her turn and hugged Hugo. Her eyes took him in, even as she seemed a little shy, a little hesitant. "What an incredible accomplishment."

"We won't stay for the awards ceremony," Dad said, "I need to get Ben back home before all hell breaks loose. Where's Ivy? Is she riding with you, Caroline? Are you staying here a while? For the ceremony?"

▲▼▲

Later, after pizza with the team in Athens, Hugo rode back to Atlanta in the Westmont van, luxuriating in the place of honor, the front passenger seat, soaking in his accomplishment. From the back, the hum of the other divers' conversations, punctuated with tired laughter. And in the front, his coach quiet, content, as he stared out at the road. Hugo victorious. Billy Joe trained him on the trapeze, taught him proper technique, the twists and turns, mechanics and adjustments, so Billy Joe was a winner, too. But Hugo knew something about tonight's achievement that he could never explain to Coach. It wasn't enough to master the intricacies of the dive. It wasn't enough to have nerves of steel in your performance. The truth of the dive, the whole self on display could never be assessed by degrees of difficulty multiplied by points, just as desire and commitment could never be quantified, only offered as a gift. You have to throw yourself off the board, as if your life or another's depends on it. And wasn't it Ben who first showed him how to take what life gives you and turn it, how to take pain and twist it, control and shape it—reverse and forward, backward and inward—how to take what you can do and transcend it? And underwater, in the sacred moment after a perfect dive, it would always be Ben he sensed first, never words of praise, of course, never any words, but something else, something stronger and more persistent: their shared heart beating.

CHAPTER 9

PERRY, MARCH 1992

Trey slapped a padded hand on Perry's shoulder and pulled him close for this beer-buzzed confession. "I owe you, man." His words hit Perry's face with a gassy heat. "I owe you big time, right?"

They were side-by-side at the bar in Jalisco's; 4 pm—after the construction workers' knock-off time, and Trey was already three Dos Equis down and halfway through the Nachos Grande platter.

Damn right Trey owed him. Perry's crew had completed the spec house at River's Edge ahead of schedule, despite a cease work order from the Atlanta Planning Commission that shut down operations in December. Some bureaucratic bullshit about flood zones, that had Perry walking the low-lying lots with an APC inspector for hours, pointing out the natural causeways and dams of the Chattahoochee River; when even that didn't allay the inspector's concerns, Perry offered some assistance on a "little construction project" that the inspector happened to mention he would be starting on his own house. And Perry managed this ... negotiating and assisting ... while still supervising his guys, who worked long days and weekends, cut no corners, spared no time or expense to get the spec done. Boy, was it a beaut: all wood and glass, perched on the steep slope of the top lot, commanding dramatic views of the clay-churning Chattahoochee.

Perry's pride was justified, too. He'd culled the land himself: several bone-rattling 'dozer days, razing the scab pines, slowing down to preserve a few mature hardwoods that would lend the lot "character." He even convinced the harried architect to re-do the preliminary drawings and figure out a way to configure the deck around a huge oak. That would be the kind of detail Huff Home buyers drooled over—another example of the "innovative, yet ecologically harmonious development" that *Southern Living* would feature in the cover article for its April edition. Half of the lots in the River's Edge development had already sold; the rest would no doubt go after the magazine article hit the stands.

Trey took a long, sudsy swallow, and wiped his mouth with the back of his hand. He tapped the counter with his empty bottle, summoning another round. "I always pay my debts, Perry." He punctuated this assertion with a deep bass belch. "So here it is: an all-expense paid trip to Colorado. Take the wife, the kiddies. Y'all can have my Keystone cabin. Snow's great this time of year, too. And we won't be breaking ground again here till after spring rains. Go on and get lost for a week."

A Novotny family getaway. Ridiculous, on first, and even second thought, a Novotny family getaway. Would never work. Not with the older kids' school schedules. Not with Caroline's courses and seminars. And certainly, certainly not with Ben back home again.

But later that night, Perry thought: *Why not? Why the hell not? Lots of families take trips each year. Hell, many go twice a year.*

Hilton Head. Aspen. Kiawah Island. So why not us? Are we really that exceptional? Are we kowtowing to what ifs: the accidents, seizures, medical crises? Time to change that. Yep. Time for a family getaway before all the kids are gone.

Amazingly, the stars aligned as Perry made the plans: Ivy and Hugo's spring break coincided with Caroline's—something that had never happened before. Hugo was done with diving for the season; no training sessions would cut into the week. And when Ivy fussed a little, saying she wanted to join her senior class lark to Sea Island, Perry told her she could ask her best friend Harper to come skiing. That left Ben. He hated cold weather; skiing was out of the question, and the altitude would probably screw up his fragile equilibrium. He'd be fine if the family left him for a few short days with an appropriate caregiver. Hugo, being Hugo, would offer to watch Ben in the cabin while the others skied, but Perry insisted that they all needed time away—even the best Boy Scout needed to let his guard down sometime and relax.

An appropriate after-school caregiver appeared—practically out of nowhere—in the form of Debbie Dothan, a Georgia State student who'd been helping Caroline with Ben a few afternoons each week, ever since the Sisters of Mercy gave him the boot in early February. Debbie had come with glowing recommendations (from Petey's mom, who had used her for occasional respite care and weekend getaways), and, so far, she'd done a good job: always on time to meet Ben's bus. Even dealt with a couple of grand mals in February. No freak outs about the seizures or the unpleasant task of giving Ben the rescue meds. She loved the little guy. Perry and Caroline left lists and instructions, phone numbers, and a stack of videos, hugged Ben tight, and said their anxious goodbyes. When the family pulled away in a cab for the airport, Ben stood at the top of the driveway, holding Debbie's hand, bouncing in place and flapping his free arm.

"I don't know about this, Perry," Caroline had said, looking back as the taxi pulled away. "Are we flirting with disaster?"

"He's in his own home, with his toys, his videos, and a one-on-one caregiver to boot. It's gonna be just fine."

She didn't argue further. She didn't have the will or the energy, and she must know they all needed this chance at normality.

After they retrieved suitcases and duffel bags at Stapleton International Airport, Perry arranged for an Alpine Shuttle to drive them the three-plus hours through the icy mountain roads to the Keystone resort area. Ivy and Harper took the third row of the van for themselves and their backpacks and didn't shut up the whole way. When the driver turned through a series of tight switchbacks, the girls screamed in mock terror. Hugo and Caroline sat in the middle seat and didn't say a word. Perry had told Hugo he could bring a friend along too, but he'd shrugged off this offer; he'd already had to leave his favorite companion at home. Caroline had a novel propped open on her lap, but she was not reading. She actually looked a little green around the gills and Perry guessed she was feeling nauseated from the travel. No one could read on these roads, the bumping, the fear of falling, the vertigo as the van zig-zagged higher and higher. Still, a thick book was always good cover, a way out of the perfunctory chats that Perry was then required to conduct with the taxi driver. Perry, the extrovert, the communicator, the go-to guy. Perhaps it was the burden carried by any child of immigrants: Translator. Facilitator. The first generation's duty to make nice with the neighbors. *Who's Dad talking to now?* the kids routinely asked Caroline when he engaged with strangers, workers, neighbors. Over time, it had become more accusation than question. But really, weren't they the ultimate beneficiaries of his charm? This trip, for instance, would never have happened without it.

Trey's Keystone home was, like the man, ostentatious, demanding of attention and, one couldn't help acknowledging, worthy of receiving it. *Cabin?* That was the word Trey had used; Perry felt stupid for not recognizing the faux humility. Six thousand square feet, a monster of a house, set apart from several smaller monsters, across the wide base of a mountain. Six bedrooms, five baths, two living rooms, massive kitchen with vaulted ceiling, granite counters, butcher block island, and a heated Italian stone floor. The fireplace in the living area was hand-laid quarry stone—each piece would have been carefully selected and placed by a skilled worker, probably someone from the old world. Bronze pokers and tongs, as well as a long-handled brush and dustpan stood in a rack, next to a large pile of wood. Amish quilts, a lustrous cherry rocking chair, a hand-crafted wood sled covered with customized cut glass to make a coffee table. None of the typical vacation home tacky—real antiques, no expense spared. Jesus, Ben could have done some damage in here.

While the kids scoped out the downstairs game room, Caroline and Perry checked out their master suite. A large Karastan rug draped on one wall, above the mahogany bed's headboard. Three smaller oriental rugs were spaced around the room. A fireplace in there, too. And outside, built into a cedar deck, a Jacuzzi seeped a steady white vapor out from under the edges of its thick vinyl cover. Beyond the deck, behind, up, and all-around, the pine-dressed whiteness.

"Could it be any more perfect?" Perry slid open the glass door to the deck. A gasp of wintry air hit them, and he wrapped his arms around Caroline. "After dinner, perhaps me and the good professor can have a glass of wine together, and soak away our troubles in the hot tub? A little vacation lubrication ..."

"That would be nice," she said and patted him on his hand, before disentangling and retreating into the bedroom.

That would be Caroline, Perry thought, *humoring me.* When had he become another child to brush off with one of her desultory pats? Why couldn't she meet him halfway? Sometimes he thought their marriage was half dead.

"We need this, Caroline," he said, following her and trying to let his earnestness win out over his anger. "We need this time together."

She stopped and turned—seemed to summon up some last piece of herself, as she leaned in to kiss him on the lips. "You're right." Her own were dry and flaky, surprisingly cold. "I am trying. Really, I am. I have been so disheartened this month, with Ben home again, and ..."

"All I want is some time with you."

She nodded somberly. "I am tired, Perry. So very tired. I don't have an ounce of reserve."

"I don't want to take from you. I want us both to re-charge." He sat on the bed, patted the thick snow white eiderdown. "Join me, Sweet Caroline. A quick nap together?"

A mid-afternoon rest, how long had it been? Ben had never slept well. As an infant, a baby, a toddler, he was wild through the night, thrashing and moaning and crashing out of bed. Days, he was constant motion. The seizures, too. Someone had to be alert, just in case. An ancient baby monitor still buzzed on their nightstand at home. But this week, for once, they could nap. They would wake refreshed, maybe hang out in the hot tub. Perry would ask Caroline about her work, how her writing was coming. No, not a good idea. He'd keep it small: innocuous talk, the snow, the mountains, the food they ate that day. They would enjoy each other once again; he would massage her shoulders at night and maybe, for the first time in a while, maybe they would make love in this large bed.

"I am sorry," she said, shaking her beautiful head of hair. "Can you let me be alone right now? Just for a while to settle in."

Jesus. Perry stood and walked out of the room. He was tired, too, tired of always keeping her afloat—emotionally. He did not need this. Okay, she did the lion's share of the Ben care, medicines, baths, and meals. But Perry worked hard, damn hard every day at his job. And still every night he came home in a good mood, and even when he didn't feel like it, he smiled and talked to their kids and asked about Caroline's day and read Ben his stories, and put him in his Depends and his PJs, laid next to him on the floor mattress, and rubbed his scrawny back, sometimes for hours, until one of them fell asleep. Why wouldn't she let them even collapse on the bed together, if not for sex, then for a good long nap?

Well, if Caroline wouldn't join in, couldn't enjoy this gift of time together, he'd take the kids to get skis. He checked his watch, still on Atlanta time. It was 7 p.m. back home; Ben would be finished with dinner, probably watching a video. Raffi, Spot, or one of his Wee Sing & Plays. Perry decided to make a quick call, check in with Debbie. He slipped into one of the bedrooms and dialed home. All was fine, Debbie assured him.

He heard the girls giggling and started to head back down to the kitchen. The wall beside the staircase was covered with Huff family photos. In one, a younger, less beefy Trey and his blonde pre-fab wife, stood proudly at a beach house, behind their five sons, all of whom seemed to have inherited the mother's fine features and slightly vapid gaze. In the others, bleached-blond boys with their shaggy-seventies hairdos, surfing, swimming, sailing, struggling to hold up their fresh ocean catch.

Ivy and Harper joined him midway on the stairs, scoping out the pictures, rating the Huff boys.

"Now this one is super-cute," said Harper, pointing to a tan, curly haired boy and licking her lips.

"Trey's youngest," Perry said, a little taken aback by Harper's brashness. "Danny. Works with his dad now. A little too old for you girls."

"I like older guys." Harper winked at Perry.

Jesus, this girl was trouble.

"These pictures are from their beach house," Perry added. Obviously. "They have a place in Sea Island as well."

"And I bet that place is covered with pictures of them skiing," Ivy said. "All this wealth and yet they're always asking themselves, *Is where I am where I want to be?*"

"Oh, don't get philosophical on us," Harper said and punched Ivy in the shoulder.

The rental agency had left a large welcome basket on the maple butcher block—fruit, cheeses, a foot-long salami—especially for Perry, no doubt. Trey was always teasing him about his old world tastes—his daily sandwich with Bavarian salami. A note in the basket read. "Enjoy the week, Perry. You deserve it."

All right, then. Perry hacked into a bright red, nut-studded cheese ball.

"Want some?" he offered to Hugo, who had found a stool at the kitchen counter and was staring out the windows at the mountains. "Hugo—do you want some of this cheese? It looks awful but it actually tastes pretty damn good."

He shook his head.

"Beautiful out there, huh?"

"Yeah."

"Slab of salami?"

"No thanks."

"Sure? You all right? You look kind of, I dunno, wiped out."

"I'm fine. Not hungry." He blinked his eyes and smiled unconvincingly. "I think I'm gonna watch some TV." He walked slowly across the huge living room, passing the girls who were still pointing and snickering at all the pictures at the base of the stairs.

Perry hacked off another chunk of cheese and kept eating it right off the counter. It was, after all, his hard-earned vacation. Even if his wife and his son were determined not to enjoy it. On cue, Caroline leaned over the railing and called down from the second floor. "Perry, call home and check on Ben, will you? Before it gets too late."

Perry's mouth was full and he waved his hand, waved her off. Did she imagine for a minute that she was the only one worried, that Perry hadn't already thought to call? There was beer in the fridge—and he popped one open.

"You want one?" he tried again across the expanse of room to Hugo, holding aloft a cold Coors.

Hugo sat on an oversized leather couch. He had turned on the giant living room TV and was flipping through the many channels. "I'm sixteen, Dad."

"I know, I know. But I'm your father and it's okay with me."

He shook his head. "I don't like the taste."

"Suit yourself."

The girls had now disappeared onto the lower level—billiards and ping-pong. Caroline had disappeared into seclusion or hibernation or some deep and private mourning. And Hugo was lost in the TV. Perry wandered over to the couch, watched his son flash through channels: A beauty pageant. Basketball. Red Sox at spring training. This should be natural, right? Father and son, side by side in front of the big screen, shooting the shit, watching baseball ... but Perry couldn't remember ever having this with Hugo.

"Leave it there," Perry said, "Red Sox," but Hugo shook his head and kept flipping, settling finally on MTV.

When they had lived in Boston when the kids were little, Perry had taken Hugo to a few Red Sox games—the two of them alone, father and son. It was supposed to give Hugo time away from Ben, who was a crying, thrashing baby, and then a demanding and consuming toddler and child. It was supposed to be a way for Perry and Hugo to bond. But even at the age of six, seven, or eight, when lots of little boys were obsessed with the game, begged their fathers to play catch, to take them to the ballpark, Hugo seemed bored with it all, going with Perry just to be kind. Even back then, he was no doubt worried about Ben, but also not wanting to disappoint his father. When Perry asked him once, after an amazing Red Sox victory over the Yankees, if he had enjoyed the game, Hugo had shrugged his shoulders.

Was it too late to build something? Ivy would be leaving for college in the fall. Hugo had only another year. Perry took a deep suck of his icy cold beer. Hugo was growing older and Perry knew less and less about him; the boy rarely spoke, except in his extended soliloquies to Ben. He had few friends, none who ever called. And except for school or diving practice, he never went away from the house. Jesus, maybe he should worry less about Ben, more about Hugo. A deep rush of cold, an avalanche of terror. He let his arm fall around Hugo's shoulder, breathed, tried to calm himself. No. Stop. Don't do this. The boy was okay, more than okay. Mature, responsible, an excellent student and an exceptional athlete. He saw his son's final dive at state again, that remarkable two-and-a-half somersault to cap his performance, the height, the speed, the arrow-straight entry. The body as art.

On the TV screen, a strangely erotic, arty man, with sea anemone hair and smudged lipstick—and a familiar song, one Hugo must have played at home—and the man stuck in a box, a coffin maybe, and sinking, drowning in the water. But not drowning, breaking out and now swimming and breathing and floating among sea creatures.

Perry pulled himself together, tried to smile, stave off his worry. "This is your band, right? I've heard this song. What the hell is it about?"

"Hard to say."

"Who is the wild-haired dude?"

"Robert Smith." His tone said shut up and leave me alone, but he offered a pitying smile. "The Cure."

▲▼▲

A couple of hours and four beers later, while Caroline slept, Perry took the three kids down the hill to find some dinner in the village. There was a light snow falling and Ivy and Harper were chasing each other around, tossing snowballs. Harper kept baiting Hugo, hitting him on the legs, the arms, the neck, before he finally shed his composure and chased off after her, picking her up and upending her into a snowbank. It was great to see Hugo lose his tight control. Have some fun. This Harper—her light-hearted and slightly off-color humor was good for all of them. She got up squealing, shaking the snow out of her long hair.

"Girls against guys, girls against guys. Come on, Ivy. Let's show them what we've got," and for close to an hour, an impromptu white war waged along the roadside.

Perry and Hugo made a fantastic team. Unpredictably, Hugo was aggressive and relentless in the attack. Perry piled up snowballs; Hugo ran and shot, snowball after snowball, hitting the girls on the neck, the back, the nose, then executing amazing aerial leaps off banks to avoid the return volleys. They all finished up exhausted, hungry, at a pizza place on the main drag.

This was how a family vacation should be, he thought as they stood in the warm wood entry hall. *If Caroline were with them, of course. All of them together. And Ben, too, if he could ever … if he were different, a typical child.* Perry asked the hostess for a table for four, the size of the perfect nuclear family. *What if Ben had never been born?* She led them to a booth in the back. *What kind of father had such thoughts about his son?* He still felt the lingering buzz of his afternoon beers, a little altitude dizziness, and the cold tingling of his nose, his fingers and toes. He needed to sit down. He needed some food. What did it mean that he could sometimes wish Ben away? Never mind that he actually tried, repeatedly tried, to find the kid a home away from home. He wanted to believe he was a good father, a great father, the hands-on, talk-to-me type that his own father never had been. But was he? Or was he trying to create some portrait of what a family should be?

▲▼▲

When they got back to the cabin after dinner, he went upstairs to check on Caroline. She was asleep, fast asleep on top of the bed. Lying against the white quilt, her greenish-gray pallor was intensified.

A bottle of her anxiety medication, cap-less on the side table. The drapes were open and the reflection off the snow bank cast a sheen across the room. Perry felt dizzy from the altitude, the two additional beers he had over dinner, the thin air. He thought for a quick moment about trying to wake her and make love. But it sounded like hard work when you said it like that: make love, forge affection, shore up the relationship. And his head ached. Too much thinking going on between them. He covered her quietly with a soft, white blanket from the closet, kissed her forehead, then found an unoccupied bedroom with a TV and a phone and called home again.

It was almost midnight Atlanta time, but Debbie said she was still awake, and yes, everything had gone just fine after the videos. Ben was fast asleep in his bedroom; after a little fuss, he'd gone off okay. Perry fell asleep watching Rocky III, in one of the Huff boys' rooms.

▲▼▲

He woke early—4 a.m. local time—his internal clock on East Coast construction time. After a long, hot shower, he decided to walk into town, see if he could find any breakfast supplies. He found a 24-hour convenience store and came back with eggs, pancake mix, syrup, coffee, milk, and bacon—the idea of a good breakfast, the blue skies, the snow waiting. He'd cook for them all, make tea for Caroline. Calories and caffeine could work wonders on any mood. Then he'd take the kids skiing, give her a day alone in the cabin, to think, without any demands. Including his own. When did she ever get that? Each plan he made for the day was like a small boost of energy and each boost re-charged his essentially optimistic core.

Three hours later, the kids were up, fed, clad for the slopes, and ready to go get outfitted with skis. Caroline finally came down around

9 a.m., poured herself a cup of coffee and said she would skip the skiing today; she would rather stay in front of the fire and read. Perry gave her a quick kiss. "Enjoy your day."

They rode a shuttle, loaded with skiers and skis, to the base of the North Bowl, where dozens of wide white trails ribboned down the face of the mountain. Above the pines, the white peaks etched the sky. Right away, the girls wanted to get as high up as possible and tackle the toughest slopes above the tree line—the black diamond runs, that even on the maps looked terrifying. Though neither of them had skied that much before, they made their plan, ditched the guys, and headed off for a gondola. Hugo, of course, was more sensible. He suggested a methodical approach, working across the basin, greens first, then on to blues. By mid-morning, he was speeding ahead of Perry, pulling up every now and then to wait with a look of amusement and apology. Later in the day, he saw the ski jump area and decided that was where he wanted to be—off with a group of grungy looking teens, throwing themselves up and off the ramps. Perry headed back to the cabin to check in with Caroline.

She was soaking indoors, in the smaller hot tub of the master suite. The jets were off, and beneath the water, her legs stretched out long and colt-like. Perry thought for a second he might climb in with her—it would certainly feel good after the bumps and falls he'd taken. But the look on her face was nothing like an invitation. Her shoulders rose above the water, and her head was bent over a book she held at arm's length.

"Did you get some good reading done?"

She looked up at him with a watery smile.

"Yep," she replied, "I drank a whole pot of that coffee you made, and I've almost finished this." She turned the book cover toward him.

"*Housekeeping*," he read. "Good?"

"Wonderful," she scanned Perry's face, to determine if she could go back to reading or if she needed to act interested in him a little longer. "Beautiful, lyrical. Loss and transcendence."

It sounded like a plot-less snooze, but he decided to let her off the hook. He leaned in and kissed her on her steaming cheek. "I'm glad you're relaxing." Maybe a full day of rest, without the kids, without Ben, soaking in the tub, without Perry, too, was what she needed. Maybe tomorrow she would kick into gear. He left her alone and went back downstairs. Drank a beer, ate some more of the gunk cheese and wandered through the house, picking up photos, trinkets, wondering if Trey could possibly be as fortunate as this house portrayed. Could anyone?

▲▼▲

On the fifth day at 6 a.m. Perry, still on East Coast time, was awake, making pancakes in the capacious kitchen. His coffee was ready, already creamed and sugared. He stood content, unshaven, exuding chlorine from his fingertips after spending two hours in the hot tub last night, talking with Caroline.

The phone on the counter rang and even before he picked up the receiver, he knew it was the sound of the other shoe falling. He took a quick, sweet swig from his mug and still caught the phone before its second ring.

"This is Perry." He checked the staircase to see if Caroline had heard. God, how he wanted not to have to hear what was coming down the wire. "Who's this?"

"Mr. Novotny, Penny Hudson, from Piedmont Hospital. I hate to call so early." Penny—hospital social worker—a regular in the

Novotny family's life since Ben's tenth birthday accident, a run-in with a hot iron—had led a teacher to call child welfare.

"What's happened?" Perry felt blood rushing up his neck. "Is he okay?"

"An ambulance brought him in an hour ago. The girl, his caregiver? She arrived right behind him—said he'd fallen down the stairs this morning. He's still unconscious. We're worried about intracranial bleeding. Brain swelling. He has two black eyes, possibly a fractured clavicle. Dr. Mingo's in with Ben now, but I know he wants to talk to you. Since I know you all, I wanted to be the first one to reach you. The girl gave me your phone number, but the thing is, Mr. Novotny—Perry—the thing is, we don't buy her story."

Oh god, what had he done? Poor Benno. Christ, he should never have left him that long.

"I'll get there as soon as I can. Is he going to be all right?"

"I am going to get Dr. Mingo to fill you in now—then you can call me back when you know your flight details. If you want to grab a pen you can write down my pager number."

When Dr. Mingo got on the line he was all business. None of Penny's practiced compassion. He talked more of the brain swelling. A possible nose fracture that wouldn't need surgery. A broken collarbone that he'd immobilized. He was worried, though, most worried about clotting difficulties—*Had Ben ever been diagnosed with von Willebrand's?* A clotting disorder. Perry didn't know. Caroline would. They'd need to keep Ben on sedatives while the swelling went down, then on painkillers as he woke up. At least several days in the ICU.

"You'll be here before he awakens," said Mingo. He cleared his throat. "This woman," he said. "This Dothan woman? I should let you know—with the injuries I'm seeing—her story is highly improbable. What do you know of her background?"

Perry looked around the monstrous kitchen. The fruit basket's withered bounty. A fucking waste. What do I know of her background? He thought about the story he had sold to Caroline a few weeks ago. Debbie had come recommended by Petey's mom. Petey, the Down syndrome kid from the park. Petey, whom Perry had pushed for hours in the tire swing. Petey's mom, whose name Perry could not remember now, if he had ever known it, had given him Debbie's name. Debbie, twenty-something, pale-skinned, dark-haired and heavy set. She'd worked previously in a group home—did he know that? He hadn't checked. She said she was completing her bachelor's in early childhood education at Georgia State. But he hadn't checked that either. She could definitely help out for a week, she'd told him. It all sounded good. It all sounded good, he told himself then. And now?

He should go tell Caroline now. But he couldn't, not yet. Not another plan falling apart. He was on the phone with the airlines when Ivy came down in pajamas, bleary-eyed and grumpy.

She stood beside Perry at the counter, taking nervous little sips from her own coffee cup. He arranged for a midday flight from Denver—for himself. The others could keep their planned return flights for the following afternoon. That meant he would have less than a half hour to pack before heading to the airport. When he got off the phone, he gave Ivy a brief run-down.

"I am going to wake up Mom. You all will come tomorrow night as planned. Tell Hugo, please." Then he added, "Be gentle."

Perry headed upstairs, armed with a cup of tea and a plan of action. "Carrie." He sat on the edge of the bed and pulled down that thick ivory quilt that covered her chin. "Caroline, honey, can you wake up?"

She tried to roll over, away from his words, he held her shoulder until she opened her eyes and had to look at him. "Wake up."

She pushed his hand off and sat up straight. "Ben?"

"He had a fall. Penny Hudson phoned. He's at Piedmont. I have made plans to go on home ahead of you. He's okay, but I need to leave shortly. The doctor says a short hospital stay. I called a cab already."

"Wait—hold on ... we'll all come."

"It's better, faster if I go ahead. I already changed my ticket. Stay with the kids, close up the house here, return the skis and all that stuff, and come home tomorrow. I'll call you from the hospital. It's better this way."

"Jesus, Perry. Don't do these things without talking to me."

"I want you to rest."

"Don't I get a say? I'm his mother." She sat on the edge of the bed and shook her head. "You don't get to cut me out."

"I'm not. Trust me on this. It's gonna be fine."

He threw some things in a duffel bag, while she kept shaking her head. But he knew she wouldn't fight him on this. When she finally stood, she wobbled a little as she went into the bathroom and shut the door behind her. He heard the toilet flush, the shower running, the glass door open and close. He imagined her stepping into a healing steam. Plane tickets, Penny's pager number, keys to the condo—he left them for her on the bed. He was trying to protect her, protect the family. She was fragile, needed insulation from the worst—the hospital scenes: their boy spread out, intubated and restrained, again. It was better this way. Away from her, he could hold it together. They'd still have a chance. He would explain his thoughts if he had time, but his cab arrived outside and honked impatiently before Caroline re-emerged.

CHAPTER 10

IVY, MAY 1992

Over the past year, Ivy and Harper had tried to arrange a mother-daughter outing several times already. But each time they came up with a decent idea, Mom found another excuse not to go: a Ben crisis—a bad seizure, a fall in the driveway followed by the requisite stitches, a hospitalization. But tonight would be different. Harper's genius, bullet-proof proposal was Shakespeare in the park. How could Professor Caroline Clissold, semi-renowned literary scholar, say no to that? Ivy had done her part well, too, guilting Mom, telling her that time was running out; in a few short months, she would leave for Northwestern.

At six sharp, on a Thursday evening, mid-May, Mom entered the kitchen, dressed and ready to go, hair pulled off her face with a black velvet headband.

"Here I am," she said, as if steeling herself. "All yours for the night." She took the car keys from the kitchen hook, blew a kiss toward Dad at the stove stirring up his pasta special for the boys, and followed Ivy out to the station wagon.

They drove across town to pick up Harper and her mom, Merilee, and Ivy forfeited shotgun to slip in back with Harper; then they headed south down Peachtree Road, Merilee and Mom making small talk up front.

"Piedmont Park," Mom said as they turned onto 14th Street. "Been a while since I've been here ..."

"Still home to derelicts and deviants," Merilee said.

"So we'll fit right in," replied Harper, punching Ivy on the arm.

Mom pulled into a burnt-out parking lot at the corner of Piedmont and 13th. As Harper and Ivy unloaded the picnic basket and bags from the trunk, some creepy guy approached and asked for ten dollars to keep an eye on the car. Mom handed him a five and said that was all she had; she added that it was probably more than the vehicle was worth at this point. They crossed Piedmont Drive together and headed toward the main entrance.

The park's reputation was still iffy but this week the Alabama Shakespeare Company was in town, pulling visitors from the burbs—Buckhead and Decatur, Candler Park and Virginia-Highlands, for a well-reviewed production of *The Winter's Tale*, Mom's favorite of the late romances. Well, after *The Tempest*, she had said. *Cymbeline*, the excruciatingly strange play from whence came Ivy's excruciatingly strange name, was a distant third on Mom's list. So why did she see fit to name her only daughter after cross-dressing Imogen, when Admir'd Miranda, ranked higher on her list of heroines? A bronze medal name for her first-born child? Sometimes, Ivy decided, it was best not to probe.

They walked the perimeter path towards the outdoor stage, Ivy and Harper leading the way, the moms close behind. Merilee was divorced and bipolar: the first label a consequence of the second? Or maybe vice versa. Harper said that she couldn't remember when her mother became truly weird. Harper's dad, Buster Reeves, a career politician who'd served two years in the Reagan White House and even made a good run for governor of Georgia, had ditched Merilee when Harper was still in elementary school. A renowned philanderer, he no doubt would have strayed, even if his first wife had not been certifiable, but Harper laid all the blame on her mom.

"Could you live with her?" Harper had asked Ivy once, after a particularly harrowing sleepover, when Merilee had kept the girls awake till three in the morning, while she knocked back scotch and sang along tearfully to Barbra Streisand's *Memories*. "Could you be married to that?"

Harper had signed up for Dr. Boggs's psychology elective during second semester and she'd become obsessed with diagnosing everyone: family, friends, bystanders. She sometimes carried a pocket-sized DSM around with her, ready for on-the-spot assessments. When she'd first shown Ivy the official mental health listings, Ivy had to agree: Merilee was a shoo-in for Bipolar Disorder II, with rapid cycling.

As they passed the softball fields, Harper whispered into Ivy's ear, "We'll have to keep a tight rein on Mom, okay? She's giddy about all this." Then promptly ignoring her own proclamation, she grabbed Ivy's hand and pulled her ahead, picking up the pace, until they were practically jogging.

"Stick together, girls," Merilee yelled after them.

They passed a shirtless, tattooed guy sitting on a stone wall smoking a cigarette, then raced across a half-mile of crushed gravel before Harper pulled up. "Shortcut—let's cross the lake here." They glanced back, decided the mothers could fend for themselves, and walked arm in arm across a shaky, snaky boardwalk toward the performance area on the other side of the silted lagoon.

"This *is* a little creepy," Ivy said.

Overgrown willows draped over the wooden slats; the girls pushed through the branches and walked further out on the lake. Below them, on either side of the platform, metallic potato chip bags and faded beer cans glistened in the reedy mud. The lagoon, the whole park, really, could use a good dredging. The low sun conjured a dirty mist from the water. Halfway across, a couple of skinny, old men sat with their legs dangling off the boardwalk. Fishing poles, a tackle box, and two half-drunk bottles of Colt 45. Ivy stalled, unsure whether to proceed and not wanting to turn back. She shot a *should we* look at Harper.

"Come on, faithful sidekick," Harper said and booted her in the butt. Ivy teetered and almost fell, but Harper grabbed her elbow tight and laughed. "Gotta be on your toes, Novotny. Gotta be ready for anything. Follow me." A ponytail captured most of Harper's dark hair, but several unruly strands fell around her face; her blue eyes glinted in the dusk as she tugged Ivy forward.

Harper paused by the two fishermen and turned on her flirt. "Did you gentleman catch anything?"

"A bad case of the clap," one of them said with a nasty cackle. The other spat into the water.

"Lovely," Harper said.

The second one took a long pull from his bottle, then mocked Harper's accent. "*Catch anything?* Now that's an original question. *Lovely.*"

"Just being friendly," Harper said. "Sorry I bothered."

"Let's go." Ivy said.

"Yeah," one of the men said as they took off. "You better get the fuck out of our park."

Across the lake, a hand-painted sign welcomed visitors to *The Winter's Tale*. A couple of actors dressed in standard Renaissance fare—black leggings, velvet tunics, long lace-up boots—handed out programs and asked for donations. The early arrivals for the performance had already settled into the flat, grassy semi-circle in front of the wooden stage. Metal scaffolding off to the left held an impressive array of sound equipment and spotlights. Harper and Ivy checked out the stage—a palace scene—then walked up the slope to find a spot about twenty-five yards back. Harper pulled a red-and-white-checked quilt from her bag, and Ivy helped her spread it out on an incline.

"Best seats in the house," she said, sitting down on the quilt next to Harper. "Now if the old ladies would hurry up with the food. I'm starving. You got anything to eat in your bag?"

"Nope—but I've got this ..." Harper pulled out a pocket-sized DSM. She was obsessed with diagnosing everyone since she started AP Psych.

"Not exactly what I had in mind ... but okay. My family, or yours again?"

"Let's start with Ben," said Harper.

"That's easy, stupid," Ivy replied, "Mental retardation. Profound or Severe, depending on his mood when he takes the IQ test."

Harper scanned a couple of pages. "Did you know that MR is not considered a personality disorder?" She paused for a second. "How's he been doing since the accident?"

"Accident, my ass," Ivy said. Ben had spent three weeks in the hospital after the ski trip. "He's still wearing a sling for his broken clavicle. His black eyes—well, they are more yellow-ish now. But he's recovered, I guess."

"What about that bitch who beat him up? What's going to happen to her?"

"No witnesses, no proof, so no charges," Ivy said. "That's Family and Children's Services for you."

"Ben knows what happened. He could say …"

"He knows, all right, but he doesn't count because he can't talk. Debbie and her boyfriend backed each other up—insisting that Ben fell. Yeah, right. Fell out of bed, down the stairs, again and again. So that's what the investigators concluded. *Self-injury*."

"They're idiots," Harper said.

"Morons." Ivy added. "Ben has issues, but self-mutilation is not one of them."

"More than morons. They're fuckers."

"Yeah. Profound fuckers." Ivy didn't tell Harper that whenever Ben heard anyone say the name Debbie, he covered his head with both his arms, warding off the blows. Thinking about it still made her want to puke.

Harper scanned the lake path for the mothers. "Do you think they're lost?"

"How could they be?" Ivy replied. "Whichever way they walk, they'll end up here."

"Do you think they're getting along?" Harper asked, though she must have known the unlikelihood of this maternal pairing. The good professor and the manic Merilee were about as different as chalk and cheese. Wherever the hell that expression came from.

"I doubt it," Ivy said, perhaps too honestly. "I mean my mom is so serious all the time. She won't do small talk. She lacks your mother's Southern niceties."

"You mean she's not a complete fruitcake?" Harper said. "I'll tell you what, when I get out of the South, I am not coming back. I am surprised someone as smart as your mother can stand it here. All fake talk and made-up faces."

"Emory gave her some hot-shot title to keep her down South ... but you're right, she doesn't really like it here. She says all the happiness and bright colors depress her."

"Well, I know she gets blue, but I'm pretty sure it's only dysthymia," Harper said, "Not real clinical depression. It's sort of sexy, dysthymia. Definitely the diagnosis I would pick for myself."

Sometimes, Ivy thought Harper used her only to gain access to the melancholic Professor Clissold. To pretend she was another mother's child. Could be that she wanted Mom's cool remove to rub off on her own overly ebullient mother. Or maybe she wanted to grow up like Mom—scholarly and reserved. Last semester, she'd cited Mom's PhD thesis on the Four Humours in her research paper on *Hamlet*. Seemed like everyone was always longing for someone wiser or more beautiful to be or to love. A good SAT analogy: Ivy is to Harper as Harper is to Mom. And where did that leave poor Merilee?

"Yoo-hoo," yelled Merilee, waving and smiling as the moms approached from the top of the hill. "What a couple of Houdinis."

"Melancholia's preferable to mania, I suppose," Ivy said.

Harper nodded. "Trust me." She lifted a hand to acknowledge and/or silence her mother and tucked her little green manual back into her purse.

"Where did y'all run off to?" Merilee said as they neared. "Find some cute boys? Smoke some weed? Don't hold out on me now."

"Mother," Harper said and touched her arm as if to settle her.

"Just joking around, darlin'. I know you're a couple of goody two shoes. I bet I can't even get you two to taste a little wine with me tonight? Even though you're both accepted to college."

She dropped the oversized picnic basket on the ground and plopped herself on the quilt. "I'll tell you what, Caroline. These girls are not the daredevils you and I used to be. But never mind, we can still have us a little party. I brought two bottles of merlot."

Ivy scoured Mom's face for a telltale look of annoyance but she seemed unfazed; her eyes were glossy and distant, and she took a seat on the quilt. Half an hour before the play began, and the last of the sun settled into a toxic orange haze behind the Midtown high-rises that bordered the park. Merilee opened the wicker basket and spread out the fare. Apparently, this was where her mania paid off. There was a wedge of brie, as well as French bread, purple and green grapes, fried chicken that she had made herself, biscuits wrapped perfectly in red-checked linens, a green bean salad, and a homemade lemon chiffon pie. Merilee flushed as she showed it all off, then opened a super-sized bottle of red wine with a two-pronged device.

"Vino?" she said to Mom. "Surely, you'll join me, even if our honor society daughters won't."

"Absolutely," Mom said, assessing Merilee as she poured. Look, swirl, smell, and taste. Judgment would (surely) come later. But whatever Mom ultimately concluded about Merilee, she must be happy about the sights and smells before her. She never had been a good cook—that was Dad's bailiwick—and more and more of the family meals lately were takeout or leftovers from something Dad made on the weekends. Last week, he'd even brought home Arby's roast beef sandwiches.

"This is a real treat," said Mom. "Thank you, Merilee. And thank you Harper for the whole idea of this night ... I know it took some coordinating, some persistence to get us out here. Sometimes I get a little stuck in my routine."

Mom could play the role of the parent Harper imagined her to be: reserved, intelligent, and chic. Tonight, she was wearing a long, silk sarong she'd had for years, an abstract floral pattern in black and purples, knotted around her waist; her top was a simple black leotard. With her hair pulled back and a black velvet choker around her throat, she resembled an aging ballerina, or perhaps an understudy for Queen Hermione in the play tonight. No wonder Harper would like to pretend she was her daughter.

Merilee said, "Well it's no secret, Caroline, that Harper is crazy about you. She's read all your articles. She wouldn't give up until she got you to agree to come out for the evening. I think she has a little crush ..."

"Mom ..." Harper started.

"Well, it's true, darlin'. You've been talking about Professor Caroline non-stop."

Harper looked as if she could curl up and die.

"And I must say, Caroline, I admire how you and your husband manage with your youngest ... the little handicapped boy."

"Ben," Harper said. "His name is Ben."

Merilee flashed her super straight, white teeth but bit her tongue. She wore pleated khaki pants and a pink polo shirt, with a strand of pearls around her neck, had beautiful teeth, nails and hair. What was the common element? Ivy wondered. Vitamin A? or D? Merilee must have ingested a whole load of whatever it was. Her hair was brown, long, and lustrous—like a Prell commercial. Her nails, also long and well-manicured and painted a vibrant pink to match her top. It was as if all the glory went to her extremities. How did she want the world to see her? Sane, happy, pie-baking homemaker? She passed around plates, then offered chicken, side dishes, even condiments.

"So Caroline," Merilee said, after everyone had started to eat. "You're the expert; tell us about this play."

Mom sat up straight, took a long drink of the wine, and found her lecture voice. "*The Winter's Tale*, usually categorized as a romance. Some scholars say these late plays are Shakespeare's lesser works, but I happen to love them. Elements of both tragedy and comedy; revenge and destruction, as well as slapstick humor and some buffoonery, but in the end, the real focus is on redemption and grace."

"Well, that sounds nice," Merilee said.

"Nice?" Harper said.

"Did I say something wrong?" Merilee replied.

"We're talking about Shakespeare, not nail polish."

"Well, excuse me, darlin'." Her laugh was loud, forced. "My daughter finds me an embarrassment. But I'll have you know that I was an English major at Vandy. I read Shakespeare, too. Maybe not this play, but all the famous ones. *Macbeth, Romeo and Juliet. Hamlet.* And life has taught *me* a little something about loss and redemption."

Ivy wanted to tell Harper it would be okay, but Mom got there first.

"Vanderbilt has a wonderful English Department, really strong in Renaissance and eighteenth century these days."

"Yes," Merilee agreed, and clinked her wine glass against Mom's. "Though Harper doesn't seem to think Vandy's good enough for her. Has to be an Ivy League. All these smarty-pants kids today, but I don't like the idea of her up there at Dartmouth."

Mom drained her glass and held it toward Merilee for a refill. "Harper," she said diplomatically, "is going to be a star wherever she goes to college. I read her *Hamlet* essay. Her analysis and critical writing were first-rate."

Harper smiled, eating up the compliment, but pushed her plate aside—she'd hardly eaten. She stretched out her legs next to Mom on the quilt. Long, lean, and graceful, careful about what she wore, picky about what she ate, she was more like Mom than Ivy could ever hope to be. If any observer watched the four of them tonight, they would have paired Ivy with Merilee, and Harper with Caroline. Ivy's legs were short and muscular. She was her father's daughter: a round-featured endomorph, in a way that worked for cute and bouncy gymnasts, but was never flattering post-puberty. Later in life, she would probably thicken around the middle and grow jowly like her grandfather. What she would give for another three inches in height and some well-articulated cheekbones. What she would do to have Harper longing for her, in the way she obviously pined for Ivy's mother.

After the sun had disappeared behind the row of magnolias at the base of the hill, Merilee filled Mom's wine glass a third, or was it fourth time? Then she sliced up the pie, served everyone a generous wedge on a real china plate, handed out ornate silver forks. Must be from her wedding set, Ivy thought, remembering a story Harper once shared about how the Halloween after her parents separated—when Harper was seven years old and her younger brother only four—their mother took her wedding dress out of storage, squeezed her post-pregnancy, post-psychotropic meds body into it, and reeking of mothballs, went trick-or-treating in full matrimonial glory all around West Wesley Road. Harper and Hamilton, costumed as a flower girl and a pageboy, gripped Merilee's veil and hurried along behind her.

The hillside had filled now with hundreds of picnickers, some had brought chairs, tables, candles—others spread out on towels and blankets. Very little empty space was left on the grass, and soon a woman in medieval fare made preliminary announcements, requested no flash photos, and asked everyone to clean up their own trash.

All was well, as the play began. Tart lemon filling, complementary sweet, white topping. Ivy finished it quickly. She heard her mother sigh; then saw her reach into her purse and pull out a small bottle. She poured something in to her wine glass and quickly drank it down. Medicine of some sort? Then she lit a cigarette and leaned back into the hill. Was she happy for a night out, a break from Ben ... or was she annoyed by this whole construct ... whatever image of mother-daughter intimacy Harper was trying to impose on them all? Ivy and her mother had never spent much time alone. Because of Ben, most likely, all his needs and all the demands on their mother's time, but who knew really? Maybe even without Ben, she and Mom wouldn't have chosen one another's company. Was it wrong to think so often of a life without Ben? So hard to imagine an alternative version—a world in which he'd never been born. As much as she tried, she couldn't develop a clear picture of her parents, herself, or especially Hugo without the little guy shaping and shading all the interactions. Who would Hugo be without Ben to care for and entertain? Would she even be Ivy, without Ben pushing her up and away? It was as if her entire existence were defined by opposition, to her brothers, to her family. And in four short months she'd be away from them all. Then what?

Ivy propped up on her elbows to watch Act I. She had read this play once, not for a class, but during a summer break when she was still trying to understand Mom's interests. She probably hadn't finished it.

King Leontes stalked onto stage. The crowd settled. The king ranted in lengthy asides about his cheating wife, berated his best friend, hurled not-so-subtle accusations. His wife, Queen Hermione, wittily deflected the barrage, but Leontes persisted. The stage light caught beads of his spittle. Where did this come from? Leontes' suspicion, the rage? He was acting like some wife beater, spewing, out of control. Ivy wanted to ask her mother, why he was so over the top? Wasn't this the stuff of a tragic hero? King Lear or Othello? But Mom lay flat on the quilt and stared up at the sky—not watching the stage—perhaps lost in the language or the still starless sky. Had she checked out already? One night—that was all Ivy wanted. Was that too much for her to give?

"King Leontes," Ivy whispered into Harper's ear. "Paranoid Personality Disorder?"

Harper thumped her on the shoulder and smiled slightly. Ivy tried to think of something else cute to say, so Harper would hit her again and with a little less restraint, leave a light bruise for her to find and trace tomorrow morning.

Before the second act, a couple wound their way up through the thick crowd, tripping on chairs and blankets, trying to move unobtrusively, but more disruptive because of this effort. The tall woman in the lead whispered to the shorter woman behind her, *this way, over here* before someone in the crowd loudly hushed them. They paused, but then pushed determinedly up the hill and planted right in front of Ivy, breaking her perfect sightline to the stage. She had to sit up, readjust and tilt her neck left to see the dyspeptic King.

Merilee coughed loudly and said, "Excuse us, ladies."

The tall woman turned around. "Oh sorry," she whispered. "Are we blocking you?"

"It's okay," Ivy responded. The tall woman had shoulder-length brown hair, high cheekbones, and a wide smile. She was a dead ringer for somebody famous. Who was it? She settled in, facing the stage. The other woman, smaller, lighter in hair color, leaned her body back against the tall one.

Ivy tapped Harper and pointed. "That woman—exact look-alike for someone famous."

"Milla Jovovich?" Harper whispered loudly. "*Return to Blue Lagoon?*"

"Shhh," said Merilee loudly. "I'm trying to watch the show."

Yes. That was it. Ivy had lost the plot of the play—staring instead at Milla and her girlfriend. Lost, too, the dialect, caught only bits and pieces of the unfolding visual drama: pregnant Hermione dragged off to prison. A newborn girl. In the foreground, Ivy was transfixed by another scene: gorgeous Milla fed purple grapes to her beloved, from a small bunch, plucked each one and laid it on the other woman's lips. It could have been an overwrought scene from *Blue Lagoon*. Deep within Ivy—a surge of desire, with the familiar top layer of shame. On stage, the servant carried the baby to the King Leontes and berated him for his jealousy. Young Prince Mamillius—the King's firstborn child and heir apparent—died from grief. And his newborn baby girl dispatched for slaughter.

Milla discarded the empty grape vine and wrapped her arms around her girlfriend, held her tight, occasionally bent forward to whisper something in her ear. What was it she said?

Mom sat up long enough to drink more wine and smoke another cigarette. Then she lay back down. Ivy couldn't tell if she were sleeping; thank god she wasn't snoring.

The Oracle at Delphi professed poor Hermione's innocence and threatened an heirless king. Then a massive guy (the actor had to be a football player) wearing nothing but a loin cloth and a bear mask chased the servant, Antigonus, across the stage.

At intermission, Mom shook herself out of her daze and said to Harper. "Exit pursued by a bear. No one can ever get that scene right."

"I thought you were asleep," Ivy said.

"Listening with my eyes closed." Mom replied.

"Doesn't that defeat the whole point?" Ivy said. "The visual production? How can you criticize if you don't even watch it?"

"Please," she said, "I'm too fucking tired for another inquest by Imogen."

Ivy wanted to wrap her hands around her mother's slender neck and shake her into the now. And she wanted to disappear.

Merilee laughed. "Fucking tired? Well said, Caroline ... I second that emotion." She reached for the bottle of wine again, refilled her own glass and then Caroline's. "Let's drink to maternal fatigue."

Harper grabbed Ivy's wrist and whispered, "C'mon, let's get out of here for a while." She patted a pocket where Ivy knew she kept cigarettes. Benson & Hedges, just like Mom. People were stirring, pouring more drinks, stretching out, standing up. "We're going for a walk." Harper said.

"Is it safe?" Merilee said, springing to her feet.

But Mom intervened, "Oh, Merilee, they'll be fine. Stay here, for god's sake. Let's have a little chat ... about the play or, if you prefer, about our beautiful daughters." She smiled indulgently, too indulgently, at Harper. Ivy could hear that her words were starting to slur.

Harper flashed a grateful smile in return, and pulled Ivy off down the hill, toward the lagoon.

"Your mom is so cool," said Harper, as she took the cigarettes from her jean jacket.

"She's so drunk, you mean."

"You want one?" Harper held the pack out to Ivy.

"Nah. Not my thing." Ivy followed Harper through the crowd. "Besides, you wouldn't think my mother was so cool if you had to live with her moods."

"She's introspective. Trust me on this. It goes with dysthymia." She pulled a cigarette out, but didn't light up yet. "Dysthymics need room for their creative expression."

"She has you hoodwinked."

They left the theatre crowd behind and wandered for a few minutes beside the water.

At the lake's edge, through a thicket of trees, Harper found the boardwalk again. "Let's head out there," she said. "Maybe we'll find the creepy fisher dudes. We could hit them up for some ganja weed."

"Are you sure?" Ivy asked. "Those guys were definitely not friendlies."

"Druggies and psychos and lezzies, oh my!" said Harper. "Don't be such a priss-ass. I bet your mother smokes pot."

Ivy shook her head.

"You're so naïve," Harper said as she pulled Ivy onto the boardwalk. "It's one of the things I like about you." She held the unlit cigarette between thumb and finger and flexed a tiny bicep. "Don't worry, if it gets rough, I'll protect you."

Harper hitched her shorts high up her thigh, struck the Heisman Trophy pose. "Who needs arm muscles when I've got turbo-speed to outrun danger? Scary men and wild bears. What the hell was that all about, anyway? A bear running around the stage?"

"*No one can ever get that scene right.*" Ivy tried on Mom's professorial tone. "She wasn't even watching the play you know. She was passed out on the blanket."

"She's got a lot going on with your brother," Harper said. "You of all people should understand if she wants a break … a little booze to ease the burden."

"Oh great. Now you're *defending* my Mom? Over me?" Ivy bounced hard on the boardwalk so Harper would lose her footing and fall. Fall into her, fall against her. Fall in love with her.

"You jerk," Harper laughed, grabbing at Ivy's arm and correcting herself, but she still lost her cigarette in the water. "You fucking little jerk."

"At your service, Madame." Ivy bowed deeply from her waist.

They walked a hundred yards out to the middle of the boardwalk, but found no creepy fishermen. Instead, they sat down, side by side, on the ragged wooden slats where the men had been and dangled their feet. Neither spoke. Ivy felt want whirl-pooling in her stomach and time running out. She thought about catching Harper's leg with her own, and swinging it back and forth, over the water. Or grazing the back of her knuckles over Harper's hand. Simple, easy, to connect with a touch, but too much, too much would be revealed. Soon they would be graduating, moving far off to different colleges, different states; they'd lead different lives. This summer, Harper would travel to Paris *avec sa mere*, then head south of the border to Mexico, *con su padre*; her parents still playing *push me-pull you* with their kids-of-divorce. And Ivy would have one last long hot spell at home, helping with Ben's care before she fled in September to Northwestern, her safety school. If only Harper could read her mind, pick up her hand, hold it, tell her she understood, tell her she knew… .

Harper stared out over the water and, as though receiving a signal dimly through the fog, finally spoke. "I'll miss you next year, Imogen Vaughan, my loyal sidekick."

Ivy looked at her, memorized her beautiful profile—the strong forehead, the dark lashes, the slight up tilt of her nose—watched her and wanted the words to be enough.

No one ever got this scene right.

"Harper," Ivy tried.

"Yeah."

"I can't stop thinking about you."

Harper turned and looked at her, grinning big. "Yeah, right."

"No, seriously. I think that I'm in love ..."

Harper held up her hand, shifted her body away. "Okay. Enough."

"Wait. Let me say this."

"No," Harper stood. "The play's gonna end. I don't want to miss it. C'mon." She paced fast across the boardwalk, not bothering to check if Ivy was behind, marched along the trail, then up the grassy hill, dodging the strewn blankets, stepping over stretched out legs, banging into picnic baskets, and not apologizing and not stopping once, until she found the mothers.

"Where were you?" Merilee shot an evil eye at Harper. "Ten minutes, you said. It's been over thirty." She pointed at Caroline flat out on the blanket. "Looks like your heroine has had too much wine. She killed the bottle and puked into a trash bag." She whispered plenty loud for Ivy to hear. "Does she usually behave like this? Passing out in public?"

Harper shrugged and sat down again, refusing to speak to her mother, refusing to acknowledge Ivy, refusing even to consider her sprawled-out idol.

Ivy sat beside her Mom, tried surreptitiously to rouse her by poking her in the ribs.

On stage, Act V: lost children found, angry lovers reunited, the dead reborn, statues moving, breathing, returning to life. Everyone (well, almost everyone) found what was lost. Only poor Antigonus eaten alive by a bear. And that little boy, the prince, what was his name? Still dead.

As Harper and Merilee packed up, and the rest of the crowd started leaving, Ivy prodded Mom again, pinched her arm hard then harder, and finally pulled her back to functioning.

"A bad headache," Mom insisted when she managed to sit up.

Ivy offered her a glass of water but she pushed it away, struggled to her feet.

They walked the long way around the lake, back to the parking lot and Mom puked again—this time into the bushes. She muttered to all who would listen. "Migraine. Came out of nowhere." When they arrived at the car, she insisted on driving, and ignored Merilee's protests. She seemed fine as she steered them north on Peachtree, twenty mph, through Midtown, past Piedmont Hospital, hands stuck on the wheel at ten and two. Half a mile farther and she turned onto Peachtree Battle, pulled up in front of the Reeves' modest white frame home.

"Lovely time, a lovely night. Let's do it again," Merilee said as she climbed out, pulling the picnic basket from the back. Harper followed her mother without a word as she quick-stepped into the house. When their front door closed, Mom did a vicious U-turn and headed back across Peachtree Street, along West Wesley, towards home. One hand on the wheel now, the other massaging her temple.

"That woman is fucking unbelievable. Poor Harper."

Ivy shook her head. "Why did you have to drink so much? It was embarrassing."

"Oh, for Christ's sake. I had a migraine. I told you."

"Mom, you passed out. You threw up twice."

"I had a terrible migraine. And you left me to run off with Harper and I did not want to talk to your best friend's psychotic mother. Of course, I pretended to pass out."

Ivy felt the tears, hot, stinging and wiped them away.

"Oh Christ. Tears?"

"Harper." Ivy didn't know how to say more. She sobbed quietly into her hands. "I wanted it to go better."

Mom shook her head. "You got your night out."

As they crossed I-75, the highway that dissected the city lengthwise, she looked at Ivy and slapped her right hand hard on the dashboard.

"Harper? You like her? Really? With all we have going on at home, with everything—Ben just out of the hospital, probably nowhere else for him to go—you, you who have it all, on your way out, off to college hundreds of miles from here, you are going to waste my time crying about Harper Fucking Reeves?"

The car veered over center line as Mom yelled, "I thought you were smarter than that. I thought you had more sense."

Ivy reached for the wheel. "Stop. You're scaring me."

Mom batted away her hand. "Did you drag me out here tonight because of some school-girl crush? Pathetic."

"Stop it. Please."

"You stop it. Stop the girlish tears and grow the fuck up." She accelerated up and over the Westmont crest, hit the downhill without braking. "Do you have any idea what Dad and I are going through? Do you think this is how I wanted to spend the night?"

Ivy yelled as the school's floodlights flashed by. "Watch out."

But Mom took her hands off the wheel and raised them above her head, roller-coaster style. "Wheee—what a night! A night on the town with Merilee Reeves. Wheee—because I have nothing better to do with my life!"

The sharp curve at the bottom of the hill coming fast. Hands waving in the air, Mom turning slow-mo to face Ivy and flashing her wine-stained teeth. Ivy reaching for the wheel again, but the station wagon was fast and resolute, careening down the hill, crashing through scrub trees and underbrush, and rolling sideways into a kudzu-lined ditch.

CHAPTER 11

CAROLINE, JUNE 1992

Caroline lay on her right side under the pale, peach-colored spread of the narrow twin bed. It had been a long-time—since back in college, no doubt, more than twenty years ago—that she'd slept on a bed this narrow, and her long, bony limbs no longer seemed able to adjust. With the advent of middle age or the cumulative weight of exhaustion—how to distinguish?—she'd grown used to a dull aching in the back of her knees. The constraints of this child-sized bed, and the cold currents of conditioned air that blasted from the vent above it did nothing to help. Nor did the fact that she'd had nothing more than an aspirin to curb the pain since her arrival at Brady's Rehab Center three days ago. She'd agreed to the detox to get a break, but hadn't really thought through what it would require. She hadn't understood how much she'd come to rely on her wine and Ben's meds.

She had asked her shrink during their first session to prescribe something stronger, codeine perhaps.

"Nothing," he replied. "Not for the first fortnight at least. We have to completely clean out your system."

She had liked how he said fortnight—the dark cave of it, the promise of a physical and temporal remove from what she'd done, from who she'd become. But the pain in her legs wouldn't wait that long.

Nothing comes of nothing, she had said back to him. *Speak again.*

And true-blue Oxford-educated man that he was, Dr. Thorne-Thompson passed the test, coming up with his own, far more impressive quotation in response. "In here, Caroline, *we speak what we feel, not what we ought to say.*"

She had liked him for his words, even if she didn't like what they meant. A refusal of her request. A refusal of relief. For the pain she now inhabited, the same pain she'd had for years and which had always been worst early mornings and which had, in fact, been the reason that she first started dipping into Ben's meds, a little relief to start each day. Was that the truth, she wondered, or what she ought to say?

Valium had not been relief as much as a thick blanket for her mind, keeping her thoughts muffled and safe inside her head when the world around her, in her kitchen, in her home, in her car, at work was frenetic and out of control. Was that, then, such a bad choice? To sip it slowly, to slow everything down, to soften her life?

She tried to find a way to curl up, fetal position, and still stay under the covers, eyes closed tight and wishing she could numb her brain back to embryonic nothingness. Anesthetize her brain out of the here and now. She'd had a tooth extraction a few years ago and could still remember the heavenly calm that she felt as she went under, a calm that lasted through the messy business of oral surgery and even into her recovery, when she woke up and looked around the dentist's office and remembered a wonderful nothing about the past hour. But now waking up meant facing what she'd done. The wine, the Valium, the wreck. Ivy. Her daughter was okay, thank god, but hadn't been to visit her once since the accident.

She would ask Dr. Thorne-Thompson again today, perhaps, more honestly, more directly, saying, I need some real relief, I don't think I can do this without a little help. Though she was aware that the good and literary doctor would be unyielding on this point, would insist that help could come in different shapes and packages, it wouldn't hurt to ask one more time.

All he would do—all he could really, according to rehab rules—was arrange for her to get rest, non-narcotic pain relief, and therapy. Talk therapy. A nurse would get Caroline an extra blanket if she got up out of bed right now, walked down the hall, and asked. Or, for that matter, so could Perry. She could call him after her session from the phone at the nurse's desk and he would—happily, willingly—bring her one from home. One of her favorites, softened and over-washed. Perry loved to have something helpful to do. If she could call and ask him for help. She was allowed to make one call a day. She had not yet used that option.

The pain radiated from her knees and by midmorning had soaked through her. Body aches, like the flu. She'd had this every day so far. This was her due, what she deserved. It was far better than she deserved: an uncomfortable bed, a freezing room, a throbbing ache in her knees, chills, and pains. And later, after her therapy, sometime in the afternoon, Perry would show up. He seemed to be taking pleasure in showing up promptly at 3 p.m. every day to bear witness to her humiliation.

"Here I am," he didn't need to say, each afternoon, *"Still working, still providing for the children, and still taking care of Benjamin."* He carried it in his tired smile, his sweaty work clothes, and his defiantly jaunty step she could hear approaching from down the corridor.

"*Hello, my love,*" he would say. She wanted to slam the door against his false cheer. Lock him out.

She must have fallen asleep because she was startled awake by a quick rap on her door as a nurse walked in, brisk and upbeat and peremptory. "Ready to walk over to Doctor's? It's eleven."

Caroline got up slowly. She was still chilly, so she pulled on an old cardigan and her slippers. No room for vanity in this place. She finger-combed her long, tangled hair off her face.

"That's the way." The nurse took off ahead of her down the corridor. Caroline padded slowly after. Down two hallways, up one floor on an elevator, and down another hall to where the three treating doctors had their offices. The nurse walked her up to Dr. Thorne-Thompson's beige door and knocked twice quickly.

"Come in," he called in his lovely, rumbly tone.

The nurse pushed open the door and walked off down the hall. Caroline stood in the door jamb.

"Hello there. You are looking a little brighter today."

She laughed—a hollow sound, a falsity.

"Come in, have a seat." He waved his arm toward the couch and two arm chairs over by a drape-covered window. "Anywhere you'd like."

He walked over to join Caroline. "How are you feeling?"

"Cold, a little achy. Actually, very achy."

"Where is the pain, mostly?"

"Still in my knees, centered in my knees, but it spreads outwards. I need something."

"Have you ever been told you have rheumatism? Arthritis?"

"No. It's not that. It's more like ... I don't know—a migraine, I think, the pain and tension starts at that spot."

"Well, I can see about getting you a heating pad perhaps. A hot water bottle."

She shook her head. "Don't bother. I was hoping for, you know, something a little stronger. Tylenol 3 maybe ... even a few Excedrin." She was embarrassed to ask this, but her knees were throbbing more at the thought of relief, demanding relief. "A little something, to take the edge off."

"Sorry. We can't do that. I will get you some more blankets though."

"Like I said, don't bother. I'll call my husband."

"You're angry?"

"No. I understand the rules."

"Okay. Good. Now besides the pain, how have the last two days been?"

"Well. I have been in bed mostly. Except for when Perry shows up."

"Do you look forward to his visits?"

She laughed again. The same empty sound.

"Dread them?"

"No, no. I don't know why he insists on coming. Every single day. It's a burden on him and, frankly, it's not really that pleasurable for me. Just a reminder of what a screwup I am."

"You're angry with him?"

"No. Just tired. Why would I be angry?"

"I don't know. Can you think of any reasons?" He interlaced his long bony fingers and smiled at her.

"No."

His pointer fingers lifted into a church tower, which he then tapped against his prominent chin, all the time holding her gaze. "Any reasons at all? Whether they seem reasonable or not."

Caroline smiled. "Doesn't a 'reason' necessarily imply 'reason-ableness'? Surely, a reasonable reason is a redundancy."

Dr. Thorne-Thompson didn't take the bait. He knew Shakespeare, but he was not a show-off, not a game player, a word parser, his steady gaze told her. Try again.

"I have no reasons, no cause to be angry with Perry."

"I am asking you this, Caroline, because, as I am sure you know, depression is often an inward expression of anger."

What did he really know? Tall, horse-faced, prematurely bald English man. He was probably ten years younger than she. He wore no wedding band. Unmarried, or unbanded, like most British men? What did he know about marriage, children ... about husbands who can't or won't give up?

"Are you angry with me now, for my suggestion? It's all right if you are. We can talk about it. *Speak what we feel, not what we ought to say.*"

She adjusted her face, smiled at him as pleasantly as she could, though she felt irked by his calm, his persistent gentility. And mostly his repeat quotation.

"I don't need you to keep quoting Shakespeare to earn my trust," she said finally.

"But it might help?" he asked.

"No." She did not need refinement or gentility. A scholarly shrink in her corner. What she needed now, after three days in the hospital and four days in this recovery center was a hard slap across the face, a wake-up call, and an act-your-age talk. Get your shit together, woman.

She hated what she had become.

"If I am angry at anyone, it's myself," she said. "Not Perry. And certainly not you. I don't even know you."

"Why are you angry at yourself?"

"Isn't it obvious? Because I am a god-awful mother. What kind of woman does what I have done? I could have killed my daughter. I'm lucky she wasn't hurt worse ... but she hates me for what I've done. What I've said. And Perry ... I've left him to pick up the pieces again. What kind of a woman acts that way?"

"One who can see no other way out of her current situation. One who is desperately tired, completely worn out, frustrated by what she must do, and by what she cannot do alone. One who has tried her best for years. That's the kind of woman I think you are."

"But you really have no idea who I am."

"That's true, but I want to find out. And I am willing to bet that you are overwhelmed, tired, depressed. Having a child with special needs—extraordinary needs—demands ..."

"You don't see Perry in here, do you? Falling apart, deserting our family, or worse yet, endangering our children?"

"This is about you, Caroline, not Perry. This is about what you have had to carry."

"He hates me."

"Really?"

"Yes. Ivy probably does, too. But Perry hates me most."

"Has he told you that?"

"He can't stand what I have become. Isn't that why he shows up every day?"

"Has he said so? What have you become?"

"A mope, a whiner. Perry is not someone who sits around and cries into a cup of coffee. Or tea. Tea spiked with a daily dose of Valium. Are you a tea drinker?"

"Yes, actually. I am."

"Could I have a cup now?"

"Well, okay. British style, with milk?"

"How about with a shot of Valium? Just kidding, yes, with milk."

He left her alone for five minutes then returned with two hot cups. Saucers too. A real gentleman. "Here you are. A cup of England's finest. PG Tips," he said. "I have my sister mail it to me once a month because I still can't find it in Atlanta. It's a cheap tea, really, but it's always been my favorite."

"Your addiction?"

He smiled, handing her the tea. "I suppose so, yes."

She took a sip and let it warm her a little, put the saucer on the side table, and cradled the white china cup in her hands.

"Perry has never drunk tea or coffee. Always a purist. Hard-working, upbeat, take-on-the-world guy. And me the big fat drag that I have become."

"Do you feel *any* compassion for yourself?"

"No. And I don't expect my family to either."

"Well, then. We certainly have our work cut out for us, don't we?"

"I don't know how to do this. Sit here, talk with you, get better. I don't see how. Especially when I am not sure I want to go back to it all."

"We take it slowly. Right now, for today, and the next few days, it's about rest. Your body needs healing. It's as if you've had surgery. Let's say a gall bladder operation. You need time to heal, recover. Be gentle on yourself." He paused, and took in the tears that were running down her face. He handed her a box of Kleenex. "Later, we will talk about you going home. Facing what's happened. We have to get you out of the woods before we revisit that path that led you in. Okay?"

She nodded. And the tears came steadily now.

"Caroline. When last we talked, you indicated that you might prefer not having to see your family for a while. Not having to put out the effort necessary to meet and greet. Do you still feel that way?"

She nodded slowly. "But I don't think Perry would abide by that."

"Not even if I explained to him?"

"I don't think so. Or if he did agree to stay away, I think it would hurt him too much. It would really hurt him to know that I asked not to see him."

"I am more worried about you. It's my job to focus on what you need to heal."

"I don't want you to make Perry even more angry. To make me feel even more worthless."

"Of course not, no. But are you sure he is angry? Could it be that he is terribly worried about you?"

"Wouldn't you be furious? If your wife or girlfriend or whoever did something like I did? I would be. I would be—if the situation was reversed. I would hate his guts. I would have to kill him." She laughed again. "That was a bad attempt at a joke."

"I could talk to him for you. Tell him it would be best not to stop by every day."

"No. I really don't want you to do that. I think, in a way, the visits help him. Make him think he's helping me."

"But you say he is not helping you by coming every day."

"No."

"Is he still bringing your sons on the visits?"

"Not every day."

"What about if we at least limit visits with the kids? It's rather much, isn't it, to have them come in here?"

She nodded.

"All right. I am going to suggest that we give you a little more healing time, more quiet time. I will talk to Perry. There will be time enough."

Caroline covered her mouth, did not speak, but still lines filled her head. *And indeed there will be time to wonder, Do I dare? And, Do I dare?*

CHAPTER 12

HUGO, AUGUST 1992

Three p.m. Hugo's thighs clung to the white-washed, white-hot slats of the guard chair, while sweat streamed down his chest. He craved water from the fountain that was out of sight, tucked into an alcove of the ancient park district field house, across the pool. Parched or not, he would have to wait. Lifeguard rules were firm and specific, spelled out in red, capital letters on the first page of that thick manual he'd had to memorize. Number one: *never leave your station.* So he was stuck—literally and metaphorically—to this hot seat until his slacker of a supervisor, Andre, decided to give him another break. And if Andre happened to forget to relieve him (which he did more and more as the summer dragged on and his flirtations with front-desk Cindy escalated) then Hugo had no choice but to wait, perched high above the deck, scanning the water's cool surface.

The second hand crawled through another loop. His grandfather's watch: a Czech-made Primak, the face scratched, but mechanicals still excellent. On the flat back, an engraving: *Jan Novotny 25-12-37.* A Christmas gift he must have received from someone special, or a luxury item he'd bought for himself? Could he have afforded such an item in pre-war Prague? Hugo never knew his grandfather, but had heard stories of his craftsmanship, thriftiness, and the fierce discipline that kept him working seventy or eighty hours a week until his heart gave out. Hugo inherited the watch and the discipline, too; he valued them both. Like now—he could put aside his needs. Thirst, irrelevant. Forget the clock. Watch.

The guard stand was rooted into the concrete deck, between the rectangular swimming pool and the small square of a diving well. The diving boards were long gone—an insurance liability in a public pool. Three days each week, six hours a day, he sat removed from the minor comforts of the drinking fountain, locker rooms, and concession stand. Beneath his standard-issue, red guard's visor, his face crisped to a painful pink. Previous summers, out back in his home pool with Ben, he'd never burned like this. Perhaps constant motion—jumping or diving, entertaining the boy all day— had buffered him from the sun's blasts. But here, the exposure was too much—the late-day sun angled off the water, targeting his weakest spots, feet, that skin on his ears that burned, peeled, and burned again.

He picked at a flake on his forearm and scanned the water's surface.

It was a strange pool: oddly placed, next to a dingy lagoon in the heart of the long-decaying park. Was that why he got the lifeguarding assignment? Piedmont: the perfect park for a misfit? When he'd told Dad about the part-time gig, early in the summer, he'd received no opposition. His coach, Billy Joe, was not enthusiastic.

"I'll practice," Hugo had promised, "Every day. Out back at home with Ben. I'll work the competition dives. See if I am not sharper than ever come September."

Billy Joe laughed, with a glint of unkindness in his eyes, "You'll get great coaching from your brother."

They hadn't spoken since.

The lifeguard's "ten-twenty rule" required him to scan in ten quick seconds—the lap swimmers, the floaters, the talkers standing in the shallows. Reach anyone in twenty. He took the requirement seriously.

"Too seriously," said Andre, who'd spent three previous years as a guard and one as a pool supervisor. "You're creeping people out, man, the way you stare." He was always bugging Hugo to lighten up. Sit back and relax.

He could have eased up—no lives at stake—no toddlers likely to slip in, no gangly six-year-olds, suddenly panicking in deep water. Most Atlanta moms took their kids to the tamer, suburban pools—Chastain Park and Buckhead, on the north, where all the girl guards worked, where the families were less likely to come across misfits and weirdoes. Piedmont had a different clientele—all adult, all male.

"Homos," Andre told him early on, "But they won't mess with you, so don't freak." A different clientele and a different staff? Or indifferent. That was what Andre advocated: don't work too hard. Don't sweat it.

Not Hugo's way. He had no choice but to look directly into the sun's glare—move his eyes slowly, slowly across the length of the pool, taking in its angles and depths, then darting them back to the starting place—a pendulum gaze all day long. Like with diving, like with Ben: break the task down, inhabit each element. Thinking too far ahead means trouble.

The first group to arrive at noon, right after the pool opened, was always the hairy, middle-aged men who pawed through a few laps in the pool, their eyes begging Hugo for encouragement. After lunch: middle-aged realtors, with thinning hair, ridiculously deep tans, slight to considerable paunches. They always violated pool rules by bringing wine coolers—red, turquoise, and orange colored drinks, as vibrant as Ben's crayons. They'd stay for a couple of hours, talking loudly about hot properties and hot boys, winking and nodding as they smoothed lotion onto each other's backs, and slapped innuendo onto their conversation. *Prime real estate, if you know what I mean, the complete package.*

Now, like every midafternoon, was the long, hot stretch. Andre was off somewhere ... hiding? Hugo needed water, and the sun sagged in the sky, carrying its heat like a burden. The swimming lanes were clear; strange shadows rippled under the surface. An old man, who didn't fit into any of the usual cohorts, gripped the gutter in the diving well. He was Asian perhaps—with short gray hair and the telltale foreigner's swimsuit: scant and colorful. His legs trailed out behind him, as he practiced an awkward flutter kick, going nowhere. Hugo let his eyes rest on him briefly, until the man returned his gaze, then Hugo skimmed the long, empty lanes again. Time struggled against the heat of the day. The old man climbed out, dried off, and left the deck. Hugo was stiff in his neck and legs, wanting a break, thirsty as hell. But training was learning to hold form through stress and challenge. That was what Billy Joe always said. Focus on the elements, drill them into your body and mind; that would keep you going, when fatigue or doubt set in.

Late afternoon. Seizure time, when Ben's brain, tired and over-stimulated, started firing, like heat lightning at the end of the day. And if someone wasn't watching, wasn't paying attention—if Ivy, who was supposed to be on duty when Hugo was lifeguarding, was not careful—then Ben could crash against the concrete. Would Ivy do the bare minimum to keep Ben safe, if not also happy? Not that much to ask, a few hours in the water with him two or three afternoons a week. All of them were supposed to be giving Mom time, space, to help her recover. But Ivy, of course, made it a big deal—with her pouts and her petty tirades. He should be at home. With Ben.

Worry double-wrapped him now. *Ben.* Was something up? For years, Hugo had translated Ben-speak: a spoon clanking on the table, an agitated bouncing, or a sudden, coy smile. When the others could not understand, Hugo also interpreted for them. Since Chicago, though, he and Ben had moved beyond interpretation; their connection ran deeper, like with twins, maybe, like shared DNA, so that even when Hugo was away, he could feel if something was wrong. Like now. He should never have agreed to this job. He should leave. Where the hell was Andre?

Maybe Hugo was no better, no more committed than the rest of his family. No better than Mom who had been completely out of it since her accident. (*Accident my ass*, Ivy had said.) No better than Dad, with his constant travel, trips each weekend to scout out new options for Ben. No better than Ivy who moaned and groaned through Ben care, then fled the first chance she got. In another couple of weeks, she'd leave for good. Off to college, off on her own—what she'd always wanted.

Hugo had to get home. *Ben could trip. He could bleed. He could seize.* Christ. Stop it. There was more than an hour left on his shift. He had to stop his brain spinning, stop the thoughts, block Ben.

Finally, 5 p.m. *Primetime.* The beautiful men arrived, laid their towels on the rough deck, alongside the lap lanes, and baked between the heat of the concrete and the final sun. Though they all looked alike—well-muscled, bronzed—they rarely spoke to one another. Or to Hugo. They'd arrived from jobs at banks or advertising firms to start their preparations for the night. What did their nights hold? Hugo watched with his trained gaze—seeing and not seeing—wanting to know and wanting not to know.

Across the pool, Andre. At last. Hugo saw him slip around the corner from the locker room. He stopped at the water fountain, drank long, wiped his hand across his mouth, adjusted his shorts. Andre knew what he wanted. With the lean, tapered muscles of the first-rate backstroker he claimed to be, Andre wore his hair in shoulder-length dreads that lightened progressively from roots to the straw-colored ends. He was born somewhere exotic—Barbados—or was it the Bahamas? Even now, as Hugo watched him walk over to Cindy, at the front desk, Andre tilted his head, tossed his hair around like an accent. He gestured like a foreigner. Atlanta men—coaches, construction guys, he knew—never used their hands this way; they kept them stuffed down deep in the pockets; their heads remained still, vaguely robotic. Hugo was not like Andre, but he was not like an Atlanta man, either. A diver would be considered too weird for their tastes. *That's not real a sport, right?* Plus, he didn't talk loud enough, or about the right things.

Finally—Andre sounded the whistle. Two long loud shrieks. Six o'clock.

The p.m. men packed up, pulled on t-shirts again, and left alone and aloof as sculptures. Hugo stepped stiffly down from his perch, picked up a few stray towels left on the deck. Cindy had already closed up the cash register, and waited patiently by the gate, as Andre loped over to check on Hugo. Only his second visit since noon.

"Hugo man, do you mind hanging out a few extra minutes tonight? I have to run a quick errand." He winked broadly.

"I was going to get a drink, then line up the lounge chairs. Do you want me to get back up in the guard stand?"

Andre looked confused. "Nah, man, the pool's closed. Relax. Have a swim. Just stick around a little longer in case maintenance comes by. Cool? I got some things I need to take care of." His eyes followed Cindy and he shook his hair again. Beads of sweat dropped on the deck. The coconut smell of lotion. He hit Hugo lightly on the shoulder. "So, we cool or what?"

"I guess. A few minutes is okay. I gotta leave soon though." Screw him and his laid-back Caribbean attitude.

Hugo placed three loungers, head to toe, head to toe, head to toe, against the chain link fence that separated the pool from the parking lot. The lot was almost empty, now. Weeds sprouted through cracks in the asphalt. The way Piedmont was going—weeds, litter, druggies sitting on the crumbling stone bridge over the lagoon—it was no wonder the mothers and children stayed away. Andre's little red Sunbird sat alone in the far corner, seeking out shade. He must have taken off with Cindy in her Jeep. For a cold beer or a hot make-out session in one of the wooded sections of the park? Is that what guys like Andre want?

Hugo carried the used towels over to the pool entrance where the facilities team would pick them up. Finally, with his tasks done, he walked towards the water fountain and gulped greedily, savoring the cool, metallic taste. He straightened up, and involuntarily, his eyes began scanning the pool again. Watching, waiting. Then again. *Ben.* He needed to get home. Checked his watch.

Relax man, Andre's lilting accent and drawn-out As still sounded in his head. *Relaaax*—said so that it turned the instruction into an insult. *And lose the squint, man, it's creepy.* Hugo scanned the pool to the diving area. Before the boards were removed, some kid broke his neck. So said Andre. A broken neck? Was Andre bullshitting? Hugo took off his watch, placed it on the deck, ran toward the edge and jumped, launching into a single, tight somersault; his entry took him straight to the bottom of the diving well, where a web of fine cracks spread out from the drain. He planted his feet, pushed back up to the surface, rolled over, floating with his eyes closed and the gentle hum of the pool pumps. *Relax. Relax. Relaaaax.* Water cooled his sunburned ears. Overhead, the sky was hazy and thick with pollution. He needed to get home. So good to wrap his body in the cool. He needed to get back, to watch Ben. He'd be bouncing in place at the top of the driveway, done with dinner, waiting for a final swim with Hugo, before they started the lengthy bedtime ritual. He would grunt his happiest *guh*, telling Hugo about his day, pulling him around the side of the house and down the mossy steps, getting ready to push him in. And Hugo would resist, making Ben almost crazy with anticipation—pulling and giggling and squealing until Hugo executed some giant pratfall. *Splash.* So simple, really, and all Ben wanted. Home, Hugo. Hugo, Home.

Hugo? Hugging tighter, *Hugo?*

Hugo is floating in a swimming pool without you, little man. Relaxing. Relaaaaaaxing and lying, Ben. Pretending to care about you but lying around. Avoiding you, like everyone does.

Hugo swam quickly to the side and pressed himself up and out of the water. He felt uneasy now. As though he was the one being watched. Had Andre come back? Maybe it was just his guilt. Or was it Ben? Trying to reach him again.

What?

He toweled dry, pulled on a t-shirt, checked again—six-thirty. Where the fuck was Andre? Hugo should just leave, leave the pool, and head home, but he'd promised. He sat down, duty-bound. How long should he wait? He couldn't leave with the gate still open. The stillness made him crazy, so he found a broom and started to sweep, spreading out a series of puddles.

Finally, Andre walked up behind, clapped a hand on his shoulder. "Thanks, man. I owe you."

Hugo straightened up. "No worries. But I've gotta run." He rolled up his wet towel, stuffed it in his backpack.

"Have a good night, man. Okay? Leave the gate. I'll lock it on my way out."

As he bent down to unlock his bike from the rack, Hugo heard a vehicle approach from across the lot. Billy Joe's white van inched towards him. Eight weeks since school let out, and twelve since they had really spoken. Billy Joe raised a hand off the steering wheel.

If you want to talk to me, Hugo thought, *stop the engine, get out of the van.*

Billy Joe opened the door and stepped out. His thin, black hair was combed back, up and off his face. His mustache was gone; where it had been, his skin was whiter, more naked somehow than even skin should be.

"Hugo. Can I have a word?"

Hugo nodded.

Billy Joe's top lip carried a few delicate beads of sweat. "How's the job so far? They treating you good?"

"All right." Hugo held his breath, tried to look Billy Joe in the eyes. What the hell was he doing here?

"Good to get some time away from the family?"

"Look. I don't want to be rude, but I need to go," he said slowly. "I'm supposed to be on Ben duty."

"I'll get to the point then. I want you to dive for me again this fall. I thought maybe I could give you a ride home and we could talk it over." Billy Joe took a cautious step. Hand held out. Did Hugo seem dangerous, like a rabid dog? Or scared? Depressed like his mother? Angry, like his sister? Wondering how he looked to Billy Joe made him feel dizzy. Hot. Sick. Nauseated. What kind of a coach would wait for him in a parking lot? How long had Billy Joe been here? Hugo put his hand out to the bike rack to steady himself. The metal still burned with the heat of the long day.

"We start diving already next week. We had a great summer session. Some amazing new talent—a kid who might even press you a little this year. I've left you alone for the summer, haven't I? But the team needs your leadership." Billy Joe moved towards him again, and Hugo reflexively stepped back, hitting the pool fence. "You needed a break. You've already done so much hard work. But senior year could be, well, a gift back to you. Don't you deserve that?"

The words clanged in his skull and kept coming, the words clanging and echoing and fading. *Diving … discipline … deserve …* words rattled his brain. Empty words. So many demands. *Hugo.* Fall, he might fall. *Home, Hugo.* I have to go. The weight of the day, the heat, the furious heat. Ben was waiting. But Billy Joe was talking and pushing him against the chain link fence. *Can you hear me? Are you okay?* Who was laughing? Heat lightning flashed. Billy Joe's lips were moving. His body was lurching, and Ben, was it Ben?—grasping and falling. Hugo.

When he came around, he was on the ground. Billy Joe hovering over him, Andre offering water. "Man. You fainted. Take it slow now."

After a while, he sat up, and a bit later, Billy Joe led him to the van, helped him into the passenger seat—hauled his bike in the back—and finally drove him home: from 14th Street to Northside Drive and on to the crescendoing hills of West Wesley. And all the way, Billy Joe talked softly of the gifts of training, ritual and regimen, the power of preparation. Hugo heard the words through the dazed aftermath Ben must inhabit; he didn't tune out Billy Joe's words so much as allow them to float. This was how it must be for Ben, after each seizure: the world going on despite him. Hugo stared out into the dusk, his eyes scanning the roadside, up and down, back and forth over kudzu mounds of dark growing darker. But a plan was forming too. A plan of his own, no one could claim it: Hugo and Ben, Ben and Hugo. All the training, the discipline, just preparation for what he will do, what he must do. His window down, and cicadas sawed the humid air, back and forth call, brother-to-brother, *shickkaw, shickkaw,* neither sound nor movement, but two in one—the vibrations of a primal tether.

PART II

DEATH BY WATER

Chapter 13

Hugo, November 2000

Hugo parks in the carport, enters the bungalow through the side door. Lois, dressed in purple bell-bottoms and a yellow shirt, doles some nasty looking meat onto two plastic plates.

"Ben did great today," she says. "Eighteen packets, zero time-outs."

"Wow. Is that a record?"

"Nah. He hit thirty around Halloween, remember? The M&M incentives. He got on a roll. Knife, fork, spoon—boom, boom, boom. Wouldn't even take a turn on the swings during his afternoon break."

She adds a spoonful of lima beans to the plates, covers them with plastic wrap. "You boys eat tonight. Don't forget again. Okay?"

Hugo nods.

Lois is better than okay. Even though she'd been caught dozing her first day on the job, when Ben tossed his sneakers out the bus window on the ride home from the Work Center, she had a sense of humor about it. Leading Ben down the steps off the bus and handing him over to Hugo, she'd said, "Home in one piece. Well ... minus the shoes." And to her credit, she's never let it happen again. Been his coach for over eighteen months now. Humor and durability are key. The pay's crap and the hours painfully boring, but Lois doesn't show the usual burnout signs: irritability with Ben, missing a day for an unexplained illness, smoking in the house. Sure, there's something a bit off about her, the pudding-bowl hairdo, her peculiar taste in clothes, and her love of organ meat. Humor and durability, and okay, oddity, are all essential.

"It's calf's liver. Y'all need the iron."

"You don't have to cook for us. That's my job."

"I know, I know. But you never eat right. All that sugary cereal. All those Cheetos."

Previous nights, she's tried beef tongue, oxtail soup, and once, a disastrous steak and kidney pie—gray gravy under a pastry shell, with gristle floating around unchecked. And if Hugo doesn't dump what she's prepared for tonight, she'll dig it out of the fridge tomorrow and put it in the blender for one of her disgusting spinach/protein shakes. Still, she's good with Ben, never embarrassed by or apologizing for his behavior. Shoot, she's the one who proudly introduced him to the whole neighborhood, taking him to knock on the doors of all the bungalows and apartments until he had a posse of young children who would play with him. Strange as he looks, cruising the cul-de-sac on his yellow trike, Ben's a known commodity. Samnang and his brothers, who live with a slew of relatives in a small unit next door, often come to use the swing set out back, and take turns pushing Ben.

Lois picks up her hat and coat, her car keys from the table. "Remember to eat." She yells into the living room. "You did good today Ben."

The little man is laid out on his beanbag, watching an ancient

Wee Sing video: *Old King Cole and Friends.* Hugo knows every word, every gesture of Jester's song now playing: the shoulder roll, the knee touch, the shimmy, shimmy, shimmy.

"How's my buddy?"

Ben smiles vaguely, and hugs himself, without taking his eyes off the screen.

"Yep, I'm home from work, but you're too damn busy to greet me right. Well, finish up this show. Lois cooked some nasty ass meat, but I'm going to make us some real man food."

Hugo tosses the liver slop down the disposal and finds a family size mac and cheese from his stash above the stove. While the water boils, he opens the day's mail—junk, all of it, except for a Statement of Particulars from Georgia Vocational Services, wanting more details about "the time and nature" of the services that Hugo provides. Screw that. Screw them. The bureaucrats are never satisfied with what he sends. If they really want more information, let them come knock on the door; let them manage a bad seizure night. He preps the mac and cheese, extra sloppy—the way they like it—fills two serving bowls, grabs two spoons and a dish towel just in case, and carries it out to Ben. Dinner in the den. Now that's a real service he provides, seven nights a week. Put that in the Statement of Particulars.

Side by side on the floor, they eat the soupy mac and cheese and watch the dramatic end, as Sonny and Jester yet again manage to find their way through the woods to King Cole's castle. The trumpet flourish. The big dance. The parade around the castle. When it's over, Hugo hits rewind and Ben rushes to the TV cart and selects his last video for the day. What else? *Where's Spot?* Over the years, Hugo has surrendered to a different flow of time with Ben. Months can go by in a blur and minutes—like those during a bad seizure—can feel like hours. How many times have they watched Spot play hide and seek? Where are those pesky penguins? Where's that alligator? Some nights, the seconds go so slowly that Hugo thinks he might lose his mind in this house and never find it again. Where is that mind? Where could it be? In the closet, under the stairs, stashed in the grand piano?

Around nine, when Ben's eyes flutter with fatigue, Hugo leads him down the hall to their bathroom for a pee and a minimal tooth cleaning. Swab, rinse, spit. Then to the bedroom, where Hugo helps him undress, and tapes him into a Depends, pulls on his reindeer pajamas. Ben lies on his mattress on the floor. *Guhs* once, and Hugo turns on Teddy Ruxpin. *Come dream with me tonight. We'll go to far off places.* Hugo lies down next to Ben and stretches one arm over him to massage his shoulder; a few minutes—they're both so tired—a few minutes more, until Ben's breathing will come slow and steady as Hugo's own.

Hugo jerks awake when Teddy Ruxpin's tape clicks off; he waits to be certain Ben doesn't stir, then covers him with a cotton blanket and slips out into the hall. In his own room, Hugo opens the window. The apartment complex next door is still humming, lights are on in many of the rooms, on each of the four floors. Wind-shuffled November air carries a strong scent—he can pull out threads of nutmeg, cumin, and perhaps cinnamon—he breathes in the fragrance of the meals that one of the Cambodian families prepares. He hears the deep timbre of an old man's voice, a chorus of trilling, womanly laughter, the clatter of pots in a sink. Scents and sounds of belonging. Sometimes, it feels as if Hugo and Ben are the new arrivals in America, and their neighbors are the indigenous people—sharing foods and swapping stories, living cradle to grave as family, an ancient, grounded people.

A woman's face appears in the kitchen window across from him. She waves at Hugo. He waves back, then he closes his curtains.

After all the years—seven or eight now, since he moved in with Ben—after all this time, his loneliness at night is as intense as ever. He's with Ben from 6 p.m. to 7 a.m. every night; and when Ben's asleep, Hugo has the bungalow to himself with his thoughts unmoored. Sometimes, he thinks he should try to build himself a different life, outside of his current routine of college classes, part-time work at the health club, and his long nights with Ben. And when Ivy calls, as she likes to do around holidays and on his birthday, she always blathers on about how he really should finish his degree—so many jobs for nurses these days, he could go anywhere he wants, such an honorable profession—but she doesn't remember, or doesn't want to remember, the reality of caring for Ben. She's off in Chicago, working as a doctor with real patients; she has a real girlfriend, too. A world of her own. She might as well live on Mars. She has forgotten how she used to run from the room when Ben seized, leaving Hugo to handle it. She has forgotten, or maybe never understood what Hugo's decisions have given to her. When she meets someone for a beer after work she certainly doesn't have to worry about who is watching Ben. About who will hold him when he gets overtired and has a seizure. About how to administer the Valium. Hugo picks up his physiology textbook from the side table; he's officially enrolled in two courses at Georgia State's School of Nursing, but he has fallen far behind in the reading this semester, with only two weeks until finals. Maybe he should drop out. It's not as if he's ever going to use the degree while he's caring for Ben. He thumbs through a chapter, unable to concentrate, puts the book aside.

He breathes, slow, regular, in and out, counts to one hundred, tries again, but his mind will not settle. He pulls on boxers and walks down the hall, three steps down into the den and turns on the TV. Nick Rewinds. Ren and Stimpy. The abusive, hyperactive Ren and his peanut-brained cat pal. Hugo and Ben have seen every episode, rolling on the soft carpet, giggling. Hugo knows somehow that Ben's slow brain finds humor, a true and painful humor, in watching all the skull-bashing blows to the discordant theme song: "Happy Happy Joy Joy."

Hugo mutes the TV, tries to sleep on the couch; the orange sectional that once furnished the family room at their home on Nancy Creek. Dad transported the couch and a beige rug and the television here on the back of his pick-up, when Hugo and Ben first moved into the bungalow. Dad often brings things—stacking corner tables, an oil painting of the Irish sea that Mom has always hated, dishes, an electric razor. Are they thank-you gifts? Or perhaps they are more like the offerings of a man going to confession, Dad doing penance—like Ivy with her periodic phone calls. Or maybe the donations are more pragmatic—investments—Dad building equity in this version of the future. Ben and Hugo's merged future. Ben and Hugo, happy as can be. What everyone wants to believe. Happy Happy Joy Joy.

When Dad says there are other arrangements we could make, Hugo nods, but neither of them take the conversation further. They both know that other options never work, that reinvented versions of the future would only harm Ben. Dad offers an out, for his own conscience. And Hugo likes to hear it to prove that even if Dad doesn't want things to change he is at least aware of what this arrangement requires.

▲▼▲

He wakes early on the couch, eyelids dry, mouth grungy. Overnight, the Nick cartoon marathon has merged with his dreams and now mutated back on the screen into a show too insipid even for Ben's expansive taste. He walks back to the bathroom, bending his head from side to side to work out the kinks in his neck. It's before seven; time to begin another day. He takes a hot shower, then dries, and wraps the towel around his waist. He pushes his hair out of his face as he looks in the mirror. Lois is right; he is too thin. His eyes look sunken. He should eat more, and eat more healthily. And he needs a haircut. He'll get one today. And a shave. A shave and a grip. He slaps cold water on his face like that guy in the aftershave commercial. It's not too late to go back to his classes, study hard, pass this semester. He puts the plug in the tub and starts the bathwater.

When he pushes open the bedroom door, Ben stirs, sits up on his mattress, hugs himself.

"Hey guy. Your breath is wicked this morning. Let's get you in the tub, then do your teeth." He helps Ben out of his PJs and removes the sodden Depends. "Come on man, tubby time."

Ben shakes his head no, gives a devilish smile.

"Don't fight me today. I've got the water running. Come on, Ben. I don't want to have to do the Dooby Treatment."

Another emphatic head shake, and Ben takes off, naked and gangly, tottering down the hall. Game on.

"Oh yeah?" Hugo rallies, even though he could do without the chase scene today. Ben rushes to his favorite hiding place. Hugo doesn't need to see his face to know the smile is wide, the tongue is lolling, his eyes are mischievous and sparkling.

"Oh yeah?" Hugo chases after him. "It's the Treatment for you, then."

Ben screeches and dives under the sheets on Hugo's bed, as always forgetting to cover his legs. A two-year old's logic: I can't see you, so you can't see me. Hugo strips back the sheet with a roar, straddles Ben, holds down his arms and gives him a good dose of the Treatment, tickling him relentlessly under the chin and arms, until Ben is hiccupping and drooling and laughing. Then he lifts Ben over his shoulder, hauls him to the bathroom.

"Get your skinny ass in the tub while I go fix us some breakfast."

He plops him in the water. Ben's tall enough now that he must bend his knees to fit. The water runs; if Hugo turned it off, Ben would knock the faucet back on with his foot. Another element of the morning ritual—off, on, off, on—so Hugo lets it flow.

"I'm gonna get dressed and fix your breakfast shake. Be right back."

Vanilla Ensure, two raw eggs, a daily tablespoon of Tegretol and a spoonful of sugar. He whizzes it up, pours it into a tall plastic cup. Ben may be small and wiry still, but at least he gets good morning nutrition. Hugo leaves the cup on the counter, goes outside to get the paper. It's brisk, the sky is clear. Another half hour before the Work Center bus appears and honks for Ben.

"Hello, Hugo."

It's Narith. The oldest of the brothers who live next door; the family's designated translator, standing behind him in the driveway.

"How's it going?"

Narith nods. "I am very well, thank you. My mother requests for you to come for dinner. Yourself and Benjamin. This evening?"

"That's really kind. Thank you. Ben's not great at sitting for a meal, though."

"He can be entertained with Samnang, perhaps?"

"All right. Thank you. I can bring a bottle of wine."

Narith nods again and disappears into his building.

172

Hugo brings the paper inside, pours a cup of coffee, and turns to the sports. Falcons are 7 and 4, with a chance at the play-offs. A few minutes more and he goes to dress Ben. By the time he reaches the bathroom door, he knows that something's wrong. Way wrong. Too quiet, none of the usual splashing, toys clanking against the tub liner. Hugo pushes the door open. The faucet drips on Ben's too-still body—submerged and distorted through the water.

No. God, No. Hugo lifts him out of the tub, lays him on the bath mat. His lips are blue, his eyes fixed, the wandering one—a milky stone. Hugo shakes Ben's shoulders—his skin warm, but his body so still, so still. Not a seizure, then; his limbs are limp, unmoving. No, god. Help. "Someone help!" He screams again. "Help, please, help!" 911. He starts for the phone, then remembers, CPR. Lifeguard training. The ABCs, airway, breath, compression. Chest compressions. Pump, pump, pump, breath, two-three-four, pump, pump, pump, breath, two-three-four.

▲▼▲

Lois finds them there. Hugo sees her, hears the ambulance arriving. Had he called? No. Namrith? Lois? He cannot think. He cannot stop, he is still pushing on Ben's chest. EMTs arrive. Two paramedics talking, words he cannot understand—then the lean woman in a blue jumpsuit pulls Hugo aside and works on Ben, all the way down the corridor and out on a stretcher. When the paramedics lift him into the ambulance, Ben's face is fixed, and one arm drops off the stretcher. Hugo climbs into the back. Before the door closes, Lois tosses him a gray sweater. As they pull away from the bungalow, Hugo sees out of the back window, Jeri, Namrith and little Samnang, standing together in front of their building. Sami waves and smiles, then covers his ears when the sirens begin to wail.

CHAPTER 14

IVY, NOVEMBER 2000

Despite a chill wind that tumbles trash around the Hertz lot, Ivy opens the roof on the Miata rental and accelerates north from the airport along I-85, Atlanta's federally funded race track, whipping through the downtown s-curves and up the 14th Street exit ramp. Right at the light, over Peachtree, then a quick left, into the buffed brick driveway of the Piedmont Funeral Parlor. She shifts gears for the incline and squeal-stops in the first of five parking spots, each reserved with a tasteful olive and taupe sign for "The Bereaved." These words seem about right for her particular, un-evolved grief.

The funeral home, perched on a ridge overlooking Piedmont Park, is stately and well-painted, more than holding its own among a row of glass towers that must have gone up over the past decade. When Ivy was in high school, Midtown Atlanta and this park in particular were haunts for the homeless, heroin addicts, and, of course, homos. They'd walk the periphery, singly, dually or even triply diagnosed, looking for their respective remedies. Today, in keeping with her arrival in an expensive sports car, the area seems spruced up, gentrified, finally "turning," the way Dad and his developer friends predicted it would.

She came straight from the airport—instead of going home to her parents—wanting to see Ben before tomorrow's service, wanting to see him alone, have time to react, without an audience. When she was a kid, it was okay to run panicked from the room whenever Ben fell from a seizure, but she's a doctor now, twenty-seven years old, returning like some hard-traveled war hero, decorated with an MD, and well into the first year of a four-year residency in obstetrics and gynecology. Having done the emergency medicine chunk of the curriculum—a sordid, five-week ordeal of bullets, bone, and yes, lots of blood—she should be prepared to hold her ground at a viewing of the body. Her brother's body. Just in case, though, she doesn't need a room full of witnesses to her weak-kneed incompetence.

The brass knocker on the solid oak door is a lion's head with a full gold mane, polished and fierce. She lifts and slams it, watches it rebound off a shiny pad. Injury and retaliation. Mr. Kalwar, the young Pakistani owner of the funeral home, with the Brooks Bros. suit and the requisite voice of sincerity, opens the door, introduces himself.

"I'm Dr. Novotny, Ben's sister. I was hoping to see him before all the formalities tomorrow."

He nods his head, ushers her into the front parlor, but once inside leans in to whisper, "I'm afraid a private viewing isn't really possible at the moment. The coroner, you see, has been *waylaid*." Mr. Kalwar's phraseology and diction suggest a British boarding school; his swank suit and fluid upper body movements read gay. He gestures for Ivy to sit down on a suede couch. "May I offer you some coffee or tea, perhaps?"

"No, thanks. I've been sitting on a plane all morning. I really want to see him." She needs to look at Ben, laid out silent and immobile, as she sometimes wished him to be, then berate herself for what such unspoken prayers have finally wrought. At the very least, she owes him an honest and private goodbye. "Could you take me back? I don't mind if he's not ... prepared. I am a doctor. "

"It's a bit more complicated than that. I am afraid your brother's body is not yet *here*. The coroner has been waylaid."

That word again. *Waylaid*, spoken softly, very *Twilight Zone*. Ivy sees it with quotation marks around it, too, and tries to make its meaning fit today's events. "What does that mean exactly?" Some kind of mortician-speak, perhaps? Or British diction? "My father told me Ben would be here." She looks at her wristwatch for emphasis. "*This* morning."

"I am sincerely sorry for the confusion. Please make yourself comfortable while I make a call. Sometimes these things take longer than expected."

Mr. Kalwar indicates the inviting couch again. His clay-colored eyes and lighter chestnut skin contrast handsomely with the starched white of his shirt collar. Clean, lean, and very smooth. She wants to ruffle him somehow, as he stands waiting for her to take a seat, smiling with his polished patience, and offering annoying assurances.

"What things? And where is Ben now?" It's not a spiritual question.

"He's still at the Coroner's Office. DeKalb County. They have jurisdiction because he died in Clarkston. They probably need to determine cause of death. Rule it accidental."

"Of course it's accidental," she says, louder than necessary. "He had a massive seizure. In the bathtub."

Although he is too young to be credibly comforting, he puts a hand on her shoulder and nods. "I understand how frustrating this must be. And may I say that I am so, so sorry about your loss, Dr. Novotny."

Ivy moves away from him to take in the parlor: Very tasteful, even if a bit exotic for Atlanta. A red kilim underlies the rich, chocolate-colored couch. This must be where he does his bit as ersatz therapist; he probably sits on one of the two straight-backed oak chairs, listens, nods, sympathizes: *so sorry about your loss.* In medical school, she learned never to use words like "loss" or "expired" in these circumstances. The first year curriculum like finishing school—how to dress, how to carry yourself, how to raise and lower your tone as needed to impart authority or understanding; students practiced their bedside manner on an array of actors who received good money to role-play tricky patients. Ivy should pass on some of the advice to Mr. Kalwar. *You lose keys, not patients. Same with expire—that's only for driver's licenses and credit cards. Be clear, be direct.* She practices it on herself: *your brother is dead, Ivy.* Adding the first name at the end is a nice touch. Personal. While touching the bereaved, she learned in the same class, is rarely a good idea—even a gentle hand on the shoulder is too open to misinterpretation.

"The funeral—can it still go as scheduled tomorrow?"

"Oh yes. Usually, they do a quick autopsy—rule out any foul play."

Autopsy? Why hasn't she understood that until now? Ben laid out in some cold metallic room, splayed and sliced, after all he has been through. Of course his end would be like his beginning: knives, masks, procedures. She'd visited him in the hospital once, after an accident, or a seizure; he was tied at the wrists and ankles with soft restraints, his head in some kind of immobilizing contraption, IVs in his bruised arm. He looked like the frog Ivy's class pinned down and dissected in fifth grade and she ran screaming from the room. She feels faint, her ears begin their telltale ringing, the way they did during her grisly ER rotation: *Novotny's going syncopal again.* She needs to sit.

"As long as we get the body over here by tonight, we'll be ready. If you want to come back, first thing tomorrow morning, I can get you in for a separate visit before the service. For your private grief."

Not grief. Not yet. How can grief begin when she hasn't even seen her brother in years? She was hoping that facing him here, bearing witness alone, might help jumpstart the process. Trust Ben to pull a fast one on her and show her up as cold and unfeeling, one last time. His blue eyes twinkling in that mischievous way, as he smiles and *Guhs. Gotcha.* She told her parents, told Hugo, so many times over the past ten years, that she was too busy to come more than once a year, too much to do, too many courses, too many demands, a new rotation. Had anyone believed her?

Her sole elective during medical school had been a course on medical history. From Hippocrates down through the works of his heirs apparent, Soranus, Galen, and Vesalius, the practice emphasized obsessive watching—recording signs and symptoms—but it was a science wary of innovation. The focus always on doctor and patient, observer and object. No room for extra actors: the prodigal sister, or "The Bereaved." No screenplay to follow. No protocol. Not even a glossy pamphlet, captioned: *Grieve like this.* Now she had to improvise. Grieve like this, Ivy: *fly home, but don't see your family. Go directly to the funeral home, the one without the body.* So much time away and still no sense of how to return home. She was never good at accepting Ben during his life, so how could she possibly come home now, genuinely grief-stricken, seeking and sharing comfort with her family? *Not like Hugo.* In the last few years, he had barely left Ben's side. Lived with him in the bungalow Dad bought in Clarkston, cared for him, sacrificed for him. Hugo, of course, was there when Ben died.

"Are you all right?," Mr. Kalwar asks, "You look poorly."

"I need a minute."

"Take your time. This is very stressful, I understand. I am going to ring the coroner's. See if I can learn anything more."

In the middle of the room, a well-lacquered mahogany table carries an autumnal-toned floral arrangement and a stack of business cards, as well as a box of tissues, discreetly encased in a miniature sterling silver casket. She pulls out a tissue and shreds it. In the far, windowless corner of the room, a healthy looking ficus tree stands so green and full that it hits her as an indictment: She's killed off four such plants in as many Chicago apartments. Each year of medical school, as she migrated north, away from Northwestern's downtown hospital complex (to Lincoln Park, to Wrigleyville, to Uptown, and finally, to her new condo and openly lesbian life in Andersonville), she bought another ficus at the Great Ace Hardware. With each purchase, each move, she told herself she'd be better, more careful about water, more diligent about room temperature. A trustworthy caregiver. But always, in a matter of weeks, the leaves began their steady, baleful drop.

Fake. The ficus has to be fake.

She left home for Chicago at eighteen. Left behind a family in disarray. College melded into medical school, medical school morphed into a residency, and her plan was to keep right on rolling, through post-graduate residency years two, three, and four, and into a prestigious fellowship, possibly followed by an academic post. One long, inexhaustible, and legally defensible excuse to stay busy. During infrequent phone calls home, she always, always asked about Ben—how he was in his home-away-from-home with Hugo—and only a few times did she see him—a quick visit before the start of medical school, then last year at his home. She'd gone to the bungalow—spent an hour or two with her brothers, but felt as if she were drowning the whole time—old furniture from the Nancy Creek house filled their place. Familiar paintings on the wall. The same brown-striped towels in the bathroom. Everything recognizable, but disorienting in its placement. When she left, Ben stood in the driveway waving goodbye and she honked and circled an unnecessary loop around the cul-de-sac. The last time he saw her, she was running off again.

The couch calls. Maybe she will not leave this place. Maybe she will wait here all day for Ben to show up, then sit vigil with the body until the rest of "The Bereaved"—the ones without quotation marks—arrive.

Mr. Kalwar returns. "I spoke to a tech who would only tell me the chief pathologist is still working and they will let us know where things stand later in the afternoon. But apparently your father has been over there to address some questions."

"What questions?"

"About the cause of death."

"Cause ... Ben had a seizure. He's had them all his life. It's not that complicated." Ivy stands and moves back to the center table, picks up one of the business cards. *Martin B. Kalwar, CFSP*, in a fine gold script. "What does that stand for, CFSP?"

"Certified Funeral Service Provider," he says. "A state licensing requirement."

"And what does a CFSP do, *exactly*?"

"Well, my job includes meeting the family, transporting the body here, preparing it for viewing, helping the bereaved with details of the service. And final disposition, of course, usually burial or cremation. In this case, your father selected cremation. I do all the paperwork. Get the cremation permit from the medical examiner, signatures from the family. Attend to whatever else the family needs."

"Well, what the family really needs in this case," Ivy says, drumming his business card on the table, "is my brother's body."

Mr. Kalwar grimaces slightly, as he walks towards her, then places an elegant hand on her elbow.

"We'll work it out, I assure you." He leads her back to the entry hall. Clearly, his CFSP protocol advises him to get testy clients out the door. "Your father has made all the necessary arrangements: the casket, the service, the cremation. The autopsy is out of my control. But I feel certain we'll be ready before 11 a.m. tomorrow. My staff will work all night if we have to."

He opens the heavy front door and escorts her across the parking lot. "Call me in the morning, and please do not worry. It is probably a minor snafu. These things happen. Really, they do."

But they don't, at least not in Ivy's limited experience. Not to other families. Not to the truly bereaved.

Mr. Kalwar bends low for the Miata door. "A beauty," he said, patting the smooth, cherry-colored hood.

"Yes." Ivy steps into the extravagant rental, feeling at once immature for her snippiness and deservedly chastised—really, who would choose a car like this to go to their brother's funeral? The engine, sensing her embarrassment, revs cheekily. She raises a hand to Mr. Kalwar, and drives off down 14th Street, hoping that somewhere soon she'll get her bearings, find Peachtree Street, and wind her way home.

▲▼▲

Hugo sits at the end of the diving board, a still life on this cloud-shrouded night: *The Diver.* His feet disappear in a milky mist above the water and his shoulders round forward and down, in fatigue or grief. Impossible to discern, in the deepening dusk and from this distance. On the back deck of the house, Ivy watches, not wanting to invade or, more accurately, afraid of what comes between them—the distance and the years—eight years since they lived together in this family home. Their time apart will come to equal their time spent together—which weighs more? How is it possible to have shared parents—a conjoined childhood—to have nature, nurture, a multitude of genes and a thousand experiences in common, and yet to feel only this: a desire to flee the moment she arrives?

When her friend, Cam, dropped her off at O'Hare this morning, she said, "Remember to breathe. Deep breaths, especially when you want to run." A pragmatic nurse with a New Age twist. Ivy hasn't spilled much about her family during their job-constrained friendship, but Cam is the kind of friend who seems to understand things not said. And since Ivy appreciates any advice she can cling to now, she grips the cedar top-rail and draws slowly from the moist evening air. Each breath does settle her, like a cool washcloth on a fevered brow. She wears a layer of nervous sweat from the early morning plane ride, and a film of grease, smoke, and shame, accumulated from the afternoon hours that she wasted at that hangover of a bar, The Hole in the Wall. She went there after stopping at the funeral home, waylaid on her way home. For more than three hours, she made small-talk with a big-boned girl from Alabama, to postpone this moment.

She wraps her arms tightly around her torso—Ben-style. He's gone, and from here on, it will be only Ivy and Hugo. The backyard seems smaller and denser than she remembers. It must have started as a crude semi-circle bulldozed into the thick Georgia pines by Trey Huff's construction crew. After he bought the house, Dad dropped a deep swimming pool in the middle of the yard, wrapped it with concrete and tile. Past the pool, he planted several low-maintenance beds, full of azaleas, rhododendrons, box woods. Beyond the beds and still inside the wire fence, a few hardwoods lean in towards the pool. Ben's pool. The leaves rustle and whisper: *where is he?* Winter comes late in the South, sometimes not until January. The trees hold onto their leaves. So many trees, and all of them—the perimeter hardwoods, even the green-black swath of pines behind the fence—watch Ivy like unforgiving ghosts.

Just breathe. If only Cam were here to escort her down the wooden stairs towards Hugo, to help her through the coming days. She'd know the right words to say to help Ivy close the distance. If only she were more like Cam—calm, confident, steady. Being home brings back the floundering mess of a girl with a chunky body and unclear desires. She wants to go back to Chicago, back to work, to patient charts and differential diagnoses—if not this, then that; check box one before moving on. She has been thinking lately of signing on at Northwestern for an additional two-year fellowship in Reproductive Endocrinology: how hormones impact body and brain. *Stay or go, fight or flight, preserve or procreate.* RE is a balancing act—learning to titrate the perfect solution of estrogen and progesterone in

183

a woman's body. A successful fertility outcome depends on timing, preparation and patience; these requirements have not been virtues in her life so far.

Across the pool, with his head bent over the water and both hands resting in his lap, Hugo could be silently praying. What would he ask God for? More time with Ben? Or freedom—for himself, and also for Ben, freedom from the constraints of his physical body and the torment of his seizures? That would be an honorable request—that Ben's soul shed his beleaguered body. In the past, Ivy prayed sometimes for Ben's death, for a gentle end, a deep, deep sleep that relaxed his palsied limbs, softened his screeches, left him laid out, with a whisper of a smile on his lips.

Ben died in the tub after a massive seizure. Mom said on the phone yesterday morning. Ivy wanted to ask, *Was anybody with him?* But the question would have sounded like an accusation against Hugo, her blameless brother. Does it matter now, does it matter *how*, Ben died? From the moment he was born, doctors said he didn't have long. The only surprise is that she feels any surprise at all—that the phone call she always expected to receive still felt completely unexpected. She *wished* him dead sometimes, yes, but still she is not prepared. She did not want this. So she grips the balcony rail and watches: one brother gone, one left alone on the board, and Ivy still the heartless observer. She could stand here all night. Maybe the cortisol hasn't kicked in yet and grief is simply stalled. Stress pulls hormones from safe harbor until they flood the body like the ancient humours. Hippocrates said epilepsy was triggered by an imbalance of phlegm: too much water—the brain drowning in fluid. The boys in the pool. Ben in the bathtub. If only grief would come, strong, cleansing, powerful enough to move her forward, down, towards

Hugo. She wants to believe that she can grieve. But she doesn't; she suspects a far more shaming truth: she is not capable of it. Hugo got the compassion; he always was and will be the good soul. Ivy chose medicine—that ancient and caring profession—as a cover, so no one would question her selfish heart.

When she was a kid, and Ben would fall—a tonic-clonic onset—she would be running away before she knew what she was doing. Before formed memories, she remembers running from his seizures. She was three, four, five and fleeing, thirteen, fourteen, fifteen, gone. Her own primitive, neural escape. Some inner voice would say *Stay, Ivy, stay,* but she heard it only when she was leaving, sometimes after she was already long gone, when the message had already become a reprimand: she had failed before she even received it. And she couldn't return, terrified of what she would find. The seizure would be over, Ben doped up on Valium, splayed out exhausted on their parents' bed, and her adrenaline finally, belatedly surging. Ivy would linger in the periphery, lightheaded and jittery for hours. Next time, next time, she would do better. Ben's last seizure—in the tub—would have snagged his brain in milliseconds. Did he know this one would be different?

She holds the rail so tight that her forearm starts to shake. *Just go to him.* The wooden steps down to the pool deck are rotting; where there used to be straight lines, the edges are gnawed, irregular under her weight. A fluorescent moss paints the risers, and the gray-white mist slings across the water to draw her down. The pool, the boys in the water, the summer heat, the lightning at night, the slips and falls, the seizures on the deck, the long minutes waiting, the dead of the wait, the fear that can stall a heart, the heart finally stopped. If Hugo senses her looking or hears the muted thud of her clogs first on the steps, then cracking louder on the concrete, he does not show it, does not look up. Maybe *The Diver* hopes that fear will turn her back, before he has to acknowledge her arrival.

His hair, longer than Ivy remembers, curls shaggily around his ears. And his frame is slight beneath his thin gray sweater. What does he see in the pool: a leaf, a twig, a skeeter bug? What does a still life feel? Siblings still alive when their brother is not. Siblings who do not know how to talk to each other. He must sense her arrival but he does not or will not look up. He always laid claim to a special sense—said he knew when Ben was in trouble, sick or needing, that he understood. Maybe it was that he listened better, was more empathic—the type of listener doctors are supposedly trained to be—to hear the meaning of silences, interpret the movement of muscle, the pulsing clench in a jaw, the flutter of an eyelid. Why won't he look at her, tell her he has been waiting all day, as she would do, and with a sigh of reproof, if their roles were reversed?

If their roles were reversed. *The Girl on the Board*: Ivy sitting alone, resolute and unmoving above the water. *The One Who Cared Enough to Stay.* Ben gone, and with him her anchor and reason for living. And, if it were Hugo, instead of Ivy, arriving after so many years, absurdly late on this of all nights—what words would she toss at him? *How dare you come creeping back like this? This is not your sorrow.*

Ben and Hugo never needed her. They inhabited a water world of games, shared a language, and so many experiences, a world they built of desire or necessity. She told herself she didn't care which it was—it didn't matter; she wouldn't join in if they didn't want her. Perhaps the fear of coming home is finding you are still who you always were: that selfish, incompetent teen.

The mist turns around her calves. *There's still time to turn back.* The pool water is brown and brackish with leaves, insects, decay.

Ben should be bouncing in clear blue water, waist deep, slapping the surface, screeching, anticipating Hugo's next best dive. No heat lightning blankets the November sky; no crickets chirp their rhythmic losses, but the night vibrates with something else. Hugo senses it too and lifts his head at last and sees her. Fear ricochets along her jaw and all she wants now, all she has ever really wanted, is to get away. *And didn't you get that?* Hugo doesn't say. The year she left was the year he stayed. The year he committed himself to Ben. *Had himself committed.* Does it matter how it happened—free choice or predetermination? She got away while Hugo made his life here. Ten paces and she stands at the base of the diving board, kicks off her shoes and bows her head like a penitent.

"Hugo." Her voice thick with want.

His eyes catch hers then move off, but he pats the board next to him. "Hey, Swiss Miss, come on out here. Come and sit with me. I wasn't sure you'd make it."

Grief or a tincture of age, time, and responsibility has diluted Hugo. He is not the hard-muscled perfectionist, the acrobat suspended above the blue. He is thin and tired; his unshaved cheek prickles Ivy's lip when she bends to kiss him. Almost a decade since they lived here together and he is a man, not a boy. And it is not only Ben they have lost but also the time and opportunity, the possibility for their childhood to be anything different than it was. She sits down near him, perpendicular to him, with her feet dangling sideways off the board. Hugo and Ivy together in the frame, *Siblings on the Board.* Wherever they go from here will always be weighted by a past of judgment and jealousies. He tosses hair out of his eyes and squeezes her hand.

"You've been gone so long."

It sounds less like a condemnation than a question, the way he says it, but she does not offer any kind of an explanation. She doesn't have one. Tears, warm and shameful. Hugo stayed. They watch the water through the mist, the darting insects on top, the murky shadows below, they watch the ghosts, they are the ghosts watching themselves long ago in the water.

"It is wrong here without him," Ivy says.

Hugo presses her palm so hard into the board that the coarse metal grates her skin. The mist wraps them up: air and water, gray, inconstant, interstitial.

"Oh god, Hugo. There's so much I wish I could do differently." He nods, but he can't understand this. Grief for him must feel pure and resolute, a swan dive cutting the water.

His voice is etched, deep. "It's like he's playing a trick, holding his breath, ducking down in the shallow end. Hiding somewhere and ready to pop up. But that was me. He never learned how to hold his breath." Hugo swipes at tears with his free hand, then rakes his unruly hair off his face. "I should never have left him alone in the bath."

She should hug him, but any gesture would seem forced. "You couldn't watch him every moment."

"I was reading the newspaper in the kitchen."

"You don't have to explain. Not to anyone. Certainly not to me."

"I can usually sense a seizure, feel it building; I am there when he falls … I wasn't listening."

"Look at me, Hugo." She waits for him to turn his face and meet her eyes. "None of this, none of it, could ever be your fault."

"You don't know what you're talking about."

"I know you gave up everything to care for him. I know you never had a life of your own."

"It was never like that."

His face is dark, angry, unlike what she has seen in him before, and it scares her. Across the pool and fifty meters back, a rusting wire fence separates the yard from the pines in Nancy Creek Park. Back in high school, if things at home got too intense, she would slip through a hole in the fence and follow the three-mile, clay path that snaked through the park, running up and down the steep banks, and crisscrossing the creek in its shallows. In memory, it is always summer in the back yard, the green so vivid, the flowers thick-petaled, tropical in size and color; the kudzu creeping up from the park, and the bleached, buzzed boys are always in the water, screeching, splashing, and spraying her with their being.

Ben is dead and Hugo is a grown man, grieving. *Stay, Ivy and find the right words for once.*

"He could have had a seizure anywhere, you know. On anyone's watch, on the bus, at his work center."

"If I had been doing what I was supposed to be doing, I could have pulled him out of the water, given him Valium. He would have been okay."

"You don't know that."

"He drowned. On my watch."

"But it could have been the seizure that killed him."

"I know what the coroner said. Inconclusive. But if I had been there in the bathroom, where I should have been, I'd have pulled him from the water and talked to him, rubbed his back and eventually, he would have come out of it. Like a thousand times before."

"Don't do this." Her heart thumps loud and she is afraid Hugo must hear it.

"I had to get away from him," he says as he buries his face in his hands. "In the end, I was just like you."

CHAPTER 15

HUGO, NOVEMBER 2000

The Eulogy Not Given:

Benjamin Karel Novotny: Benjamin, Ben, Buddy, Boy, Little Man, Lurch. From the moment you ripped into this world you shook it. Took things the way they were and poked at them; pressed and prodded to shape what was not into what it could be. You lived each second as yourself—your knock-kneed, wobbly, chlorine-scented, bouncy, drooling self. Your life one big Carpe Diem. Seize the day. You taught me how to look at things through your slightly blurred lens, with your slightly scrambled brain. Scramble the world. Shoes go on the feet—why not out the window? Who says a telephone can't swim? What did Dad want with those keys anyway? God, I am going to miss you. Dragging around your lazy left leg, laughing at your own pratfalls, trying to tell me so much with one

varying "guh." Good, great, more, yes, okay, thanks,
I love you, good night. Got to go. I didn't know it
was time. Did you not want me to know? What am I
going to do? Who will link arms with you when you
take off in your slanted run towards the next game?
Who will hold you when you seize the day? Seizure
day. I left you in the bath alone. Did I let you go
or did you leave me? What will I do without you to
shape my world? Who am I when I cannot be your
brother identical wannabe with you wherever you go
Hugo?

On the grass lawn, just to the side of wrap-around porch of the funeral home, Hugo watches his family leave. He starts to raise his hand for a ride home, or maybe just a goodbye, but no one seems to notice. Anyway, his intentions are dark and unformed as the heavy, gray sky that moved in during the service. Goodbye requires more—resolution or rage—and since he has neither, he pockets his hands in his borrowed, gray slacks, rolls his shoulders against the building wind, watches and waits as the cars clear out of the parking lot.

His family first. Their departure, of course, a hurried and disjointed thing, which at least brings some comfort: familiar discombobulation. A great word, dis-com-bob-ul-lation, syllables popping off in all directions. Perfect for the Novotnys. Dad and Ivy lead the mourners in the faded blue pick-up truck, that rattles and creaks as it dips at the bottom of the driveway, then roars out into the Midtown, midday traffic. His mother, meanwhile, follows behind them, far more sedately—but just as obliviously—in the passenger seat of a silver Accord, piloted by June Stein, who is an Emory professor, another fifty-year-old feminist with a doctorate in what is it? Anthropology or maybe Archaeology? Mom has few friends, but those she does have are divorced or widowed, as if she already considers herself an honorary member of one of these clubs. June maneuvers the Accord to the front of a line of cars waiting in the driveway to exit onto the street; it idles just long enough that Hugo catches Mom's profile through the glass. Almost haughty in grief, she stares straight ahead like an aging ballerina or a wronged queen. The black-coated funeral attendant has stopped the traffic flow on Piedmont Street and waves June's car out onto the street.

After the family, the convoy of friends—maybe thirty cars—moves slowly, resolutely, onto Piedmont. The last to leave the parking lot, the Clarkston Work Center bus, is filled with the able-enough who traveled with aides. The bus that coughs and splutters as it pulls away, a giant yellow period at the end of the funeral procession. Poor Lois is not on the bus; Ben doesn't need *his* job coach any more. She came alone in her car to the funeral—Hugo saw her, clad in an orange print dress, standing at the back of the ersatz chapel. She escaped early, it seems, without talking to anyone in the family. He will never see her again and he feels this as a subsidiary loss, a faint echo of his deepest sorrow.

A funeral home attendant picks up a sign from the driveway and carries it up the hill, along the driveway past the house and towards the utility outhouses at the back of the property. Only Hugo is left. Well, Hugo and Ben, of course. In life as in death, conveniently left or obliviously forgotten. Isn't it what Hugo wanted anyway? Isn't that what he chose—to be with Ben? So why bitterness? He does not like this new and growing sense of being wronged; it does not belong to him. He shivers; the storm that threatens from the north will arrive soon. How is he supposed to go now? Even if he had a ride, it wouldn't be easy. He wishes Lois had offered him a ride, so then the two oddballs could have left together, missionaries without their mission. They could have driven somewhere—anywhere—in her clunker of a car, back to the bungalow or to Lois's home in North Georgia. They could have drunk cheap beer or better yet, free moonshine, at her hillbilly mother's trailer home and told stories about Ben, on and on, until some meaning or purpose emerged from their pickled memories.

He turns up the collar of his thin gray jacket and walks around the empty parking lot, trying to think clearly. He could use an overcoat. He shivers and stomps his feet on the asphalt. Good thing he asked the funeral director to dress Ben in his best sweatsuit, along with a rainbow bandana tied around his neck. Ben always, always feels the cold. Hugo bites his lip, wanting some feeling, anything *other* than cold or emptiness or worse yet, bitterness to take him over. This empty parking lot. What remains? Ben and Hugo, Hugo and Ben.

Near the main house, a red brick path meanders to a fountain in the middle of a small lawn; Hugo paces over to it quickly. Several dormant rose bushes on either side, prickly sentries, wait for his next move, but Hugo has no idea why he walked here. The fountain is shut off and the pond covered with several slimy lily pads. Large drops of rain target the lilies; he sees them hit before he feels one on his cheek, two, three then several more. Wide, angry blotches mark the shoulder of his jacket. He hurries along the path, past the fountain, through the front garden, before looping around behind the house, where a covered walkway leads from the back entrance of the funeral home to the ugly, functional outbuilding. The crematory. He raises his shoulders, pushes his hands deeper into his pockets and walks quickly past it, circling back to the main house, its ornate front porch. He climbs up the five wooden steps and takes shelter. This house is a miraculous survivor, his father said yesterday, one of only a handful of antebellum homes in Atlanta. Hugo reads the historic marker, drilled into the clapboards to the left of the front door. He has no clue where to go next. Or how to get there.

His car is still at the bungalow, where it has been over the last two days, while he's moved through this—this crisis—in other peoples' vehicles. An ambulance first carried him and Ben—already dead—from the bungalow to the hospital, his father's pick-up truck from the hospital to the old family home on Nancy Creek. If he had his car now, maybe he would get in it and drive, as far as it could take him, until he ran out of money and gas. Then he would keep on walking. Walking, hitching, hopping on a train. Where would he end up? In New York City? He tries to conjure up a scene, young people huddled and rushing on a wet street, tries to blend in. Hugo disappearing in a crowd. Hugo finding a studio sublet. He could get a job waiting tables, finally finish college. He could start again. Alone. Away from all of this. He tries to conjure a future he might want. He spits over the railing onto the sidewalk, then watches the rain slake the bricks. But he can't leave Ben behind. Not here, alone, waiting for the crematory.

What a god-awful word. Just like the morgue, where he and Dad spent most of yesterday. Awful words, awful sounds—like someone throwing up. He spits again. Dad trying to get Ben's body released for the funeral. Trying to get him out of there without an autopsy. The final insult, that they should cut Ben open. Hugo would throw up, but his stomach holds nothing. He can't remember when he ate last. Probably not since dinner with Ben. Before he died. Death by water. Death by seizure—that's what everyone wanted to believe.

That is what Dad's hours of arguing and pleading got the coroner to write on the death certificate. *Cause of death: massive seizure, etiology unknown.* Otherwise, there would've been an investigation. Otherwise, Hugo—who had left Ben alone—might be found responsible. Ivy told him last night not to blame himself, but he knows what happened. And he will go on knowing, as sure as if he were to go to his parents' for the reception now, some of the guests would ask, "What will you do next, Hugo?"

What next? He could return to the bungalow, pack up all his shit. Dad will no doubt sell the home and Ben's clothes will be donated to some charity. Lois, poor, poor Lois, who looked so out of place at the funeral, will move on, find other work with other special-needs clients, feed them her patented liver and spinach shakes. Lois of the strange dietary habits and the massive heart will find another job; her adaptive functioning is plenty good. What will he do? He kicks at the porch railing, kicks it again, and a chunk of painted gold wood chips off. He begins to cry but the tears seem irrelevant in the rain. He paces the porch, back and forth, what to do, where to go, how to get there. He could call his parents. Or Ivy. They would all be so embarrassed to have left him. They would blame each other. Or not. Maybe they would forgive one another, call the oversight understandable, given the week's events. He could start walking and see what happens. How many times had he left Ben before he finally chose to stay with him? Each time Ben went to a new group home was a kind of death. They had struggled until Hugo finally got it right, until he made the promise to stay with Ben. Does death end that commitment?

He walks back inside the funeral home, into the chapel area, where Mr. Kalwar is down on one knee, picking a piece of lint from the carpet. He straightens up when he senses Hugo, turns around and smiles, perhaps with just a touch of annoyance.

"Did you forget something?" Then, more graciously, "Your jacket is soaked. Can I get you something? A towel, an umbrella?"

"The cremation—when does that happen?"

Mr. Kalwar checks his watch. "Soon—usually an hour or two after the service."

"I want to see it."

Kalwar stares at him. "Well, there is a small observation room ... but there is really nothing to see."

"I *need* to be with him."

"Listen, I know this loss was terrible for you. Can I call your father, perhaps?"

"Ben was my brother," Hugo says. "We lived together."

Kalwar adjusts one couch cushion, pats another, still looking at Hugo "All right. Let me call Amar—out back. See how long before they are ready to start."

▲▼▲

The crematory itself has none of the rich aesthetic of the main house where the service was held; it is a purely functional space, spartan, white, antiseptic in feel. Two tall men—the ones who directed traffic earlier in the day—sit at a plastic card table in the front area; each holds a hand of cards and neither looks up when Mr. Kalwar escorts Hugo in.

"This is the deceased's brother. Here to observe."

The older man nods, plays a card. He fans out his hand on the table top with a victorious smile, then stands up slowly and leaves through a side door. The other man piles up the cards, shaking his

196

head. Mr. Kalwar leads Hugo through another door, up three steps and down a long and windowless hall. They enter a tiny white-walled chamber, with a thick glass window that looks down on the furnace.

"If you pull the chair up close to the glass, you can see. There's actually nothing awful or frightening about it. But, well, it's stark. That huge steel contraption—that's the cremator. Just a few more minutes probably, and Amar will begin. You will see the casket come in on wheels; it's a hydraulic trolley, so one or two men can handle the coffin alone. Amar will push it into the cremator. The process will take maybe two hours altogether—another hour to cool."

"Okay."

"If you change your mind or need anything, please let me know." Mr. Kalwar sets a hand gently on his shoulder, as he heads back out into the hallway. "To your right and down the hallway: a restroom, a drinking fountain, tissues. If it becomes too much, you can always walk away."

Hugo stands at the glass, rubs his eyes, preparing himself to witness. He was not there when Ben died and he must be here now, must see this through. *Wherever I go, Hugo.* The large double doors swing inwards. Amar and the other man push the casket into the chamber. If they know Hugo is watching, they do nothing to acknowledge him, except perhaps to perform their work without talk, without smiling. Hugo spreads his hands on the glass, leans in to watch. The trolley rolls to the lip of the furnace. Amar sets the brake, moves to the side control panel. The mouth opens, fiery and ravenous. Hugo wants to feel the heat, but the divide is thick, holding him back, a deaf, dumb witness. The other man pushes the casket onto the conveyor. Head first into the flames: how the seizures would take him, brain then body. Hugo would have taken those seizures from Ben. When he was a kid, Hugo would beg God, just give the next one to me, my body can take it. Next, the middle section, his body, then the casket tapers—Ben's palsied legs. The steel mouth of the cremator clamps down. Inside, blistering, splintering, fire—varnish wood cloth skin flesh bone—Ben alone burning. Hugo alone behind cold glass, watching as their soul is consumed.

▲▼▲

Later, when the fire has cooled, when the rain has stopped and the clouds are moving out, he leaves the funeral home, starts down the driveway. He checks his watch, close to 5 p.m.; his family is certain to miss him by now, over four hours since the services ended. The ashes, in a large plastic container, fit under his arm. At the bottom of the driveway, he turns left and walks up 14th. The street cannot manage the leaves and the debris from the storm. He gets soaked by a passing car before jumping onto the low stone wall of the Piedmont Driving Club, then he continues south along the side of the street, hopping over driveways and curbs to avoid the clogged drains. He walks the park's periphery until he finds the back entrance, turns into the shrouded access road.

This was the route he had always taken, on his bike, that one summer, when he'd worked here as a lifeguard. And still tonight, along the sides of the dark road, as if they have not moved in the intervening decade, dozens of cars parked with the men huddled together inside. He passes them, now as then, eyes ahead, without slowing or looking.

Around the last corner, a winter moon hangs pale above the old pool house. He walks to the pool gate and rattles it. Locked for the season. That summer, he would ride his bike here for his lifeguard duty, sit on the stand and bake in the day and, when the evening flourished with heat lightning, he would pedal home back to Ben. Now, he looks through the chain link fence. He takes his hand off the container under his jacket, lets the two sturdy buttons of his suit coat hold it tight against his chest. His dress shoes are big and slick-soled; but he is still strong enough to pull himself up quickly, while his feet scuttle behind. He swings his legs over the top and cradles the ashes against his chest, with one arm as he drops down onto the hard deck.

Nothing has changed but everything is different: the pool is covered with a dingy tarp; chairs and tables gone, but the old bath-house and the concession stand fit his memory perfectly. What had he wanted that summer he worked here? An escape from Ben? From his family? An introduction to another type of life? None of it had made sense. All of it had weighed on him heavily, until he couldn't breathe. The heat, the long days, the heavily-muscled men lurking through the afternoon. All the demands and desires that pressed against his lungs. He walks the edge of the pool, walks the full perimeter, back to where he'd begun. The guard stand. That summer had been the beginning of the end. The heat, the demands, Mom checked out on wine and painkillers, her stay at the psych place. Ivy leaving for college, Dad working, working, working on a solution. Hugo had chosen here—right here—to make a life of Ben. He had found a calling and its name was Ben, and Ben had called out to him each night from then until now. With his arms and his eyes, whenever Hugo came home from his lifeguarding job, Ben's arms hugged himself, signing *Hugo, Hugo*, and his eyes said, *oh joy*, and they chose each other. Didn't they? Didn't they? Together they tackled the heat and desire, that long summer, and together they took on doubts and seizures that wracked their mind and body.

Hugo committed to a life with Ben. Holding his hand, holding him up in the water. What now?

The tarp has collected rain, leaves, and a few sodden pieces of trash in the middle. All around him the air is wet and cold. Dampness crawls through the thin soles of his shoes. The air smells, too, of mold, death. He takes off his sodden jacket, sets the ashes on top of it, then steps out onto the tarp. It sinks under his weight; the pool's icy water filters up through it and puddles around his feet. As he moves further out across the pool, towards the diving well, water rises over his shoes, his socks, the chill climbing up his ankles, his shins. Diving and Ben, diving and Ben. How he had craved the discipline that could take desire and shape it, make it manageable, make it worthwhile. How easy it would be now to let go. To slip his body through the space between the wall and the tarp. To swim to the bottom of the diving well. How long then until the water would swallow him? He is a diver and the boards are gone, a lifeguard and the life is gone. But below the water, swimming and twisting backwards and turning, slipping undercover, under the tarp, under the dark and the rain and the night, his lungs would catch on fire and in the fire he would be spinning again, forward, backward, inward and reverse, lingering in the sacred moment he has always loved, the silence after his performance is over, but not yet, not yet, judged.

CHAPTER 16

CAROLINE, NOVEMBER 2000

People do not say it—*What a relief it must be*—but Caroline knows many think it as they walk into her home, pause at the kitchen counter where she sits on her stool, kiss her on the cheek and say how very sorry they are, before dropping off their food offerings. *A relief to have him go first.* How dare they think it, when they know nothing of his life, except perhaps what they saw this morning in the photo collage or heard in Ivy's eulogy? How dare they, when they've scarcely acknowledged Benjamin. But many, many times over the same years, hasn't Caroline had those exact thoughts? Hasn't she, alone in her car, or in bed late at night, next to a somnolent Perry, whispered the inverted parent's prayer: *please, please, let my child go before me?*

Her funeral garb: gray pantsuit, silk blouse, and a double-knotted scarf to hide her ... wattle. Ha! Benjamin—after he'd grown far too long to do so comfortably—would sprawl across her lap, push aside the scarf or jewelry camouflage and strum her neck. *Wattle, wattle, wattle,* Hugo would shout, until even she, the human guitar, had to laugh. *Wattle,* from Old English *wadel,* meaning bandage. Exactly the point, right? She needed one to hide the sagging skin. *You're no spring chicken, my love,* her mother might have said, if she were here. What else would she say? What comfort could she offer? What if she'd lived in Atlanta all along, ready to offer Caroline and Perry a helping hand, an afternoon—or better yet, a weekend off? Wouldn't that have made a difference? During the toughest years when they'd tried again and again to place Benjamin—all those years, all those homes, all the pain. No one outside the family ever knew how to care for Benjamin; no one knew what they were undertaking. Except Hugo. Where is he, anyway? Probably upstairs, avoiding the crowd, the hubbub. He hadn't wanted to speak today; said his sister was better with *that public stuff.*

June pulls up a stool next to Caroline. She's one person Caroline can stand talking to today. She lost her husband seven years ago in a car crash. She carries her loss like a gem, polished and hidden in her coat pocket.

"I'm sure you don't want to eat, but you probably should try something."

"Perhaps later." Caroline says. "I can't stand the thought of food right now."

On the counter, a casserole of stuffed and swollen manicotti, a bucket of fried chicken, indistinct side salads, and a platter stacked with brownies. If she could get rid of it all: the plates and trays, the clinking and the clanking of serving spoons, the chattering of neighbors, the platitudes of parents from special schools, the sad eyes of her graduate students, the overbearing smell of flowers. She should make herself step outside, onto the deck, just to breathe. But Ivy's out there with someone she doesn't even recognize—a large woman, smoking a cigarette.

She nods towards the porch. "Do you have any idea who Ivy's talking to?"

"No idea. Do you want me to go find out?"

"It's all right. Sit with me."

"Of course." June picks at a massive brownie then pushes it aside. "She did well today, the eulogy."

"Yes."

"I got the sense that she really captured his essence. His humor, his joy. That story about Perry's car keys was so touching."

Caroline tears up. June takes her hand.

"Are you sure I can't make you a sandwich? The English Department sent a huge tray of cold cuts."

She tries not to grimace. Why are funerals always centered on eating? Because giving food is the most tangible way of caring? Is this true in all cultures? June studies the *Kung! San*. How does it go in Botswana, where they have no hams or chicken to offer, no trays of sweets for the grief-stricken?

"A cup of tea, at least?" June asks, "With a touch of milk?"

"Okay." The scarf squeezes her throat. She should loosen it, but doesn't. Not vanity. Just effort. Too much. Every movement today feels like too much. Is it grief or relief that keeps her immobile and breathless? How similar they sound, how they work together, one hand squeezing and the other letting go.

As June crosses the kitchen to fill the electric kettle, she's intercepted by Valerie Cooper, whose son was a swimmer at Westmont Academy; Craig went off to Stanford on scholarship, Valerie will tell you, any chance she gets. June seems to listen patiently. Still more people with cakes and pastries wander into the kitchen. *Sorry, so sorry*, they murmur to Caroline. *If there is anything at all we can do.* Where were they ten years ago?

Burly rednecks and wiry Mexicans from Perry's construction crew tromp in, wearing ill-fitting suits and cheap shoes. They find Perry in the living room and hug him like a long-lost brother; he pours shots from a giant bottle of Jim Beam. In the far corner, a cluster of Emory faculty, Frank Beardsley, longtime chair of the department, and even her good old boy nemesis, Floyd Cuthbert, sip wine. The two groups, the construction workers and the academics, don't mix. Perry moves among everyone, greets and circulates, hugs people, pours drinks; suit jacket off, tie loosened, he works the place like a politician. The black pants—a little too big around the waist—bring out the boyish quality he's never lost, and yes, she still loves that in him. But she loves him from her distant stool: aloof and brooding, he would say. Crisis, like aging, makes people not better, not different, just more so. She wants the strangers gone: is that too much to ask?

Ivy comes back in through the screen door with some tag-a-long—a woman, who, despite the cold, is clad only in black jeans and a black t-shirt. *Dyke*, Caroline thinks, and hates herself for this hateful naming, but her mind goes even further. *Bulldyke*. The woman is as wide as she is tall—why would anyone with a grain of self-respect dress like that? It's one thing for Ivy to *like* other women, but this current object of her attention is more akin to an ugly, over-weight man. She must be one of Perry's women-in-the trades interns who showed up to pay their respects. Ivy centers herself in front of the French doors to begin another Benjamin story, no doubt, some accident or injury, a tall tale told to cast a sympathetic light on the teller. What sort of tale is best for a funeral? Or a seduction? Ivy must find her family's deeds and dysfunction useful tools in her conquests. But today of all days?

June returns with tea and reclaims her stool.

Caroline wraps her hands around the mug, nods towards Ivy.

"Look at her. She hasn't been around at all to help. And now she's entertaining?"

A true blue anthropologist, June observes but doesn't judge. Unlike Caroline, whose mind is, always has been, ready to categorize and rank.

"Where's Hugo?" June asks.

Caroline shrugs, scans the room again. Maybe he's upstairs napping. Unlike his sister, he's probably keeping a low profile, avoiding the spotlight, avoiding scrutiny. Or maybe he went to get his car, to drive around for a while, be alone, be with his thoughts. Poor Hugo. How will he recover? Caroline loves her kids, all three of them, of course, though it's a lie to say her love for each is the same. Imogen Vaughan, fiery, successful and, yes, selfish, claims a huge portion of her heart, but she has always pushed against her parents. Hugo, the soft and forgiving second child—so much simpler to love. Benjamin blasted onto the scene—his birth like that line from Pericles: *as chiding a nativity/As fire, air, water, earth, and heaven can make/To herald thee from the womb.* Her special son required a special kind of love. Was it still called love when it sucked you dry?

Michael Drayton, director of the Clarkston Work Center, approaches with his blazer slung over his arm. He brought a small busload of his folks to attend the funeral. They'd all sat together quietly on the left side of the chapel, but none of them had made it to the reception. Michael tells her that they've all gone back with their aides to the center. He hopes she understands. She's so glad so many of Benjamin's friends came.

"I have to get going, too," Michael says. "But I wanted to say again, how sorry I am. How sorry we all are. We are going to miss Ben." He bends down to hug her.

She's grateful that Perry put a line in the program thanking all of the staff at the center; any donations will go there, to benefit its job training services.

Caroline calls after him, "Did Hugo ride the bus back to Clarkston with your folks?"

"He certainly could have. Shall I phone the Center and ask?"

"Don't worry. He probably went to get his car. He'll show up."

Several more people say their *sorrys* and *goodbyes* and *if there is anything we can dos*.

June whispers, "Turn your stool towards me. If you get tired, lean in to me and cry. People will leave you alone for a while. This week, when what you most want is space, everyone will pester you like crazy. Next month, when all you want is good company, you won't be able to track down a soul."

So many days what Caroline craved was time alone to sit, not only time away from Benjamin, but from her entire family. Perry had taken it upon himself to try to give her that. He had tried to take Benjamin away, and she had agreed. God, what a mess they had made of it. They had not known when they started the whole search for a group home exactly what they were starting. She had wanted time and space and Perry had wanted to please her. They had entered the process like fools, the pair of them, thinking they could find a nice-looking building with bunk beds and a few young girls with common sense to run the place. What fun Benjamin would have. Like summer camp. Were they delusional or desperate? So many disappointments and failures. So many false starts over the years, until Caroline gave up. She numbed herself and tried to just get through. She had been so tired, so worn down, during the terrible years of Ben's adolescence. Overwhelmed by Benjamin's needs—any mother would have stumbled—any mother would have faltered. It was Hugo, in the end, who took on the task and finished what Perry had been unable to do. Hugo taking all of it on, when it wasn't his to take. She knew it was not right to allow him to care for Ben. Was Hugo even capable of saying this is what he wanted? Could he make such a choice? Had she, in the end, failed not one, but both of her sons?

The phone rings; someone answers in the living room. Then Perry's voice calling out, "Anyone seen Hugo?" He comes into the kitchen and repeats his question. His eyes dart around the room. "Anyone?"

Caroline stands and grabs his shirt sleeve. "What's going on?"

"That Kalwar guy just called from the funeral home. Hugo was there, long after we all left, I guess. Kalwar said he seemed overwrought. Wanted to make sure he got home all right. You haven't seen him yet?"

She shakes her head. "I thought he took the bus—back to Clarkston."

"No. The bus left when we did, right after the service." Perry's already walking towards the door, putting on his suit jacket, pulling keys from his pocket. The rain has stopped, but it's dark. Cold. "I'll go find him. I'll drive out to the funeral home, back out to the bungalow if I have to."

She says. "Please. Wait. Talk to me."

But in true Perry fashion, he's already gone.

CHAPTER 17

PERRY, APRIL 2001

Puffy-eyed and rumpled from seat-sleep, with a headache thicker than his two-day stubble, Perry waits in the non-EU line, behind business travelers fiddling with cell phones and a few college kids tethered to their music. Kids? Make that young men, guys close to Hugo's age, exploring a new city and culture, learning through living. Or just living for Christ's sake. That would be enough. What if Perry and Caroline had insisted Hugo go away to college, what if they'd ignored his protests and sent him out into the world? *What if, what if, what if?* Perry shakes his head against the pounding recrimination. Now's not the time to think about how things could have been different. He is here—Ruzyne International Airport—and he has a task: find Hugo, bring him home.

A square-faced customs officer scarcely glances at Perry's passport before stamping it, and waving him through into the thrum of Terminal 2. No comment on the Novotny name. No, *welcome to the land of your ancestors.* Just another American tourist, searching for roots. Perry stuffs the passport into his backpack, which holds two plaid shirts, several pairs of boxers and socks, an ancient Boston University windbreaker, and a stick of Old Spice. Money? Credit cards? Pocket pat for the momentary assurance of his wallet. Then he straightens up to check out the surroundings: spacious, modern, all glass and steel, no remnants of Cold War concrete. A decade since the Velvet Revolution, and the airport's a bustling international hub, showcasing the best the West has to offer—McDonalds and W.H. Smith Books, Mrs. Fields and Starbucks. Multi-ethnic travelers push past him in both directions. Signs overhead direct in Czech, German and, thank god, English.

His teeth are grimy and his mouth sour from the three or four cups of airline coffee he downed prior to landing. He'll need a place to clean up before the next step of this half-cocked search and rescue. *Christ*—no toothbrush or toothpaste. What was he thinking? *If he had been doing that, he wouldn't be in a strange country, embarking on another Perry-grination.* Her voice again, but at least he stops himself from composing his worn-out response: *it's gonna be just fine, Caroline.* No one in Prague to lie to but himself.

And Hugo. He must believe in the chance of Hugo, in this city. So get moving, get a move on, stop the whiny shit. First stop, Tourist Information, marked with the familiar, lower-case *"i"* (put aside your ego?); he grabs a map from an un-staffed booth. Next, a currency exchange where a teller takes five of his crisp hundred-dollar bills and gives back *korunas*, thousands of them, cheap comfort to stuff his wallet. Further down the terminal, he uses the funny money to buy a travel toothbrush and a tube of unfamiliar German paste, as well as a Fodor's, from a snaggle-toothed *Babicka* (authentic or tourist attraction?). Then, in an ultra-mod restroom—wave-on faucets, rocket-fueled hand-dryers—he freshens up, pops four Excedrin to keep him going.

Doesn't matter where, right? Caroline said. *As long as you get away from me?*

He should call her. Let her know he's arrived safely. He fumbles in his pocket for the Nokia, but when he flips it open ... dead. Anyway, it's still middle of the night in Atlanta. He'll wait until he finds a hotel later today. Let her enjoy a day without him.

A twelve-foot-high glass wall separates baggage claim from the hum and hustle of buses and taxis. He pushes through the revolving door, into a mixture of exhaust and morning drizzle. As he waits in the short cab line, he opens the guidebook. *Welcome to Prague. The City of a Hundred Spires, with fairy tale vistas in every direction.* He thumbs past the lyrical introduction to get to basics. *Information for tourists: 1. Don't change your money at the airport.* Well, he'd screwed that one up already. *2. Negotiate cab fares before you depart; taxi drivers run many scams.* Good to know. *3. Watch out for pickpockets, especially in tourist spots.*

"Taxi?" A thin man, in a brown shirt, with a droopy brown mustache—too sad to be retro—opens the passenger door of an ancient Skoda. *AAA Taxi* signage on roof.

"Yes. *Dekuji,*" Perry tries.

"Destination?"

"Destination?" He's momentarily confused.

"To where you are going?" The driver doesn't smile, but his English has a polite polish.

"Prague," Perry pulls on a memory. "Zitna, Number 28. *Prosim,* is that the right pronunciation? *Pro-seem?*" He probably sounds too eager, too desperate to please; the very qualities that Caroline has come to despise in him. The driver accelerates out of the pick-up zone.

Getting Around Prague: Ruzyne to city center, about thirty minutes. Perry doesn't talk. *Why bother? What is he even doing here? What are you hoping to achieve, Perry?* His thoughts are starting to echo her words and he pushes the book aside and covers his eyes, tries to block her out. Block her out? When had it gotten to this ... after all they've been through together? All he'd ever wanted to do was keep her happy, keep his family together. Tears, hot and dry—blur his vision. Dry tears—impossible, of course, but so too is being in Prague—being anywhere, being alive when his boys, Benjamin and Hugo are not. No. Stop. Hugo could be here, right now, waiting to be found.

Maybe you need to let him go. Caroline said as they'd argued in the kitchen yesterday. *He had good reasons for leaving us, you know.*

Perry's response: a fist slamming on the counter. *Don't you think I've considered every possible reason he might have?* Their eyes met across the countertop and he hated her. *What kind of father would I be if I didn't try to find him?* He didn't add: *what kind of mother gives up looking for her son?* But she heard it, of course she did.

Half an hour later, the cab pulls up in front of a seedy porn shop, displaying in its window a variety of pink feather boas and leather straps, a few empty cardboard boxes, and a giant, blow-up bimbo—platinum wig, big tits, and a plastic carrot rammed into her surprised mouth. Perry shakes his head, when the driver turns for fare.

"This can't be the place."

"Number 28, just as you say," the driver points at black numerals on the plaster wall. "700 Korunas."

With no other address, nothing else to go on, he pays the guy, too much probably, since he didn't pre-negotiate the goddamn fare, then steps out onto a narrow, dirty sidewalk, hauling his backpack. The cab pulls away, leaving him clueless on *Zitna*. Which could be the title of his life's story. What does it even mean—*Zitna?* He definitely remembers his father's voice, the soft wavelike rush of the palatalized Z. The number is the hazy part—Perry's memory of his father's translation of a strange language years ago. Before him now, number 28—a run-down building—façade in bad need of work, plaster, cracked and chipped; the gutters look shot, and the roof—hard to see from this angle but sure to be a mess. Where his own father grew up? Which unit? Today, porn is pimped out of the first floor, for Christ's sake. *Nice*. Upstairs? Offices or apartments—blinds down, so who knows? He peers in the store, past the bimbo: It's cluttered, with cardboard boxes, several shelves of videos, busty blondes pinned on the walls. A display case midway back holds god-knows-what and, on top, an old-fashioned cash register. Who would shop here? The window offers no operating hours, and the front door—padlocked. Should he come back later? *Excuse me,* he might say to some sleazebag clerk, *I am looking for the Novotnys? Do they still own this building? Do any of them live here?* The whole notion as ridiculous to him as it must have seemed to Caroline. He is decades late for a genealogical exploration and probably way off course for locating his son. He should turn around now and head home. Admit he was wrong. Apologize for leaving, tell her he's failed yet again.

He *is* sorry. Sobs claw inside his chest wanting out. Forehead against the grimy glass, he kicks the foundation, kicks again, almost breaking his fucking foot. A chunk of plaster breaks off. Fucking failure father fuck-up. How could he have let it get to this? A woman in tall boots side-steps him, like he's drunk or crazy, keeps walking. His eyes follow her down the street. Grief gargles in his throat. He spits bile—sour coffee, the chalky Excedrin—onto the sidewalk. Wasn't that supposed to be Caroline's malady—the black bile of melancholia? His own imbalance, she said, was too much blood, relentless cheeriness. Well, where the hell did that go? Look what it got him. Look at him now. He needs to get a grip. Straighten up. What a fucking mess. He checks the watch—his father's first, then his, before he passed it on to Hugo, now his again: a tangible, ticking connection. Primak. *Where are you Hugo? Why did you leave me the watch?* It's 4:12 a.m. in Atlanta. Caroline still asleep; he adjusts six hours ahead, turning the tiny gold spindle. Six hours lost just like that. If he could just turn it back, recapture the past days, weeks, months ... What if he'd sat with Hugo through the funeral, driven home with him afterward? What if he went back further in time ... What if he never let Hugo take it all on? Like a real father, like his own, he could have just said no. He spits up again.

He should try to settle his stomach. Eat. Maybe find someplace where he can sleep off his headache too. Food first, then sleep. He crosses the street, dodging four lanes of zippy cars, walks half a block to the first place he sees: *Café Europa.* Though he's the only customer, the young waitress acts annoyed by his arrival, more so when he requests a table and service: *Espresso. Food. Some pastry, perhaps?* She takes her time delivering coffee and *kolacky*, the size of a half-dollar, stuffed with a little jam—apricot maybe; he'll need a dozen more to feel even vaguely satisfied. How to ask for something more substantial? Bacon and eggs. Do they eat that here? He opens up his guidebook. History and Culture. *Prague—Praha—means threshold; a city built where the mythical Princess Libuse had a vision of a man building a home.*

Building a home, not running from it. Perry left his home, his wife, his work to come here, based on the notion (*a wild speculation,*

213

Caroline said) that Hugo might be somewhere in the Old Country. Yes, wild grief was his real guide, pulling him over the threshold—he had nothing else to go on ... no visions to tell him what to do. Only... the night of the funeral he'd gone to the boys' house—Hugo's Honda still in the carport, and Perry's heart revved. In their kitchen, the keys dangled on a hook by the back door, soggy cereal dotted the kitchen counter, lights blazed throughout the house; the TV on in the den, too—Nickelodeon, of course—manic cartoon characters darting across the big screen, volume high, hysterical laughter. SpongeBob—a crazy new character Ben adored. He turned it off, walked through every room calling *Hugo, Hugo*—opening doors to both bedrooms, then the bathroom—water still in the tub, a tussled mat on the floor. *Hugo?* He peered into closets full of plastic toys, clothes, stuffed animals. Finally, he walked outside again, round to the back of the house, past the swing set, and approached the storage shed. His heart accelerating again, with each beat, a specific and accumulating dread. *Please, please, please.* He pushed open the door. *Hugo?* Dark, cobwebs in his face, but he stumbled around and found a pull cord, a fluorescent tube flickered on a broken-down tricycle, several shovels and rakes, a dirty hose snaking across the floor. Nothing, nothing in the shed but yard tools, and plastic playthings. He knelt on the cold, cracked concrete and sobbed his temporary relief.

The police interviewed the staff at the funeral home, the owner, Kalwar, who'd last seen Hugo walking away, at the end of a hard November rain. They re-interviewed Perry and Caroline, too, asked all kinds of questions about Hugo's mental state. *Any signs of depression? Any reason he would want to disappear? Any thoughts that he might want to hurt you?*

They instructed Perry on measures he could take ... and for days and weeks after, he followed the protocol, did what the authorities advised: re-traced the route from the funeral home to the bungalow, searched and re-searched the boys' home, looking for something, anything, notes, letters. Hugo had left everything at the bungalow—paperwork, bank account, computer, car key. Did he have a current passport? Perry couldn't find one. Had Hugo come home to get it before he left the city, the state, the country? Perry talked to everyone he could think to ask. Set up email lists and contacted friends, his diving coach, Westmont alumni. Got a story in the *Journal/Constitution*, as well as the local *Northside Neighbor*. Posted flyers. Offered rewards. For three months, Perry lurched at each phone call, each message left on voicemail; he followed every lead, every scent of a possibility.

Then, in April, a break: a maintenance worker at Piedmont Park opened the pool gates to prep for summer season. There, at the edge of the one-time diving well—Hugo's wallet—swollen and warped with nothing inside but a Clarkston library card and next to it on the cold concrete, the Primak watch, the one that had been his grandfather's. The maintenance worker called the Atlanta Police Department, and the next day, Perry identified watch and wallet for the detective—showed him the engraving on the back. His father's name. Perry took the watch in his hand to feel a connection. The time stuck at 12:37. Like his grandfather, Hugo had always been careful and precise; he would only have left the watch for a reason. A message, a clue, or perhaps a demand: *If you really want me, come and find me.*

Okay. Here I am, Hugo. *Praha*. Outside your grandfather's old building. Grab your things, I've come to bring you back home. But all Perry can hear now is laughter in the city's name: *Pra-ha-ha-ha, you will never find him here.*

He waves his hand for the girl.

"*Ano?*" she says. "What is it that you want?" A good question, though she makes it sound as if Perry's seeking something unsavory—a sweaty stint in the porn shop across the street. All the young people in Prague speak English, the guide says. It also claims the post-Soviet generation is friendly, outgoing, and eager to please. In the girl's flat affect, Perry senses not only disappointment, but also distrust. What he had left behind.

He points to his cup, adds a quick, "*Prosim,*" so she doesn't think him a rude American. Then before she turns away again, he adds clumsily, "That shop across the street ... Number 28 ... when does it open?"

She shrugs. *Dirty old man,* she does not say.

"Not for me." He blushes. "I just need to know if anyone works there still?"

"I have seen people there, not so regular. Old men." She says "Maybe you like Club K5—on Korunni Street. More Americans."

"No, no," he says. "I am looking for my son." Which, of course, clarifies nothing, and the girl turns back to her coffee machine.

"Wait ... does Zitna have a translation? In English?"

She takes a drink from an imaginary glass. "Whiskey," she says.

If Zitna is a bust, what next? His parents are long dead, his children either dead or gone, and Caroline will leave him soon. Leave their house. Leave the memories of their family. She will certainly move out of Atlanta. Head back up north? Boston, and memories of easier times. *After all we've been through,* he might argue for the sake of arguing, *can't we just stick this out together?* She said yesterday that he'd been leaving her for years. *Why can't you own the fact that you want to leave me too? That we're no good for each other anymore.* He'd never allowed himself to contemplate it during the years they'd struggled; hadn't made room for it. He had to keep things going, keep Caroline upbeat through the hard, hard work of caring for Ben. *Divorce* just means people should have tried harder. *Failure* is a better term, more accurate for the end of a marriage. Even *widower* seems closer to the truth, because it is, after all, the loss of a spouse. Lose a parent, an orphan. Is there a word for a parent who loses a child? Why can't he think of a word for this, the greatest of the three losses?

The waitress sets down his second espresso.

"Can I ask you something else?"

The girl's lip curls back in disdain, as if he's about to proposition her, right now, ask for a hand job in the coffee shop.

"When a parent loses a child, what would you say? What would you call that parent in your language?"

"I do not understand." Her eyes azure, alarming in their stark focus.

"If a child is lost. What is the parent? What word in Czech?

"I do not know," She shifts from foot to foot. "Perhaps we say, umm, *neopatrny?*"

"Could you spell it for me, please?" He opens the Fodor's to an inner page and sets it on the table.

She pulls a pen from her apron pocket and writes it in a slanting forward script, adding a slanted accent on the y, the way his father did with Novotny.

"Thank you," he says and smiles, what she must see as a wide, too white, American smile. "I will take five more of those little cookies, and the check too. Whenever you have a moment."

▲▼▲

By 11 a.m., Václavské Náměstí is buzzing; mopeds outline

the perimeter, pedestrians crisscross the square. Czechs hand out flyers: Mozart concert Saturday in St. Ludmila's. Dinner for Two at Ristorante Margarita. Spa excursions to Karlovy Vary. A girl with a pink crew cut offers Perry a button that says, in English, "It's Legal to Love." *Demonstration tonight,* she tells him, *Peace Square. Come show your support for the gays.* His mind flips to Ivy, back in Chicago, living her very private life. She has not officially come out to her parents—no pink crew cuts or rainbow flags—but the family has always known. She must know that. Coming out at this point would almost seem embarrassing. Like overkill. Maybe he should visit her in Chicago and let her know he knows; relieve her of the need for any big disclosures. Maybe he could meet her partner. Her lover. What's the right word? After he finds Hugo, yes, he will go see her. Summer in Chicago is supposed to be beautiful. He pushes through the dozens of street carts that line every side alley. Vendors hawk vases and goblets in deep blues and greens and reds, all the hues from an older world, complex and rich and layered. Hundreds of stringed puppets dangle from rails. Everywhere Perry looks, marionettes wave and kick and laugh at him.

His father made him a puppet—so many years ago. It had been waiting, wrapped in tissue paper, under the Christmas tree, when Perry was far too old for such things. Perry tore off the paper, expecting a Red Sox Jersey, or perhaps, *please,* a catcher's mitt. Instead, "Kašpárek," his father said gruffly, "a very clever clown." Perry thought he had hidden his disappointment, but probably, he had been just as careless and unimpressed as any American kid his age would have been. His mother pulled him aside a little later in the day. *Papa worked for days. Carving, sanding, painting. Couldn't you at least pretend to like it?*

Kašpáreks are everywhere today. They outnumber all the other puppet characters: the kings and queens, the washer women. Perry stops at a cart and picks out one in a red suit—something about the mischievous blue eyes, the dunce cap and the awkward puppet limbs, the chipped right leg, remind him of Ben. An old man takes his money and wraps the puppet up in several layers of tissue, hands it to Perry in a plastic bag. *Help me, Papa,* Perry thinks. *I wasn't always the most grateful son to you, but please help me find him.*

▲▼▲

At the tourist center, on the edge of the square, the woman behind the desk is cherry-cheeked, friendly; her English perfect. She recommends a hotel in Vinohrady, a short walk, she says, and a nice residential part of town.

"Affordable," she tells him, no doubt taking in his unshaven face and student's backpack, and balancing those factors out with his middle age, adds, "but also quite quiet. You won't get a lot of teenagers running around late into the night." She highlights a walking route. "Less than two kilometers," she says.

He coughs. "Oh, one more question. *Prosím,*" and opens his guidebook. "Can you tell me what this word means?"—he points to the waitress's handwriting inside. *Neopatrny.* "I was wondering if there is an English translation."

"Well—it depends on context, yes? But usually I would say it means careless or perhaps… imprudent. Does that make sense?"

Perry nods. Yes, it makes sense. The waitress was right when she'd used that word. Hugo was right to run away. Would Caroline be right when she left their home too?

He leaves the office, walks along in a flow of tourists, pushes through a crowd accumulating at the base of the clock tower for the hourly parade of the apostles. The Orloj dates back to 1410. When Perry finds Hugo, perhaps they would come back here together, take in some of these incredible historical sites, explore the craftsmanship that was evident everywhere he looked. Not now. He checks his map, finds he's walked in the wrong direction, so he turns around, reroutes towards the hotel.

The room is basic all right: no bathroom or television, but a clean, unfussy double bed. He strips to his boxers, splashes water on his face, and brushes his teeth with the strange-tasting (anise?) paste. Then he pulls the puppet out of the plastic bag, unrolls the tissue paper and takes a good look—the coxcomb hat is hand-knit, with a tiny bell sewn into each of the two points; the eyes painted bright blue, glint with a foxy intelligence. Perry hangs Kašpárek on a hook next to the sink and climbs under the quilt on the bed. His body wants sleep, but the caffeine kicks at his brain. Later today, he will walk back by Zitna, knock on some doors, see what he can find out. Maybe he'll find a lawyer, try to interest the local police. My son is missing, I think he might have come here. Who is he kidding? He has no idea, no information, nothing to go on. An ancient watch was not a clue. It was at best a suicide note. Isn't that what Caroline wanted him to see? His wanderings help nothing. He is a man always running away. Is that what she's believed for years? He rolls to his other side, his legs twitching, headache pounding. The puppet's blue eyes meet his. Fool.

PART III
EVEN SO

CHAPTER 18

IVY, 2007

"What self-respecting dyke plucks her eyebrows?" Cam stepped out of the shower, wrapped a thick blue towel around her chest, and stood behind Ivy, scrutinizing her hack-job in the steamed-up bathroom mirror.

"Since when have you considered me self-respecting?"

Cam finger-combed her hair into its familiar and spiky disarray. "Probably since you decided to date someone of your approximate age, weight, and intellect." Her grin looked even more lopsided than usual in the mirror as she reached for her deodorant.

"Approximate?" Ivy asked.

"I'm a little older, a little thinner, and truth be told, quite a bit smarter." Cam stroked Secret under each arm, then planted a kiss on the back of Ivy's neck.

Ivy critiqued her plucking; an overworked spot in the middle of the right brow gave her a disjointed look. Cam's brows were sleek accents for her wide-set fern eyes. The first time Ivy had met her, over eight years ago on the labor and delivery floor at Northwestern

Hospital—she a time-tested nurse, Ivy a scrub-green resident—she'd been pulled in by those eyes. Set a little too far apart, they gave Cam's face its mischievousness. The elegant line of her brows was the perfect antidote.

Ivy had never seen her pluck. Was it possible that her brows grew that way—fine, arched, and mysterious? Ivy felt envious, as she always did around naturally petite and graceful women. She wanted to know all Cam's secrets, her feminine wiles, and pull them out of her, one by one.

"Want some help?" Cam said. "You're butchering yourself."

"I'm getting the hang of it ..."

"You'd do better with pruning shears. Hop up."

Ivy sat on the counter. Cam dropped her towel, took the tweezers in her right hand, cupped Ivy's chin in her left. "Don't move, doc. This is going to hurt like hell."

Slight of bone, scant of muscle, despite three workouts each week at the YMCA, Cam probably weighed twenty pounds less than Ivy. She was seven years older, too, but liked to round up to ten, so she could play sage. Not much of a stretch really, since the emotional gap was wider than the chronological one. And though Ivy felt confident she could top her on any standardized test, Cam was more intelligent in all the ways that mattered: common sense, family relationships, spelling.

When they'd first met at the hospital, Cam was as cute and straight as the red-gold braid she always wore suggested, and happily married, it seemed, to Bobby, a lawyer in her father's firm. Ivy was still entangled with her former medical school professor, Jill Pellegrino, a humorless physiologist, with serial research grants and minimal teaching responsibilities; the relationship was dying a slow death.

From the haven of professional lives, Cam and Ivy flirted with each other, sharing little bags of almonds and snippets of personal lives, an intimacy possible only because Ivy's increasing attraction to Cam was conscribed by the randomness of their five-minute encounters at the Level 5A nurses' station. Adorable and unattainable. Ivy's desires to be her and to bed her were impossibly conflated.

Then in November 2000, the world shifted: Ivy lost her brothers. Cam comforted her in the aftermath of Ben's death, and then Hugo's disappearance and the worst time of all, the waiting, the months and months of waiting, with nothing resolved. She watched without judging when Ivy started fucking around with a Chicago cop, and a super-butch UPS gal. A few months later, Cam took Ivy out to dinner and confessed that she, too, had met someone—a karate black-belt and Nordic Goddess named Heidi Sorenson. The way Cam's eyes flashed when she spoke her name, Ivy knew that she ... or rather her husband ... was a goner. And sure enough, a month or two later, ravaged by the push-pull of old commitments and new desires, Cam left Bobby, cut off her lovely hair, and began a two-year passion-play with Heidi. Ultimately, Heidi played her uber-dyke part well, breaking Cam's heart, as well as her collar-bone, in what Cam always insisted was an accident. Something about a wayward roundhouse kick.

Finally, last spring, when they were both single, they met by the lake to talk and walk, and after a long stroll around Montrose Harbor, made the *Decision to Give it a Try*. The idea that you could enter a relationship by choice was a new one for Ivy. Love had always seemed like an accident before, an out-of-control truck bowling her down, dragging her along the road for a while, and leaving her battered and bruised and miles from where she needed to be.

"So, what do you think?" Cam had asked. The evening had

steamed up a soft, white mood and she was red-cheeked as they stood side-by-side looking at the water. The possibility of an us seemed blurry, like the cityscape to the south. "What do you say, Imogen Vaughan Novotny?" Even Cam's voice was querulous. "You and me and the old college try?"

Ivy laughed and kissed her quickly on the cheek and looked across the lake for some assurance.

"Don't mock me," Cam said. Her eyelashes filtered the mist into the finest pearls and Ivy knew how much she wanted this. Wanted her. She wasn't mocking, she hoped her second and lingering kiss assured, more embarrassed by the idea that love could be such a deliberate undertaking. And, yes, worried that asking for something, someone, so deliberately was tempting fate. Weren't wishes and wants safer left in hibernation?

▲▼▲

"Gotcha!" Cam said, pulling Ivy back to now with a hard yank, followed by a triumphant flash of the tweezers. "You have the thickest hairs. Like sutures." She showed off her sample—brown and coiling—half an inch long.

"My grandfather's legacy. Jan Novotny—bushy-browed Bohemian boat-builder. Have I ever told you about him?"

"Oh, perhaps a few times." She continued her work, switching to the left brow.

"Am I repeating myself already? Not a good sign. My grandmother's legacy. Early onset senile dementia. Mary Catherine Vaughan. Have I told you about her?"

The plucking hurt, but only a little, and truth be told, Ivy enjoyed the feeling. A cute, naked girl, causing manageable pain.

"Ouch. Now that's enough." Ivy hopped off the counter. "I know you need your space, your privacy, to do your ablutions. So, I'm going to head back to my condo to get some work clothes. See you Wednesday night?"

Cam held Ivy at arm's length and eyed her handiwork. "You should move in here," She said. "Stop all the back and forth."

"Let's talk about this later."

"Wait. I can't let you go half-plucked. You look sort of ... unstable."

Ivy wanted to swoop her up, take her back to bed, and steal from her, and yes, she even wanted to live with her, but she checked her impulses, said, instead, "That is what keeps you intrigued."

CHAPTER 19

CAROLINE, MAY 2007

After Benjamin died, she'd had no time for grief. Or relief. His life was over—suddenly, but not unexpectedly for her special boy, because every seizure over twenty-three years had felt like a death rehearsal—and part of her felt that afterwards, she was entitled to both sadness and freedom from the constant worry.

Then Hugo was gone.

That endless winter in Atlanta, every move, every effort felt as if she were pushing against a tide of judgments: what had she been thinking, allowing Hugo to carry the load? She had put herself first. What kind of mother …? If anyone had asked her which was harder—Ben's death or Hugo's disappearance (no one did, because it would have been an unthinkable question)—she would have answered that not knowing where to go, what to do, when to give up, was far worse than death. Death—a heart can suffer, a mind can sort, a body can release. With Hugo gone, she was trapped living but not alive. Her marriage—stretched and tested and already fragile from the years—might have endured death. It couldn't withstand loss.

Two weeks after the funeral, Ivy went back to her life in Chicago, called regularly at first, but then went quiet. Perry began a series of missions to find Hugo, following leads as undecipherable as tea leaves: A phone number written in Hugo's physiology textbook. A brochure for a sports medicine program in Arizona found in his underwear drawer. The wristwatch he'd inherited from his grandfather and left by the Piedmont Park pool. While Perry chased phantoms, Caroline stayed in their home where every room brought a jolt of pain. The *Wee Sing and Play* videos from the early days still filling the basket in the den; the leaf-coated swimming pool; upstairs in Ben's room, two bare mattresses, side by side on the floor. Like walking into an electric fence.

So she packed what she needed—clothes, important papers, books—and loaded the Honda. A separation, she told Perry, the day he returned from his failed trip to Prague. She didn't modify it with "trial." If he was surprised, he didn't let on. If anything, he sounded relieved. How could they have stayed together? They would have reminded each other at every turn, every coming and going, of their weakness, the choices they'd made along that way, the blind eye they'd turned to their sons' lives.

She drove north, two days up I-95. Alice Seward, her mentor from long ago, had offered her place on the Cape. Alice's kids were both married and living on the West Coast; she rarely went out to Truro anymore. Caroline was welcome to use it for as long as she liked. She paid Alice a modest monthly rent, enough to cover the utilities and taxes, and Alice asked nothing more of her.

When she first arrived, the hoary landscape matched her mood— bleak, gray, endless. The limbo she deserved. There were weeks in the beginning when she didn't leave the cottage. If she managed to do anything, she might make a cup of tea, read a book in the green-checked armchair in front of the fireplace. On her best days, she would call Perry for an update. *Any news from the State Department about Hugo's passport? What about that Atlanta detective?* After the first year, she stopped asking and he stopped reporting. Lately, when they spoke, it was about safe topics. His nonprofit had signed an agreement with ARC Southeast to build ten new small group homes for people with disabilities in the Atlanta region. She liked the students at Coastal Community College where she taught two classes—older, hardworking, and far more driven than the Emory undergrads. *How's your writing?* Perry would usually ask. Plodding along. At the end of every conversation, they touched on Ivy, who spoke more often to Perry than to Caroline, but not much to either of them. Perry said she'd come around. Caroline was not so sure.

Her life on the Cape—six years on—held many of the things she'd often wished for when she was weighted down with parenting, caring for a child with so many special needs: time to walk for hours in the morning without having to run home worried that something had happened in her absence. Time to meet a friend in a café—linger over a cup of tea, talking about Marilynne Robinson's *Gilead*. Time in the evening to sit in a rocker on the porch, hearing only ocean whispers. Her life had room for these things now, but the room was still thronged with loss. Not so much a new life as a shadow life.

Still, on mornings like this one, she was not unhappy. Her teaching gig had wrapped up for the semester. Pale gray light seeped into the cottage through the frayed linen curtains in her first-floor bedroom, waking her early. 5:30 a.m. She padded barefoot across the wood floor, scuffed from years of sand and salt, the careless habits of children, not her own. In the kitchen, she filled the old-time kettle, a chipped red, stove-top whistler. While the water heated, she filled a bowl with cereal—something organic and local from the Truro Fresh Market—and added fruit. After a second cup of tea, she rinsed her bowl and mug in the sink and dressed for her walk.

Last fall, she'd read a sign on the bulletin board at the market, asking for volunteers to walk dogs at the Cape Cod Animal Shelter. The poster showcased a grizzled old mutt with sad eyes and a blue bandana around his neck. The caption read: "I'm waiting for you."

The cashier at the time—a well-pierced, pregnant woman asked Caroline, "You want a dog?"

"No, no—this says they need walkers."

"Yeah. Real bad. I worked there for a while. Can't now. For obvious reasons. You should try it. The dogs are, like, unbelievably grateful. Makes you feel good."

She'd driven to the shelter, filled out the required paperwork and started the next day. At first, she stuck to the nature trails not too far from the shelter, a half-hour loop, but when she got more confident, when she realized the shelter didn't care how long she kept the dogs out, she began to bring them to the beach.

▲▼▲

Today, she drove the five miles to Wellfleet to pick up her pair. Two mutts—Gunnar and Gretchen—last left of the previous summer's G-litter. They knew Caroline well, barked as soon as the entry buzzed opened, got crazy when she leashed them up, barely waited for the car door to open before they hopped up into the backseat. She opened both windows in the back, so each dog could breathe in the misty morning.

Back home, she parked at the top of the crushed gravel drive.

Alice Seward's cottage sat on a bluff, above Little Hollow Beach, an indent in the Cape's long, arthritic finger. This morning, the bay churned gray, blending into a fallen sky. She let the dogs out of the car, wrapping a leash around each wrist. They pulled her down a narrow path, through the dunes. *Easy guys. Easy.* She didn't try hard to hold them back. How could you restrain such enthusiasm? When they hit the beach, Caroline turned south toward Parnet Bar. A light headwind. No one in sight either direction but at the water's edge, a trail of footprints disappeared with the incoming tide. Most mornings she had the beach to herself. After a half-mile or so, after the dogs had got their initial crazies out, she'd let them off leash. These two listened well—at least when there were no other dogs around—and she had treats in her coat pocket too, just in case.

Midway down the beach, two horseshoe crabs gripped the sand, their hard shells like giant, brown ticks. Gunnar sniffed at one, tried to turn it over with his paw. Gretchen steered clear. Smart girl. These dogs were energetic but manageable, would settle into being great companions.

Should she adopt them? The thought came in like a wave. Receded.

Still too soon.

She walked further, hopping over a few tidal gullies, until they reached the end of the promontory, where she let the dogs off leash. While they darted in and out of the estuary, she scanned the hemline of shells, collecting several purple-tinged quahogs for Neil. Her friend. Sometime lover. What was the best word to describe their relationship? His wife had died of breast cancer six years ago—the same month as Ben, in fact—and at age sixty-three he'd closed his Newton medical practice, without regret, he said, and moved to

Provincetown. Caroline had met him at an Ann Patchett reading at the Fine Arts Center last fall, and afterwards they talked about *Bel Canto*, which they both loved, and *Truth and Beauty*, which they didn't. He asked her out for coffee. He lived in an apartment above a gallery on Commercial. He didn't mind the long and barren winters, didn't mind nights alone to read, rain-soaked days to paint in his extra bedroom. They'd found a routine of dinner on Fridays. Sometimes a play, a concert, or a reading. On occasion, they spent the night at his place, full of his books, favorite paintings that he'd kept, and several photos of his wife and their family. She never brought him back to the cottage—and he seemed to understand, never pressed for more. Neil's three daughters all lived in the Boston area and visited him often during summer months. He said they were glad to hear he had companionship but wouldn't want him to remarry. Not yet. Caroline replied that she had a daughter, who probably wouldn't give a damn either way.

After thirty minutes romping in the water, the dogs returned to Caroline, tongues lolling, chests heaving, sand caked on their underbellies. She leashed them up again and turned towards home. The shells clinked in her coat pocket; the dogs didn't pull anymore. The wind at her back, the sun beginning to burn through the mist. She'd rinse the dogs off with the outside hose, rub them dry, and take them back to Wellfleet. She felt bad when she had to shut them back in their kennel. But she liked the feeling of no one counting on her.

Midmorning. She was at her desk and had the rest of the day before her for edits. She'd finished a series of articles over the past two years and recently merged them into a book. *Women Wanderers: Exiles and Migrants on Shakespeare's Stage*. University of Chicago

Press would publish it this fall. The revisions were time-consuming, but the hours went faster, easier than when she was writing new material. And she was almost done. She was presenting at Chicago Shakes Symposium next month and still needed to finish her lecture on *Sophrosyne: Hermione's Saving Virtue.* Three weeks away. She thought that she might try to call Ivy. Maybe later in the day. She'd already left a couple of messages that had gone unreturned. Why was it so hard to earn a moment of her daughter's time?

Maybe she could ask Perry. If nothing else, he always picked up her calls. As she did his. What was left from their marriage was an unspoken promise of being available to talk, a reliable kindness, concern. One thousand miles between Perry and Caroline, one thousand between Caroline and Ivy. Another eight hundred between Perry and Ivy. If you marked each of them on a map with a push pin, drew lines connecting the three pins, you'd have a long-legged triangle. The geometry of separation. When did separation become estrangement?

She would call him early afternoon, when he wrapped up work. Ask his advice about her upcoming trip to Chicago. Whenever she called he was busy—he traveled a lot, finding financing for the group homes he was building—still moving, still building, shaking hands, doing what he did best, and she supposed she admired him for his constancy, his drive, his determination. Even if he never stopped long enough to figure out what he was pursuing.

That was her bitterness talking. She didn't need to be bitter; she could let him live life his own way now. She didn't need to shut him down. She didn't want to play that role anymore—naysayer, fun-buster. She sensed that he worked at this pace, working hard all week, traveling part of every month, still searching on his free time because he believed that one day he'd find Hugo. One day ... it would all be just fine. She sensed too that if Perry stopped moving, trying, the despair might drown him, the way it had almost drowned her.

▲▼▲

Four p.m. on the dot and she put aside her editing, made tea, poured herself a cup, then dialed his cell. He answered on the first ring.

"I was just thinking of you. How are things?" He asked.

"I'm fine. Are you home—in Atlanta, I mean?"

"Yeah. We're getting ready to break ground on the new project north of Marietta—off 575, so I'm going to be around most of the summer. Keeping things moving."

She told him about the end of the school year. The dogs. He loved hearing about the dogs, seemed to find it amusing that Caroline woke early most days to exercise strays, the Caroline who used to beg for just another thirty minutes sleep.

"And the book?"

Her book ... the publication date getting closer, she told him. She was starting to believe it might happen.

"That's amazing," he said. "You got it done. I always knew you would. Send me a copy. No, send me a bunch."

She couldn't help but smile at his enthusiasm, his faith in her. Through all those years could he possibly have believed she'd finish? All those starts and stops, flurries of activity, marked by months of mere survival.

"Well, it took me long enough."

"Only a decade or two. Not so bad considering. Anyway, I'm proud of you, my love."

He coughed, realizing his overstep ... changed the topic. "So.

Is it summer out there yet? We had a hot week here. Over ninety yesterday."

"Not even close. I wore a jacket this morning when I walked the dogs ..."

As the conversation was winding down, she brought up Ivy. Trying to keep it light. Had he talked to her lately? Any plans to visit Chicago? No, not in construction season, at least—but he hoped to get up there for Thanksgiving or Christmas—get her to take a real vacation from work and show him around the city. She hadn't committed yet ... you know how she is. Said she might be spending it with Cam's family. Said she might be on duty. Perry would go either way—show up and bang on their front door. Something would work out.

"It's just that I'm going to be there for a conference soon and ... I was wondering ... Does she say anything about me visiting?" Caroline felt ridiculous. "You know, whether she'd want to see me? I still haven't met Cam."

"Oh, you should definitely visit," he said. "No matter what Ivy says, just show up. Cam's great. They balance each other, you know."

"I don't want to force myself on her. You know that's not my way. And I don't want to push her further away."

"Don't overthink. Just go." he said. "That's what parents do."

She felt the words like a punch in her solar plexus. Couldn't get a word out.

"Caroline?" When she didn't say anything, he added, "But do what you understand."

She exhaled. That was his point, right? Caroline always had done "as she understood." And Perry believed that she'd never got it right. She was the parental screw-up. The reason the boys were dead and gone, that Ivy might as well be.

She wrapped up the conversation quickly, wished him well. Went upstairs and filled the tub. She'd soak and unwind before heading out to see Neil.

CHAPTER 20

IVY, JUNE 2007

"We need to talk," Cam said, interrupting Ivy's breakfast of granola and the *Sun-Times* sports page. It was early Thursday morning, in a summer that seemed full of promise: the Cubs playing great, as they always did before the All-Star break and the inevitable August collapse, the weather cool enough to sleep with the air conditioning off and windows open. A breeze shifted the lacy curtains. Across the Crate & Barrel table that had followed Ivy through her bachelorette pads, Cam sloshed milk into her mug, clouding her tea. And Ivy's mood.

We need to talk. The words sounded ominous and, like Cam's fixed smile, filled Ivy with foreboding. Cam's natural grin pulled left of center, a little goofy and far more trustworthy than this morning's polished attempt.

Symptoms of co-habitation showed on the tabletop, now stained from more use than it had encountered during Ivy's single life. It was the only piece of furniture she'd moved into Cam's cottage. Cam had inherited this home from her Nanny Fitzgerald and it was still fully and fussily decorated with the items you'd expect of an Irish grandma: spindle rockers, lace curtains, and cross-stitched pillows. Living here was cozy, sometimes just shy of stifling.

Cam sipped her tea. Ivy felt her waiting for something.

"Talk? About what?"

"Family things." Cam buttered a slice of toast. "No need to panic though." She offered up another smile—her nursing variety, all tolerance and understanding.

"I have procedures this morning. Can it wait until tonight?"

"Sure." This time, her lopsided grin, the one that made Ivy want her, whatever she was saying, whatever demands she might be making. "But skip your run and get home early."

Ivy's gut jostled with a familiar guilt, even when she knew her conscience should be clear: no affairs, no fatal attractions, in over a year of this relationship, including three full moons living together in the hand-me-down home. But the past was like a blackmailer, returning with reminders of old mess-ups, as if to say, you'll never escape yourself, Novotny.

She deposited her cereal bowl in the sink and filled a travel mug with coffee. Pager, Blackberry, wallet, and workout bag. She eyed Cam for clues. With her hair drying into its spiky slap-dash, Cam spread a dollop of strawberry jam across her toast, put down her knife and blew a kiss as Ivy left. "Be good."

The flagstone path meandered through the back garden, past the peonies that Cam had neglected to cage, through a patch of purple foxgloves and hollyhocks that reached Ivy's shoulder. By the one-car garage, the roots of a gnarly crabapple tree lifted the stone pathway, while the low-lying branches almost blocked passage. She pushed back a particularly offensive branch until it snapped.

Windows down, AC off, Ivy left Evanston, headed south and east along Ridge Avenue, through Rogers Park and Edgewater, crossing Sheridan and onto the Drive. She caught a glimpse of the lake, displaying her most placid self: blue, serene, and trustworthy. After living in Chicago for sixteen years, more than anywhere before, Ivy knew the lake, for all the dazzle and charm, to be untrustworthy. Four seasons a year, she ran along the waterfront, five days a week, forty minutes a day, her inviolate time with her inconstant friend. Sometimes she'd come in soaring good spirits, expecting synchronicity, and find the waters roiling, anxious, and gray. Other times, the lake teased with her poise. This morning, all was well—the waterfront teemed with joggers, cyclists, babies in strollers, dogs and their walkers; at the Foster Avenue beach, a cluster of old folk swayed in T'ai Chi sync.

After Ben died, after Hugo … she'd returned to Chicago mid-January. Iron-gray skies wrapped her condo building. Inside, the radiators hissed her back to an empty life. She had found running shoes and headed to the ice-edged lake. As she ran, she hated Ben for dying, hated Hugo even more for disappearing. And perhaps she hated most of all her parents' inevitable inability to preserve their own relationship. Wasn't it cliché for parents to separate after losing a child? She ran that day, hard and long across slick sidewalks, over crisp mud-caps, into headwinds that tried to rip off her jacket, while the water insisted, you're still here, you're alive.

And she was alive, happy even, in her life with Cam.

Still, this morning … *We need to talk.* As she drove past Montrose Harbor—the place where their relationship began—Ivy figured out what Cam wanted to discuss. All her smiles and patience over breakfast had been a set-up: she was softening Ivy up for another Baby Talk. Talks 1 and 2, a few weeks back, had resulted in arguments and

240

tears and Ivy was not ready for another re-hash. Barely a year since their *Decision to Give It a Try*, they had been moving fast, pushing the relationship, as if it were a gifted child in need of more challenge. Officially "partners" now, they were living that short phase of lesbian life that precedes fusion. Ivy had met all of Cam's large Irish-Catholic family already, dutifully presenting different versions of herself, depending on the relative and Cam's instructions: Cam's roommate, Ivy; Cam's work colleague, Dr. Novotny. And while Ivy liked the image they cut of a happy well-suited, professional dyke-duo, gainfully employed, done with aimless dating, a visual and logistical and temperamental match, Ivy thought they had accomplished plenty. Couldn't they enjoy this part a bit longer—evenings on the couch, half-watching bad TV while undressing each other, the three-hour brunches on shared days off?

Ivy's job requirements (arriving at the medical practice by 6:30 a.m. weekdays) pretty much ruled out a.m. exercise, so her runs were evening affairs, mandatory for debridement of the day's stresses. If Cam thought she could interrupt a workout to talk babies again, she had another think coming. Ivy would call her midday, plant the seed that she might have to stay late at the office to *catch up on some charting*. Or something more ... emergent? A patient had suffered a miscarriage. *Suffered a miscarriage.* A hell of a euphemism, but one Cam would swallow sympathetically. She was, after all, almost forty. She counted pregnant women on the sidewalks, while Ivy's thirty-three-year-old head still turned for sleek dykes on their even sleeker racing bikes. Ivy wanted to train for a triathlon; Cam wanted to start charting her temperature and tracking her pre-ovulatory surge.

Never vague or indirect about her desire to have children, Cam had told Ivy—back when they'd met at the hospital, and Cam was still straight and married—*I'll have kids one day. Probably not with Bobby, but I'll have them.* Ivy had assumed she was joking about her husband, in the way that married women always needed to do with lesbians, putting down their men as oafs and ne'er-do-wells, trained only to take out the trash. But now Cam was approaching her reproductive D-Day, and living with *Ivy*, wanting kids with *Ivy*, telling *Ivy* that she couldn't delay much longer. Well, she'd have to wait. Ivy would run tonight, run along the lake, run fast and hard and alone, joining in the solidarity of so many singles.

Now, at Belmont Avenue, all the boats in harbor formation, and sunlight moved, dancing off decks and hulls, shimmering down so many silver masts. The brown slatted docks spread across the water like Hs. Hugo. Hugo. Hugo.

Still running away from commitment?

He frequently kidnapped her thoughts, coldly assessed her actions, and disapproved of what he saw. After the funeral, he'd never returned to the family home. At first, Ivy had wanted to believe he'd gone for a week or two, needing time to grieve his way. After a month, she told herself he'd contact them again soon, in a clearer way. He'd let them know. Three months later, a Piedmont Park maintenance worker found Hugo's wallet and watch on the pool deck. As if the two items he'd left meant something: That time and money no longer mattered to him? In what world, in what kind of place would that ever be true? That he was disinheriting the family? Had he gone on, gone forward from that night? Or were these items a sign that he was done—the final checkout?

Her parents had developed their disjointed responses to his disappearance, Dad kept moving, searching, visiting every place he could think of. Mom said, *he'll come back when he's ready, let's leave him be.* As if Hugo were a moody adolescent, hiding in his room. As if that had ever been true of him (though it had been of Ivy). *I must find him,* Dad responded, disregarding Mom's input and continuing his next quest, this one the inverse of his last, running all over the country, to bring his son back home. Ivy must have seemed equally predictable: escaping again, back to Chicago, sole sister, soul-less sister, better off alone.

Always so melodramatic, Hugo said now as Ivy approached North Avenue beach. *You have a partner who loves you, wants to build a life together. Will you leave her too?*

▲▼▲

It was close to six forty-five by the time she entered the professional building, got on an elevator. On the 14th floor, a long line of women snaked down the hallway to the doors of her practice. Reproductive Endocrinology patients were compulsively early and rigidly compliant with their fertility protocols, arriving here before 6 a.m. each day, as if promptness and obedience would get them what they so desperately sought, what was so beyond their control. In the reception area, the first patients received paperwork for their morning procedures. Emelin, the front desk worker who always wore the hospital's cheap blue blazer over a clinging blouse, managed multiple patients with polyester manners. Her stern eyes and fixed smile said she had no time for exceptions and excuses: *Wait your turn, please, ma'am. Green forms go to labs and pinks to ultrasound. No, you cannot talk to your doctor yet.*

Ivy nodded at Emi, swiped herself into the back suites and sought out the temporary calm of her office, sat at her desk and dug up the files for this morning. Three patients, back-to-back-to-back

243

hysterosalpingograms—real-time x-rays of the uterus and fallopian tubes. Though she was only in her third year of practice post-fellowship, she'd done enough HSGs for a lifetime. Ten a week, fifty weeks a year, over two years on the job would put her at more than a thousand. A veritable endocrinological superhero, *Hysterosal-Gal*: see her clad in sea-blue scrubs, waving a giant syringe full of dye, scouting out unsuspecting tubal blockages that threaten fecundity everywhere.

Cam thought it funny that these wannabe-moms would place their wants and wombs in Ivy's care. *If only they knew how little interest you have in babies*, she said during one of the baby talks. Ivy defended herself: *RE has always been about the science for me. The hypothalamic-pituitary-ovarian axis, adjusting and balancing and computing. The ratios of FSH and LH, the levels of estrogen and progesterone, and the challenge of tweaking them all to achieve desired results.* Cam had replied edgily. *You're not really that out of touch, right?*

Ivy pushed aside the files on her desk, walked to the window. Cam wanted a baby, okay, but she was operating from her own set of fears. Cam knew the stats: at age forty, her monthly fertility rate was already down to ten percent, her risk of having a child with Down syndrome one in three hundred fifty, her risk of miscarriage twenty-five percent. Stats and facts and "something inside" told Cam it was time to get started. To Ivy, though, they meant the opposite: *Don't test the odds; don't ask for trouble.*

If she angled her neck just so, she could see a stretch of lake—cool, blue, removed. Then a tiny white boat, a red triangular topsail. A predictable intrusion. Hugo in her thoughts.

Don't ask for another Benjamin? Isn't that what you mean?

Yes. Okay. Ivy had seen what a tiny slip in the genetic blueprint could mean for a baby, for a family. What it had meant for Ben, for Mom and Dad, and for Hugo, too, especially for Hugo, even if he never saw it himself. And since he'd been gone, she'd had the discussions, many discussions, with couples who had learned that their baby will have Tay-Sachs, Turner's, or Angelman's. *What would you do, Dr. Novotny?* They'd often ask. *Only you can make that kind of personal decision,* she was trained to say. *But what would you do?* Ivy would sit with them; she'd listen and let them cry, hand them the tissues. She might even try to say something meaningful, but the truth was she had no idea—no idea what she would do, what they should do. So she cannot, she will not, put herself in a position to find out what decision she would make.

Besides, Hugo wasn't around to talk it through anyway. He'd left her alone with these decisions.

You left us first. His perennial trump card.

Linda peered around the office door. "First patient's prepped."

Ivy changed into crisp scrubs and surgical clogs and entered the stark procedure room—the AC at a steady sixty degrees, the room well-lit, the instruments in pristine packages, laid out on a stainless tray. The patient, prone on a gurney, wearing the hospital's trademark blue-gray gown and the blue head wrap that made everyone, even the prettiest women, look round and puffy-faced.

"Kayla, how are you? I know Linda has talked with you about today's procedure. Any questions for me before we get started?"

She shook her head.

"You're feeling relaxed from the medicine we gave you?" Ivy erred on the side of over-medicating. She wanted her HSG patients loopy on Valium before she even began.

"I'm okay," she replied. "Just a little nervous."

"This will go fast. The Valium relaxes you, but if you need something more, let me know. I don't want you lying here in pain. Okay?"

Kayla's husband stood by her head. "She's brave," he said, looking queasy and fragile himself.

"Are you all right?" Ivy asked him. "You can wait in the lounge if you prefer. Linda can get you, as soon as we're done."

Kayla through her haze: "He needs to be here with me."

He nodded, but his face was chalky.

"Keep talking to her, keep her company." Ivy didn't want a fainting, but she also wanted the patient as relaxed as possible, if having her man close by would help, that was fine. The fallopian tubes can close from stress and tension alone.

But a few minutes in and Mick, the x-ray tech, behind the glass screen called out, "Two patent tubes."

The husband bent down to kiss Kayla. "Good job, honey. The tough part's over."

Not true. If the tubes were open, if the male's sperm count and motility were good, and the patient still hadn't gotten pregnant in three years of trying, then they were probably beginning a long and difficult path.

▲▼▲

Ivy got home close to 9 p.m. Cam had eaten and was watching TV in the living room. In the kitchen, Ivy served herself a bowl of pasta, poured a glass of wine, then joined Cam on the couch. The fresh bite of basil, ripe tomatoes and garlic, the perfectly cooked pasta, cold Sauvignon Blanc. This whole tableau, the late dinner, cuddling on the couch, an "ER" re-run on TV, composed the perfect argument against kids.

But Cam turned off the TV. "We need to talk. Remember?"

Ivy's glass clinked against the table top. "Babies."

"What? No. About your mom. She's got some Shakespeare summit at U of C next month—gonna stay at a hotel in Hyde Park for two nights, but she wants to take us out to dinner."

"You spoke to her?"

"I answered the phone, so yes, we talked. Is that so strange?"

"She never calls the house phone. What did you say?"

"That we'd love to see her."

"Well, you could have checked with me first."

Cam picked a piece of lint off Ivy's pants. "She said she's left several messages at work, called your mobile too, but you never called her back. What else could I do? And I want to meet her in the flesh. The brilliant, brooding professor. It's way past time."

Cam's smile, to be fair, was not smug, but something about the way she sat there talking made Ivy want to slap all that not-quite-smugness right off her face.

"You had no right to make that decision without talking to me."

"If you picked up your phone occasionally, she wouldn't have had to go through me. Besides, you're all she has left."

"*All she has left?* Was that her line or yours?" Ivy stood up and cleared her plate. "The last thing I need is you two tag-teaming on me."

She would call Mom back tomorrow morning. Better yet, she'd head upstairs right now, stoke up the laptop and shoot off a quick email, tell her that she simply did not have time to see her next week—crazy amount of work to do—when what she meant was that she had no desire to re-live all their losses.

CHAPTER 21

CAROLINE, JULY 2007

Ivy had not answered any of Caroline's phone calls, which wasn't surprising. Then two weeks back, she'd sent Caroline a curt and dismissive email: work was busy; she'd have no time for a dinner. Caroline was hurt but told herself she was not the type to foist herself on her daughter, that was not, never would be, her style.

Still, as she climbed into her rental car at O'Hare, a tiny Toyota something, she turned on the GPS, found herself entering Ivy and Cam's address. After an hour in stop-and-go traffic on the highway, and another fifteen minutes on side streets, she pulled up in front of a small brick cottage on a quiet, maple-lined street, the number—1809—above the red door. She parallel parked under the large tree canopy, opened the car window. The sidewalk was empty; the houses, each one charming in an old school way, close together on small, irregular lots. She could hear a lawn mower, but saw no one except an older man, the next house over, trimming a box hedge. She took a few minutes to calm herself. She was here. What to do? If anything. She could drive away and try to be content with this—seeing the home where her daughter now lived. Maybe she should call Perry. He'd give her the permission to go ahead, ring the doorbell, show up uninvited. Disinvited, really, because Cam had said on the phone, yes, come, and Ivy had overruled her.

She reached in her purse for her cell phone. Started to dial his number. No, she didn't need Perry's advice today. She was still pissed at him for his passive aggressive criticism of her parenting: *Do as you understand.*

Okay. She would.

Two in the afternoon. Friday. Ivy would be at work. Caroline could leave a note. No pressure. So why did the walk through the patch of a front yard seem so daunting?

What's the worst that could happen? Perry would say.

She found a pen and her notebook, pulled out a piece of paper. *I arrived in town for my conference. I know you're busy, but if your schedule opens at all—even if it's just for coffee—I'd love to see you. I miss you. Mom.*

She folded it in half, crossed the street, opened the small gate and walked into a garden overfilled with lupins and hollyhocks; roses climbed a trellis on either side of the front door. This house—just shy of cloying, not what she would have imagined for Ivy. She could picture her daughter in a downtown high rise with a doorman, or one of those faux London townhouses so popular with young professionals in the Boston area. This place must be all about Cam's influence. Or maybe Caroline knew even less about her daughter than she thought.

Three steps up to the door. She was bending down, about to slip the note through the brass mail slot when the door opened.

"Can I help you?" A slender woman in jeans and an over-sized t-shirt looked down at her with wide eyes, an almost-smile.

Caroline stood, took a step back. "You must be Cam."

"Yes. Caroline? Wow … I'm so glad. For a minute there I thought you must be a Jehovah's Witness." She opened her arms. "I was just heading out for a walk, but come on in. Please."

"I shouldn't have stopped by uninvited. I had time and I thought well, I could leave a note. Is … is Ivy home?"

"At work, I'm afraid. Your daughter's a very hard worker." She tilted her head—crazy red hair going every which way, a lovely grin. "But come in. We can talk. We can call her if you want and tell her you're here and to come on home."

Caroline's heart skipped. She had wanted this, hadn't she, wanted to see her daughter? But she didn't want to make things worse.

Cam read her thoughts. "It's okay. She'll be glad you showed up. Maybe she'll even skip her evening run. That would be a first."

Still so rigid. Ivy had always been one for planning and preparation, runs and routines. She flashed on the young girl—first or second grade—who insisted on bringing her homework to Boston Medical Center when they'd had to rush in with Ben, sat doing math problems in the waiting room, with all the crises whirring around her. The teenager who'd insisted on taking summer school classes, even when she had straight As, and the college kid who'd stayed on campus every summer to work in labs. The daughter who'd never let her guard down.

Cam made tea in the tiny kitchen and carried a pot and two cups and saucers out on a tray. They sat in the living room, on matching blue floral armchairs. The room, the house, the tea setting, and Cam—all so dainty.

Cam asked questions. When was Caroline's lecture? The topic? Maybe she could come and hear? Were non-academics allowed? She didn't say anything about Ivy joining her.

Caroline answered, even as her mind was spinning. Taking in the doilies on the side tables. Many photos of people she didn't know. A large, red-haired clan reappearing in different configurations. Cam's relatives? What if Ivy walked in now and found Caroline sitting here, sipping tea? Would she feel deceived? Angry? Trapped? Coming here, coming inside was a mistake. Ivy always wanted control. Maybe Caroline should leave. Get out while she could.

She asked for the bathroom.

Down the hall, in a closet-sized room with a sliding door—barely space for both toilet and sink—she washed her face, pinched her cheeks. Bags under her eyes. Vertical wrinkles above her top lip—the result of too many cigarettes in her early years or too much sun and wind over the past few. Both. She felt old and frightened, a familiar desperation in her gut, and longed suddenly for the ease of the benzos, the softening grip of her worries. That seeping-in sense of *who cares?* But she did. She'd always cared. And wasn't that what Dr. Thorne-Thompson, her psychiatrist way back then had helped her recognize? That the drugs had been a way to escape how much she cared, a shield from what she saw as her failures. As a wife. As a scholar. As a mother. First to Ben, but also to Hugo and to Ivy. She opened the tiny medicine cabinet above the sink, found Advil, a cherry Chapstick. Not what she craved, but she helped herself to both. Fifteen years sober. Six years since the boys were gone. Shouldn't she be beyond this place?

Maybe there never would be a place beyond loss.

When she sat back down across from Cam, she took another sip of tea. "So, how is my daughter? You said she's still working too hard, pushing herself? Sounds like Ivy."

"Overall, she's happy, though hard to read, I'm sure you know.

But I think she's in an okay place—we're in a good place together. Yes, she works too much but we also have a good life together here. A few friends right here in the neighborhood. And my family adores her. She doesn't believe me when I tell her that, but they do."

"Your parents are close by, then?"

"Not too far. River Forest—western 'burbs. About forty-five minutes from here. This was my grandmother's cottage—all the furniture and belongings, too. I was lucky enough to take it on because my siblings are all married with kids. So, we see my family for holidays, birthdays, and stuff. You know."

Caroline felt a pang in her chest. Her life on the Cape was quiet, conscribed. She read and wrote; she took long walks on the beach. She enjoyed good food and local culture, her time with Neil, but they didn't live together. She hadn't told Perry about him. Probably she never would. She wanted her life this way—predictable, quiet—she'd earned that, hadn't she? Deeper down, though, beneath the calculated calm, she wanted her family again. Walking with the kids beside the Charles. Ben and Hugo sharing the stroller, Ivy and Perry walking ahead, prattling on about something. A chance to do better.

"I am glad she has you," Caroline said. "She was always so independent. She probably had to be, you know because of Ben. And since she left home, well, she's never wanted to talk to me much. Especially since the boys."

Cam nodded and refilled Caroline's teacup. "She's not trying to shut you out ... I mean, I can see how it feels that way, but she does care about you. I know she does. She finds it easier, I think, to stay busy, to keep her mind off the past. But she'll come around."

Not a single picture of Caroline in this place. Maybe she was petty to notice. She felt her needs and her hurts surging inside. She

252

shouldn't have come, put herself and Cam in this position. What if she started crying here? For years now, she saved all her tears for the tide. Nights on the beach when she could let go and weep. She should go.

She stood, "Will you tell her I stopped by? Or is it better not to?"

Cam reached for Caroline's hand, "She'll come around. She's way less cautious with me now ... she talks to me some about the boys. And, I mean, when we first met she was dead set against having kids. But she's considering it. If I have learned anything with Ivy, it's not to push too hard. She needs to be the one to choose."

Caroline squeezed Cam's hand. "I'm glad she has you."

After the front door closed, Caroline stood in the tiny garden. She could smell the flowers, lavender and something sweeter—gardenia? Hear the light hum of an insect. The afternoon was warm, but not uncomfortably so, but as she walked toward the car, she felt disoriented and unsteady. She pushed open the gate, crossed the street, made it to her rental, got into the front seat, and her body began to heave and moan as she gripped the steering wheel. She'd wanted connection with her daughter but coming here only made their estrangement more obvious to Caroline. Ivy and Cam were talking about having children—Ivy had been "dead set against"—Cam had said, but now ... And none of this, not a word, between Caroline and Ivy about the fear and joy, the doubt and the possibility, the hope and even the despair that came with being a parent. Parked on the side street, she sobbed—without tissues, without holding back. Tears, more tears, and her nose dripping, snotty. She wiped her nose on the back of her shirt sleeve and started crying all over.

When she finally stopped, she started the car, opened the windows, and entered her hotel address into the GPS. She shouldn't be this shaken up. *What's gone and what's past help, should be past grief.* Some scholars read Paulina's aphorism to mean that grief should be left in the past. But Caroline suspected it meant something different: That there was a state of being beyond grief, bigger, deeper, unfathomable.

CHAPTER 22

IVY, OCTOBER 2007

Cam held out Ivy's fleece jacket, propped open the front door with her foot. "Just quit the nay-saying and let's go."

Ivy had envisioned them spending this mutually scheduled day off taking a long walk along the lakefront, followed by an even longer afternoon nap, and then maybe a stupid action movie with lots of popcorn, melting M&Ms, and making out in the back row: The kind of day their increasing number of friends with children envied. The kind of day that made working long hours and weekends worth it. Instead, they were heading downtown to have a "frank discussion" with Cam's father.

Since July, when her dad had first forgotten to come home from work one evening, Cam dissected his every move in daily conversations with her mom. The house phone would ring, either late at night or exceedingly early in the morning. The woman was uncanny for her poor timing. Cam would lie flat out on the four-poster bed, receiver under her chin, picking at her cuticles, and always, always, uh-huh-ing along patiently while her mother documented evidence of her husband's diminishing mental capacity: lost garage remotes, an angry outburst over scrambled eggs, forgetting the way home again. Cam never complained—all part of her daughterly duty, apparently, to listen, acknowledge and sympathize—but Ivy registered her own impatience, sighing and staring at the alarm clock, and finally walking out of the room, as Cam sank into the familiar rhythms of each call: *I understand, Mom. That must be so hard. Of course, I'll talk to him.*

On the long walk from the cottage to the train, Cam admonished Ivy to enjoy the crisp air, make the most of the day together. She pointed out all the hardwoods in fall festival: linden pyramids of solid gold, maples pressing their fiery handprints up against the sky. Ivy did want to breathe in a better mood, surrender to the autumn beauty, but an old resentful part clung on tenaciously as the leaves.

"I know it's not what you planned, but having you along to talk to Dad will really help."

"How?" Ivy caught the annoyance in her voice and tried to soften it. "If he even remembers me, he's bound to see me as an interloper. You'd be better off doing this with Kevin or Mary Beth. That's what siblings are good for, right?"

"He'll listen to what you have to say. You're a doctor."

"And he's an old school lawyer, Cam. The MD doesn't work on them."

They walked along silently for a few blocks, then, as they crossed Asbury, thousands of fallen gingko leaves fanned across the sidewalk; their strange orange stink-berries popped and spattered under Ivy's shoes. The smell of vomit. "Christ, why would anyone plant these?"

"Frank Lloyd Wright loved them. There are hundreds planted in Oak Park, near my parents'." As they continued, she added, "Listen,

I'm aware that you're not happy about this—you've made that abundantly clear. But having you along helps *me*. That's worth something, right? And we can have lunch together. When do we ever do that? There's this great old diner by the courthouse. Salisbury steak and mashed potatoes. Dad always used to take me there for his one-on-ones. Quality time, you know?"

The elevated train headed into the city, first sinking south of Fullerton, then swallowed whole by the tunnel at North Avenue, where the shuddering and jerking and noise cut off all conversation. At Jackson, they emerged from the sub-station into the bright busy bluster of midday on State Street.

"This way." Cam looped her arm through Ivy's as they walked west a block, past the federal building, towards a rather decrepit storefront, squeezed between two glass towers. Cam read and re-read the sign on the door and peered in through the dirty window. "Well," she said, "So much for the Salisbury steak. It's closed." She tapped against the glass. "Permanently." She looked around as she got her bearings, recomposed. "But there's another place up the block we could try. We continue, comrade. Dejected but not defeated."

North along Dearborn for a couple of blocks. But the second diner option was also gone. In its place was a newfangled trattoria, showcasing a busier-than-thou, early-lunch crowd: tall men in fine suits stood at a counter ordering tri-salad plates to go, while still yelling instructions into Blackberries. Cam and Ivy stood for almost five minutes at the check-in station before a blonde, elongated woman smiled perfunctorily, then led them to a cramped table, next to the window.

"At least we'll have a view," Cam squeezed in.

Ivy picked up a thin, grease-dotted paper menu from the tiny table. "Any suggestions?"

"Never been here. It all looks generic. Chicken Caesar, chicken parmesan, chicken focaccia." She put her sheet back as if losing her appetite for this restaurant, for the outing. "I wonder why the diner closed. So good. Old style, you know? All the federal judges and staff ate there. Dad loved to meet and greet all the regulars."

"Probably not much of a market these days for midday meatloaf."

"We're still in Chicago," she said. "A guy's gotta eat."

"Well, yes. But look around. No *real* guys here."

"So where do the old timers go? Dad needs a bossy waitress—someone to serve hot beef, extra gravy, plenty of bread for the table. He could starve to death downtown these days."

"And that would be a shame?"

"Jesus, Ivy. He's eighty—about to be told he has to give up the work that he loves. Couldn't you at least try to be sympathetic?"

"Sorry. Stupid attempt at humor. I'll do better." Ivy did want to do better, but sometimes the prickly part deep inside wouldn't play along.

When the waitress returned, she ordered chicken something. Outside on Dearborn, the stop and start of yellow cabs, an implacable CTA bus hogging the inside lane, and sidewalks full of people dressed in black. It could have been some massively disorganized funeral procession.

"Is it always so hectic downtown?" Ivy asked.

"How would I know? I don't usually eat here, either." Cam paused. "Unlike you, I don't plan to have any regrets when my parents are gone."

"Don't lecture me about my family, please."

"Why not? Because your family's exceptional? Lots of people have pain but they find a way to grieve and move on. I've known you for a long time, remember? I knew you back *then*. Saw you struggle to keep a lid on it all, see you still trying. I know you have a good heart, but I also know how stubborn and self-protective you are. Your mom and dad both reach out to you—but I've yet to see you make any real effort towards either of them. What's it gonna take, huh?"

"Do you know they never once visited me when I was in college? Missed my graduation because of some Ben fiasco."

"What will it take for you to forgive them?"

"Why do you care about how I handle my parents? I'm here with you, visiting your Dad, as commanded."

"I want us to have a family. A functional, communicative family. Is that so hard to understand?"

"What if I can't do that?"

Disappointment dulled Cam's eyes. "Can't, won't? Which is it Ivy?" Her fingers tapped Morse code on the table top.

When Ivy didn't answer Cam slipped out from her seat. "Bathroom. Don't go anywhere," she touched Ivy lightly on the shoulder. "We're not done with this conversation."

Where would Ivy go? Practically penned into this overcrowded, overpriced hellhole. Not to mention trapped in Cam's family drama. On the sidewalk, a compressed crowd approached the trattoria, then stopped en masse to stare. Twenty sets of eyes, peered in the window, as if condemning Ivy's thoughts, then looked up in unison. Tourists: lots of heavy cameras on long neck cords, blue jeans, windbreakers, and all heads turned skyward. Perhaps an ArchiWorks route. Ivy had taken one of their group tours, years ago during the summer between college and medical school, when she'd had time on her hands. She'd spent days exploring the city, instead of going to see her parents, her brothers. Hugo and Ben lived together out in Clarkston by then. They would have welcomed her with eager eyes and cheeky smiles and silent communications. *She's baa-aack,* Hugo would have teased. *And look how antsy she is. Already got one foot out the door.*

Financially independent, professionally employed, romantically involved, but still stuck in perpetual angst whenever her thoughts turned back to the boys. Dead and gone. Or perhaps dead and dead. She didn't know. Would probably never know. That must be what Hugo wanted—his act of revenge: That the family would have to live on without finality. If that was his want, it was incredibly cruel. Hard to imagine of the good soul. She willed herself to think of something else. Anyone else. But then a glimmer of red caught her eye across the street. And there he was. Loping southbound on Dearborn, with hands in his pockets, his shoulders rounded forward against the wind, wearing army shorts, a baggy white T, and a red bandana rolled and tied Ultimate-style around his head. *Reverse Babushka* he might say if Ivy caught him.

If she could only catch him.

Standing quickly, she knocked over her water, pushed away the tiny table and hurried past all the other diners, past the hostess and self-serve counter, past some dubious old guy blocking the revolving doors, wondering if he should come in and stay or move on. *Move,* she wanted to scream, *out of my way, idiot.* But the words stuck in her throat, as reason and desire battled in her brain. *Hugo? Here? Hugo? Now?*

By the time she'd spun onto the sidewalk, words she could have spoken, words she should have spoken, back then, when it still mattered, were gone. Like Hugo. She stood by the circling door, feeling as empty and irrelevant as she'd always been. Of course, that wasn't him. All the *if onlys* revolving: If only you'd been smarter, Ivy, more patient and loving. If only you had gone home more often. If only you'd spoken to him when it really mattered, then perhaps he wouldn't have fled, and you wouldn't still be chasing phantoms down city streets.

Struggling back through the cramped tables and into the tiny spot in the back corner, Ivy sopped up the spill, first with her napkin, then Cam's. She needed more, a stack, and where was the fucking waitress? Her chicken-whatever floated in ice water, leaching an oily green tincture across the plate.

"What happened?" Cam asked when she returned.

"I knocked over my water. Obviously."

She sat down again. "What is with you today?"

"Nothing's *with* me. But this food's lousy and I'm ready to go."

Ivy wondered for a minute if she should tell her about Hugo—another phantom sighting. Instead of fading over time, Hugo was getting more powerful: Appearing amidst a group of rowdy fans at a White Sox game. Running a road race downtown on Bastille Day—look, in front, picking up speed at the two-mile mark and disappearing around a corner. Walking south on Dearborn, red bandana flashing, before he melted into the crowds.

Cam flagged down the waitress, paid up fast, and they headed out onto Dearborn's mad-scrabble pedestrian flow. She led them toward her father's building. At the plaza out front, she stopped by Chagall's Four Seasons mosaic—a huge colorful rectangle—and stretched out her hand, let her fingers smooth over the tiny tiles on the long easterly side. She traced an angel's wings, then she walked slowly around the boxcar. On the west side were several large wheels—cart wheels,

wheels of fortune, Catherine wheels—and floating on them and around them women, more angels, children, lots of children, jumping and flying amidst the skyscrapers, the lake and the sky.

▲▼▲

They got out on the thirty-third floor of First National Tower and entered the dark walnut world of Williams, Connolly & Dolan. Walnut paneling reached from ceiling to floor, with no knobs, handles, or hinges to be seen. The receptionist took their names and made a quick call. She asked them to take a seat in the waiting area. A minute later, a tall, elegant woman walked into the lobby.

"Hello Camilla," she said, as Cam stood. They leaned forward to hug each other quickly. "And you must be Dr. Novotny," she said, extending her hand. "I'm Elesha Wright, Mr. Dolan's secretary. I'll take you both back—this way. I'm glad you're here. It's been tough this week."

"Time for him to stop? Mom thinks it is."

"I'm afraid so," Elesha said. "You'll see." She led them along a thickly carpeted hallway, turned right at the end and rapped on a door before opening it.

Ivy had first met Cam's father at a ball game years ago—several more times at family events during the past 18 months of coupledom—but she still felt shocked when she saw Eddie Dolan seated behind an enormous desk. Instead of the rangy outdoorsman she remembered, the man who rose falteringly today was frail and gray, a shrunken version of himself.

"Daddy," Cam said, moving quickly forward to hug him.

"Cammie," he said. "What brings you here?"

"We came to talk with you. Remember Ivy?"

262

His eyes, a pale, weepier green than Cam's, carried only his age and a good amount of confusion. He looked back to Cam.

"She's a doctor."

Ivy extended her hand—hug or handshake? And moved closer. "It's good to see you again."

He whispered at Cam, "I hate doctors."

"I thought she could help us with some of the decisions, Dad. She's my partner. Part of our family."

"Is this your mother's idea?" He waved his ghost hand. "I am not falling for this. I am not falling for it. I won't do it. No, I won't."

Elesha chimed in. "Everything's okay, Mr. Dolan."

"Maybe I should leave," Ivy said.

"No," said Cam sharply. "We agreed to stick together." Then, to her father, gently "Dad. Please. Trust me."

He held up both hands as if to push Ivy away. "Get out," he said, "go on, get," and twisted both his hands in circles.

"I'm making this worse." Ivy tried to smile. "I'll call you this afternoon. After you get things sorted out here."

▲▼▲

"Where were you?" Cam asked when Ivy picked up her office phone early the next morning. "I called the house, then your cell. Over and over. Why the hell couldn't you answer?"

Cam explained that she'd spent the night with her parents in River Forest, then done the two-train commute to her clinic. It was housed on the second floor of a ramshackle gray stone, on the southern edge of Uptown, had an air conditioning unit that clanged louder than the El.

"I can barely hear you." Ivy said. She truly hated the abject state of Cam's office. Her employer, a federally qualified health care center, never raised staff salaries or made building improvements, but each year, kept expanding services to include more poor women in its rainbow patient demographic: blacks and whites and Asians and Latinas, Medicaid recipients, uninsured immigrants, new arrivals, old-timers, young artists and ancient politicos.

"Hold on," A small clang, then a big bang, and the AC was quieter. "Better?"

"Yes." Ivy took a deep breath. "Look, I'm really sorry about yesterday. About running out. That was a lousy thing to do. How is your dad, anyway?"

"He's okay," she replied. "Anyway."

The line held their silence.

Another loud clang. Then an awful grating sound, like metal being dragged down the street.

"Shit," Cam said. "I think the AC gave out."

"Can you open some windows?"

"They don't open. Painted shut. This is not Northwestern. We don't have an entire maintenance crew at our beck and call. Our patients are going to stew in the back rooms if this thing is broken. I have got a whole morning of appointments and it's already steamy in the back."

"Sorry," Ivy said.

"You're always so forthcoming with apologies, Ivy, after the fact."

"Your dad was freaked out. I freaked out. But I guess leaving like that was not the right solution."

"Leaving like that is never the right solution."

Could Ivy grant her that? If she could, maybe they'd be done with this fight, good to go on for another few months. She rolled a pen back and forth on her desk, push and pull, give and take, stay and go: what relationships required. It was the silver Sheaffer ink pen Hugo had given to her for high school graduation. What relationships required. When his job was done, he checked out. Even his leaving was resolute: no notes, no calls, just gone. Maybe the way Hugo left was *exactly* the thing to do.

"So why didn't you at least call me? Like you promised?" Cam said.

You got scared by the family shit. Hugo said. *Tell her the truth.*

But she was never a good soul like him.

"I had to run, had to clear my head. Then, I headed over to Valkyries, watched the Bears game. I needed a drink. I needed to think."

"To drink and to think?" Her tone was ice.

"I must have turned my phone off and I supposed I never turned it back on."

"That's the best you can do?"

"I'm trying to tell you ..."

Linda, the duty nurse, rapped on the door, peered in and said loudly, "Number one is ready to go." Ivy nodded at Linda, held up a finger. "Listen. I have a procedure in a few minutes. Can this fight wait?"

"Go back to work."

▲▼▲

Ivy stood at the sink, ran hot water over her hands and scrubbed hard, soaping, brushing, soaping again, and rinsing. The first time Cam and Ivy made love, Cam had climbed on top and lay very still, her pale body rising and falling with Ivy's breathing. Ivy's heart thumped under the light and steady pressure, wanting more, wanting to be held in place.

"Me and you," she had whispered. "What an idea."

▲▼▲

Later that night, Ivy drove north to Nanny's cottage, which sat dark and silent among all the bustling neighborhood homes. Eight p.m. on Friday in Evanston, family time: inside all the well-lit frame houses on the block, dinner was over—moms on couches sipping well-deserved wine, kids chilling in front of flat screens, dads clinking dishes in the sink.

Once inside, Ivy hung her jacket on the coat tree and skulked from room to room. No Cam. No messages on the answering machine from Cam. She must have decided to spend the weekend at the Dolans' house in River Forest.

She longed to be back at work, where a propulsive force moved her from one exam room to the next, finding new problems behind each door, problems that could keep her busy, keep self-accusations and memories at bay. That had certainly been Dad's way, don't stop, don't think too hard, keep on with your mission. He no longer chased Hugo but he still worked non-stop, transforming lost hope into new projects—building homes for kids with special needs. Maybe that's how he kept Ben with him, Hugo alive.

She headed upstairs, sat on the four-poster bed, and started up her laptop. Tapped out the fourteen letters—*Hugo Jan Novotny*. Ivy had looked before, so many times on nights like tonight. When she'd first tried this search years ago, she'd got five finds. Now, when she hit enter, the list was long: over 200,000 results. She leaned back

266

against her pillow, with the computer in her lap and settled in. The first was a YouTube video of some Hugo Novotny doing tricks with a yo-yo in South Moravia—three minutes and twelve seconds of amazing twirls and control—she watched it all, and the thing was, he did start to look kind of like her brother, compact body, wide eyes, high cheek bones, even though his hair was long and oily and dark, instead of blondish-brown. Even though he was ten years too young. Hit number two was a Prague filmmaker in his seventies. Three, four, and five linked Ivy to the work of a prolific physics professor in Chile; a snapshot from a university directory showed a balding somber man with thick glasses. She flipped through twenty or so hits until she felt a headache gripping her temples.

Ivy. When she typed and entered *Imogen Vaughan Novotny,* she was everywhere, resume, education, work address, patient reviews, head shots and group photos, race results from 10Ks, FACOG and ASRM conference presentations, gay and lesbian functions, softball team stats from several years back, donations made to charities and PACs. All the stats. All the facts. The facts meant nothing. The truth Ivy didn't want to see was there, too, the truth between every search result: if Hugo were still alive and wanted to find her, he could.

He hadn't.

Eleven p.m. Cam would be asleep in her old twin bed, encased in her family home. Ivy roamed. Drank a beer, ate cold pasta from the fridge, paced the living room, tried TV. The Daily Show, then Colbert. But close to midnight she gave up, pulled on a jacket, and started walking. Had she lost Cam? The night was cool, a strong wind coming off the lake. When she reached Lighthouse Point Beach, she turned south, kept walking.

Not much activity on the lakefront path at night. A couple of homeless guys under trees. A group of younger men smoking weed on the Foster Beach basketball court, swearing, laughing, as she hurried past. She should be cautious out here late at night—early morning now—but she wasn't. No. She felt agitated, reckless, dangerous. If someone approached her, god help him.

She passed Cricket Field, looped the grassy mound at Montrose and then scrambled over the giant concrete steps onto the night-blackened beach. South across the harbor, Navy Pier jutted into the water, nameless high-rises etched the sky. A city of three million and no one out here with her. It had to be two in the morning. She'd be so tired for work tomorrow—she should keep walking south. Maybe then she'd arrive ahead of her patients. But probably not. Some were probably lining up already with their requisition forms, eager to give blood, get scoped, await consults, review tests, and be sent on their way with plan adjustments and another dose of hope.

Who was Ivy to prescribe hope? Who was she to try to build families?

She zig-zagged the sand, dodging empty beer bottles, chicken bones, an umbrella skeleton. At the water's edge, waves tossed plastic bags—flashes of white in the gray tumble. She took off her running shoes and socks, rolled up her jeans, and waded in. The water was cold, her feet freezing then numbing. The lake rolled gray and grayer. She stared until her eyes made out a thin black horizon.

Welcome.

Had Hugo followed Ben? Found a body of water somewhere near or far from home and drowned himself in penitence and grief? She wanted to know. Had to know.

Ivy. Ivy. They now called to her.

For so many years, she had wanted nothing they had to offer.

Longed desperately—not for their humor, not for their wordless connection, not for their sub-cerebral love.

Ivy, Ivy—here in the water.

"What do you want from me?" Her voice lost. Her body shaking, her balance failing as she stumbled another step forward. She shouted louder this time, shouted it into the gray. "Why can't you leave me alone?"

Breathing was not easy in water this cold. Crying impossible. "What did I do wrong?" The lake churned against her body. She tripped on something and fell fast, forward, the shock of the cold. All the accidents, the falls and the fractures, the white-knuckled seizures, the fear that started her running away, the terror that kept her locked in her bedroom. The young girl hiding under her quilt, the teenager locking Ben in his bedroom alone, the older sister leaving for college and never looking back. Her feet thrashed under water, found the silty bottom. She found her footing, stood up. Found the self-serving, self-saving weakness, that had always protected her, that now pulled her out of the water, breathless and frigid, over the rocks, and back up the footpath—seven miles north through the night—back to the cottage, back to the home she shared with the woman that she loved.

CHAPTER 23

PERRY, APRIL 2008

He hadn't wanted to sell the Nancy Creek house. Held onto it as long as possible—seven years now—believing that while there was a home there was hope of a homecoming. He had played out the scene so many times that he knew every detail: An April morning. Azaleas blooming alongside the curving driveway, the white-bracted dogwoods at their peak, promising good things. A knock on the door (he'd thought this through and there would be a knock) and there ... in blue jeans and a ratty gray t-shirt, hair shaggy and a guilty grin on his face, Hugo.

Each year on the anniversary of both Ben's death and his birthday, Perry became especially tense. His ears on super-sensitive mode, hearing every pop and crack in the neighborhood. Was someone coming down the driveway? Footsteps? A thump on the door? He jumped when the phone rang late at night. He still couldn't sleep without checking the mailbox at the top of the drive, hoping for something—a postcard, a note—anything that told him to hold on. Some nights when he slept, he pulled his boys to him in an embrace—everyone talking at once, Ben gurgling his happy sounds, Hugo translating, and Perry asking questions, how, where? He'd wake up hugging his pillow, wet with tears, and remember he was alone, still alone, in this house far too large for one man.

Seven years. How long should a father hold on?

After 9/11, he'd learned that some families had their loved ones declared dead within days. Sure, they had reason to seek finality: they needed closure, access to bank accounts. Decisions had to be made. With Hugo's disappearance, waiting another day, another month, was not only hope—it was penance for Perry. How could he go on with his own life when Hugo had sacrificed his?

Oh, he'd researched the law. *Death in absentia:* a legal state of being. Or not being. A person could be considered legally dead when the following conditions were met: (1) Missing from their home for seven years. (2) Continuous and inexplicable absence. (3) No communications from the missing person with those people most likely to hear from them. And, (4) a diligent but unsuccessful search for the person. All four met. Still, he wanted to hold on longer—what did time really matter to him now? He had nothing but time to give to his boys anyway.

But he couldn't afford the house. Property taxes alone—upward of eleven grand—plus the utilities, lawn care, pool maintenance. All came to a sum larger than the income he received from Thresholds— the nonprofit housing development corporation he'd started and now ran. And though he still sent Caroline five hundred bucks every month to help with her rent, he could barely make ends meet on the sixty thousand a year he paid himself. He knew she was hurting too, financially. She had to be. Though she paid Alice Seward only a fraction of market value for her place, a part-time teaching gig wouldn't buy much on Cape Cod. They'd both benefit from the sale of the family home. So last week, April 9, Ben's birthday, he made the call.

And now, he waited at the bottom of the driveway for the listing agent. An old friend: Susan Watson, a/k/a Petey's mom. Pete, at thirty, lived with his roommate Scott and their PA in a two-bedroom apartment in Thresholds Clarkston—the first group home Perry had built.

She pulled into the driveway right at 4 p.m. White Lexus SUV. Sparkling new by the looks of it. Opened the door, stepped out and gave Perry a hug.

"Hello, handsome. It's been too long."

"Ms. Susan." He nodded at the vehicle. "Looks like you're doing okay for yourself."

"All show." She was dressed in a turquoise suit, hair done in the southern lady way, shoulder length, loosely curled, too blonde for a grown-up. She flashed a fresh turquoise manicure under his nose. "Check this out."

"Well, you look the part, that's for sure."

"You know real estate. Money talks. Even louder for women."

He walked her into the house, turning on the light, pointing out the best features and seeing the flaws through her eyes. The stains on the carpet in the entry hall, the missing bannister rail on the stairs. Left into the kitchen, the cabinets battered from the hectic family life that had once filled this house: laminate countertops stained from Caroline's tea, a couple of cigarette burns.

"Hmm." Susan walked towards the oven wall.

"The microwave shorted out last year."

"And the conventional oven?"

"Haven't used it since Caroline moved out. Fridge still works though." He opened the door to show her the six-pack of Pilsner Urquell he'd kill off tonight.

"Well, whoever buys this place is going to put in a new kitchen. It's what people do to make the home their own. So, don't worry about how things look now. We're most likely looking at a gut rehab here."

He let her roam the upstairs herself, scoping out each of the four bedrooms, the master suite with the Jacuzzi (jets no longer working) and the kids' shared bathroom. No need for him to go back into those rooms with the handprints on the walls. The kids' school photos.

Then the yard—the pool, empty for the last few years, a few inches of water on the bottom, leaf gunk shellacking the walls. He disclosed the problem—a crack in the liner that would need some serious money to fix. The diving board would probably need to come down, too. He showed her the fault-line, right at the fulcrum. Could snap anytime. She nodded, made notes on her pad, asked him to show her the pump room.

"A buyer might fill it in, I'm guessing—cheaper than replacing it." She looked across the back yard. "It would be quite spectacular to landscape this whole area—patio, outside barbeque area, lawn all the way down to the woods."

Perry grunted. His house, his yard, the pool that he'd built. The boys in the pool.

He walked her back up the wooden steps to the side gate and led her round front. "Do you have a sense of asking price? I want a quick sale."

"Can you show me inside the garage? Then we can talk numbers."

He lifted the door manually (automatic opener broken years ago by Ben's shenanigans). The old station wagon was parked in the middle, two trikes were parked by its side.

"Obviously, I'll get the Buick out of here," he said.

"Probably a good idea to clear out the whole garage—freshen it up, show off the space. What's in all the boxes against the wall?"

"God knows. I haven't looked in them for years. But I'll go through it, get rid of the junk, I promise."

After the walk-about, they sat at the kitchen counter on two stools. He offered her a beer or a Coke, but she said she was fine. He opened a Pilsner, drank it fast as he showed her the folder he'd dug up from his filing cabinet. Labeled simply HOME, it contained the original blueprints for the house, the sales contract with Huff Homes, and the first mortgage with C&S Bank, a line of credit he'd taken out in the late nineties, and dozens of warranties.

"Impressive record-keeping. It's great you have all this … but you can probably let go of the warranties. Anyone buying a place this big, this much land in this neighborhood, will be ready to invest some real money."

She showed him some comps—a place on Ridgewood Road, two houses past the McClatchy compound. "I'm thinking we'll list around $1.2 million … for a quick sale."

"Seems like a hell of a lot if the buyers plan to renovate."

"It is. But the lot is special, all the land, backing up to the woods. And this Ridgewood place—a much smaller lot and less square footage—4,800 compared to your 5,100. It sold for $1.6 last year."

Over a million? He hadn't kept up apparently, because this was better than he'd expected. He could pay off the line of credit, give Susan her commission, and still split $800,000 plus with Caroline. Though neither of them had saved much for retirement, this would be a damn good cushion. He would call Caroline tonight, let her know he was finally ready to do it. She'd asked him about it over

274

the years but had never insisted. She understood why he had held on so long.

Susan said she'd write up a contract tomorrow, bring it by in the evening. "This place could go quickly. But you are going to have to do your part. Start with the boxes in the garage, the clutter inside the bedrooms—show off all the space and potential. I'd recommend painting at least the entry hall and the kitchen, maybe the bedrooms too, in neutral tones: light gray or linen white. Maybe your crew can get it done fast?"

"No," he said. "I'll do it myself. I need to keep busy. Besides, Caroline may want a chance to come down and go through all this stuff." Even as he said this, he remembered how fast she had left. How little she had taken. How unconcerned she'd been about what remained.

▲▼▲

Later that night, he sat in the family room, drinking his fourth beer. The Red Sox were crushing the Mariners, 14-3. Every player except the pitcher had a hit—not even interesting to watch at this point. He knew the beer was making him maudlin, but he didn't second guess himself when he turned off the TV and dialed her number.

"Hello Perry."

"Did I wake you?"

"No. Just grading papers. It's that time of year. I was about to finish up and take the dogs out. Last call before lights out. What's up?"

"Met with a realtor today. Do you remember Petey from the park? Down syndrome kid. All grown up now, of course. His mom, Susan, Susan Watson, she's one of the best with Buckhead Brokers, apparently. Sold over fifty million last year. Anyway, she came and did a walk through."

275

"Wow. That's big news."

"Yeah. It's time. She says it could go fast."

"Susan? Was she that blonde woman—always wore pink track suits, even in the summer?"

"That's the one. She cuts quite an elegant figure these days. Fit, well-dressed. Clearly making a lot of money. Says she can sell our place for upwards of a million."

Caroline whistled.

"Yeah. Crazy. We could both use some cash, though, right?"

"Yes." She hesitated. "Are you really okay with this? Where will you go?"

"Doesn't matter. I can find an apartment anywhere. But what if he were to come back ... and no one were here? Or worse yet, what if a stranger opens the door?"

"Oh, Perry. Honey. You've done everything, everything anyone could do to find him. And if he wants to find us, he can. It's not like we're going to disappear once we sell the house. Our names, addresses, pictures—all of it is available online. It has been all this time. You know that."

He pushed himself up and out of his chair, walked outside into the cool night with the phone pressed against his ear. Listening to her voice, soothing him, telling him it was okay.

"The azaleas are incredible this year. All up the drive ... remember?"

"I bet it's beautiful."

"You always hated spring. The colors."

"Did I?" She laughed. "I don't remember that. I must have mellowed—I wouldn't mind seeing some flowers in my yard right about now."

"Any chance you could come down? There's lot of stuff to go through. All the kids' stuff. Tons of boxes in the garage."

"God. Junk we moved from Boston and never unpacked. If you just want to toss it all, you have my blessing."

Perry walked toward the mailbox. "So you don't want to look, just in case?"

He turned around at the top of the drive, looked down at the house. One of the floodlights was out, but he could still make out the asymmetrical outline, the steeply pitched roof, and the half-timber/stucco fill. What had made Trey Huff build a house like this in Atlanta, 1980? It didn't fit in with any of the colonials favored in this part of the city. But god, when Perry and Caroline pulled into that driveway for the first time, the joy of the huge yard, the house bigger than they could have imagined. The kids tumbling out of the car, racing across the grass, all three of them soon rolling down the slope.

"There's stuff in the kids' rooms too. Ben's videos, all his puzzles and blocks," He coughed, cleared his throat. "I'm not sure I can ... alone."

"You sound ... muffled. You okay?"

"I'm fine. Fine. It's just letting it go seems so final. It's a beautiful night here." He swiped at his eyes with the back of his arm. "Christ, Caroline. I am a wreck."

"I'll come down. The semester ends in another what, two or three weeks, and I can drive down to help you go through it all."

"You sure. I don't want to ..."

"I want to. Okay?"

"Yes. Thanks. Bring the dogs. I don't think they can get out of the backyard."

▲▼▲

After they said their good-byes, he opened the mailbox, brought inside

277

the flyers and bills and other detritus, set all of it on the counter and grabbed the last beer. He popped off the top and took a long pull. He hadn't meant to break down like that with Caroline. He shouldn't have called. But … if she didn't understand, no one could. He ruffled through the mail. The Westmont alumni magazine—addressed to Ivy. He still needed to tell her to give them her address in Chicago; he'd already asked her about twenty times. A bill from AT&T. Another from Atlanta Gas Light. He threw them in his to-do basket. So many to-dos piled up in there. It would be good to get out from under all these monthly obligations. He pushed aside another piece of junk mail—some frozen yogurt place opening at Paces Ferry offering a free 6 oz serving—then, there, at the bottom of the pile, a small white envelope.

His arms tingling as he picked it up, recognized the once-familiar script. When he saw the sender's name, the return address, he crumpled onto the floor. He held the envelope in his lap as he sobbed, unable to open it, his body wouldn't function. But finally, finally, he pulled himself together, got a paper towel to wipe his eyes, prevent his tears from blurring the message, as he read and re-read every treasured word.

He glanced at the clock, 11:32, and reached for the phone.

Chapter 24

Ivy, April 2008

After Cam had retired to the bedroom, curling up with the soft porn of a Title Nine athletic-wear catalog and a cup of mint tea, Ivy kissed her good-night, then hurried along the nail-pocked floorboards to her office. She'd have to give up this slope-ceilinged enclosure when a baby came. But tonight, the space was all hers. A room of her own to indulge in her late night ... proclivities. This was part of their understanding. In bed, Cam would skim the first few pages, dog-ear the spread where perhaps Makenna, PhD in electro-physiology, wore a Won't-Back-Down bikini while surfing ten-foot waves in Maui. Cam usually fell asleep after a few pages and never bought herself a thing. She needed her rest now more than ever: sometime mid-May would be her first insemination.

In the office, Ivy rubbed her eyes and cracked her knuckles, sitting upright and anticipatory in the secretarial chair. Cam had major misgivings about the web—it freaked out way too many of her patients with omissions and downright lies, she said. She was right. Ivy, in fact, routinely told her own anxious patients not to get their medical info online. She knew the risks and pitfalls, but it didn't matter; for her, web-surfing was a stress-reliever. Meditative miscellany calmed an over-active mind, prepared her for sleep, even as she tended the smallest ember of hope.

Tonight: *Novotny. Diver. Atlanta.* Which brought up his name and the score: 632.8—yes, he was still holding the Georgia high school record. From there, she deleted one search term, replaced it with another: whatever memory thread pulled up from the hippocampus. *Bandana. Jan. Prague.* She clicked on a long story about Jan Hus, the reformer; she read half a Wiki summary of Jana Novotna's tennis career, stats, tournaments and her long-sought Wimbledon single's victory in 1998. *Degree of difficulty, tricycle, Monosomy 21.* She hit enter and the house phone rang.

Jesus. Too late for solicitors. She dashed into the bedroom to answer before it woke Cam.

"Hello?"

"Sweetheart, it's Dad."

Alarm clock read 10:49. "Is everything all right?"

"Yes. Yes. Sorry it's so late, but I had to call. Mom's on the line too."

"Hello, my love."

"What's going on? Tell me. Please."

"Everything's okay." Dad.

"Ivy ..." Mom's voice shaky, quiet. "Is Cam there?"

"Is one of you sick?"

Cam sat up, turned on the lamp.

"No. No. It's Hugo." Dad again. "Hugo. He's alive. I was going through a stack of mail—late tonight, after the Red Sox game. I almost missed it. A letter at the bottom of the pile. I could have missed it.

But the handwriting. I knew and then return address. John Newman. Do you see? He's anglicized it. Jan Novotny? But he's alive, living in Toronto. So, I called your mom immediately and well, of course, we had to let you know."

"Read it, Perry," Mom said. "Let Ivy hear."

Ivy sank back against Cam's slight body, pulse thumping, brain processing. Hugo. Alive. Hugo. Now?

"You there, honey?"

"Today? You got this today?"

On her nightstand, that picture: Hugo and Ben, blurry, out of focus, standing in the shallow end of the pool. The boys she'd loved and left behind. She touched Hugo's nose, Ben's goofy smile. "What if it's some kind of sick joke? Someone who knows what we've been through. There are people ..."

"The handwriting is his. The card—it's made by residents of one of the L'Arche homes. Listen, listen."

Hello Old Man,

April 9th. Always a moody day for me. For you too, I bet. I took Jester for a walk after work. He's a strong black mutt and he jerked my arm so hard—must have smelled some food scrap—that I tripped on a root, fell flat on the sidewalk, scraped up my wrist. Anyway. Right next to my hand—on the grass verge, a splash of red. A bandana. The kind Ben wore around his neck every day to soak up drool, food. Still knotted, as if it slipped up and over his head. I picked it up, held it to my nose, imagining for a second that swampy smell: damp cotton in the hot sun. But it had a chemical odor. Maybe it had covered the mouth of a handyman. A yard worker. I looked around. No one nearby. We headed home. My home for the past

4 years. I live and work in a community. People with and without disabilities. Good years, but lately, I've wanted a sign. Is where I am where I should be? Today. Ben's birthday. A bandana day. A sign. Yes. This is my home; these people are my family. But I haven't forgotten you, Dad. Haven't forgotten any of you, my first family. Someday, I'll visit. If you'll have me. H.

"Amazing, isn't it?" Mom said. "I don't know what to say ... so much swirling in my head right now."

Ivy sat up straight now. Cam touched her cheek, wiped off a tear.

Mom and Dad, laughing, crying, talking over each other, what to do ... how to respond ... Dad wanted to fly up there tomorrow. Atlanta to Toronto. He could be there by noon. But he listened while Mom said her piece. We can't just barge in—it might scare him off. We start slowly. Write back. You should write back, Perry. You're the one he contacted. The old back and forth. Ivy couldn't keep up, couldn't follow it. And they didn't ask her opinion. A thrumming in her ear. Pulsatile tinnitus. Venous hum. Words thrumming and humming. Hugo. How? Hugo. Where? Hugo. Alive. Toronto. Now.

He'd built himself a life; he had a new family. And she didn't have to wait for Mom and Dad to figure it out, to reach agreement on what to do next. Ivy loved Cam and had almost lost her, but found her again and maybe soon they would have a baby and live as a family in their too-cozy home. She had waited and waited, searched for a right word, the right sign, some understanding. Now she had her answer. Don't wait. Don't hold back. Go to him now. Not to bring him home. That's where you've had it wrong all along. Go see his place, learn how he lives and works. Meet his family. No more homecomings for Hugo or for Ben. But tomorrow, first thing, she and Cam would pack up the car, grab their passports, drive north and east, a stop maybe in Detroit for lunch, then across the border by late afternoon. Before the end of the day, before another night passed, there would be a homegoing.

Acknowledgments

Thanks to my parents, Sue and George Justicz, for their enduring love and their belief in me. To my brothers, Alex, Nick, Max and Dan, for the gifts of joy, humor, and support. We had each other's backs when we were kids growing up in rural England; that's even more true today, when we are separated by thousands of miles.

To the amazing group that is Writers' Bridge: Lynn Sloan, Jan English Leary, Mary Beth Shaffer, Arlene Brimer, Dragana Djordjevic-Laky (we miss you): your advice and cheerleading and confidence push me and inspire me. I am so grateful for your wisdom and friendship. Many thanks to Fred Shafer, whose love of good writing is infectious and whose gift for teaching is unsurpassed.

Todd Cooper, my bestie since we were whippersnappers at Westminster, thank you for every kindness you show me as we work through this life together; I am beyond blessed to have you. Alex Kotlowitz, Maria Woltjen, Larry Wood, Gwenan Wilbur, Nancy Blum, Mary Hurley—thanks for everything you've done to encourage me and help me finish this book and get it out in the world. You are wonderful friends.

Special thanks to Ragdale Foundation and Virginia Center for Creative Arts for much-needed residencies that gave me time and space to dig in and push through the difficult parts.

Sandra Dawson, thank you for trusting me with your art, my friend. Julie Chyna and Tamara Wilm Johnson, and my wonderful sister-in-law Virginia Marston Justicz: I appreciate your careful editing and ongoing support.

Marc Estrin and Donna Bister at Fomite: thanks for pushing me to make this book better and for sticking with me when the rewrites took forever. I appreciate your help and I am so thankful for the place you have made in the publishing world.

And finally, the last and biggest thanks go to my family: Mary Margaret Rowland, my true love (jen ty), and Thomas and Lilly, our best creations.

Fomite

About Fomite

A fomite is a medium capable of transmitting infectious organisms from one individual to another.

"The activity of art is based on the capacity of people to be infected by the feelings of others." Tolstoy, *What Is Art?*

Writing a review on Amazon, Good Reads, Shelfari, Library Thing or other social media sites for readers will help the progress of independent publishing. To submit a review, go to the book page on any of the sites and follow the links for reviews. Books from independent presses rely on reader to reader communications.

For more information or to order any of our books, visit
http://www.fomitepress.com/FOMITE/Our_Books.html

More Titles from Fomite...

Novels
Joshua Amses — *During This, Our Nadir*
Joshua Amses — *Ghatsr*
Joshua Amses — *Raven or Crow*
Joshua Amses — *The Moment Before an Injury*
Jaysinh Birjepatel — *Nothing Beside Remains*
Jaysinh Birjepatel — *The Good Muslim of Jackson Heights*
David Brizer — *Victor Rand*
Paula Closson Buck — *Summer on the Cold War Planet*
Dan Chodorkoff — *Loisaida*
David Adams Cleveland — *Time's Betrayal*
Jaimee Wriston Colbert — *Vanishing Acts*
Roger Coleman — *Skywreck Afternoons*
Marc Estrin — *Hyde*
Marc Estrin — *Kafka's Roach*
Marc Estrin — *Speckled Vanities*
Zdravka Evtimova — *In the Town of Joy and Peace*
Zdravka Evtimova — *Sinfonia Bulgarica*
Zdravka Evtimova — *You Can Smile on Wednesdays*
Peter Fortunato — *Carnevale*
Daniel Forbes — *Derail This Train Wreck*
Greg Guma — *Dons of Time*
Richard Hawley — *The Three Lives of Jonathan Force*
Lamar Herrin — *Father Figure*
Michael Horner — *Damage Control*
Ron Jacobs — *All the Sinners Saints*
Ron Jacobs — *Short Order Frame Up*

Fomite

Ron Jacobs — *The Co-conspirator's Tale*
Scott Archer Jones — *And Throw Away the Skins*
Scott Archer Jones — *A Rising Tide of People Swept Away*
Julie Justicz — *Degrees of Difficulty*
Maggie Kast — *A Free Unsullied Land*
Darrell Kastin — *Shadowboxing with Bukowski*
Coleen Kearon — *#triggerwarning*
Coleen Kearon — *Feminist on Fire*
Jan English Leary — *Thicker Than Blood*
Diane Lefer — *Confessions of a Carnivore*
Rob Lenihan — *Born Speaking Lies*
Douglas Milliken — *Our Shadow's Voice*
Colin Mitchell — *Roadman*
Ilan Mochari — *Zinsky the Obscure*
Peter Nash — *Parsimony*
Peter Nash — *The Perfection of Things*
George Ovitt — *Stillpoint*
George Ovitt — *Tribunal*
Gregory Papadoyiannis — *The Baby Jazz*
Pelham — *The Walking Poor*
Andy Potok — *My Father's Keeper*
Frederick Ramey — *Comes A Time*
Joseph Rathgeber — *Mixedbloods*
Kathryn Roberts — *Companion Plants*
Robert Rosenberg — *Isles of the Blind*
Fred Russell — *Rafi's World*
Ron Savage — *Voyeur in Tangier*
David Schein — *The Adoption*
Lynn Sloan — *Principles of Navigation*
L.E. Smith — *The Consequence of Gesture*
L.E. Smith — *Travers' Inferno*
L.E. Smith — *Untimely RIPped*
Bob Sommer — *A Great Fullness*
Tom Walker — *A Day in the Life*
Susan V. Weiss —*My God, What Have We Done?*
Peter M. Wheelwright — *As It Is On Earth*
Suzie Wizowaty — *The Return of Jason Green*

Poetry
Anna Blackmer — *Hexagrams*
Antonello Borra — *Alfabestiario*
Antonello Borra — *AlphaBetaBestiaro*
Antonello Borra — *Fabbrica delle idee/The Factory of Ideas*
L. Brown — *Loopholes*

Fomite

Sue D. Burton — *Little Steel*
David Cavanagh — *Cycling in Plato's Cave*
James Connolly — *Picking Up the Bodies*
Greg Delanty — *Loosestrife*
Mason Drukman — *Drawing on Life*
J. C. Ellefson — *Foreign Tales of Exemplum and Woe*
Tina Escaja/Mark Eisner — *Caida Libre/Free Fall*
Anna Faktorovich — *Improvisational Arguments*
Barry Goldensohn — *Snake in the Spine, Wolf in the Heart*
Barry Goldensohn — *The Hundred Yard Dash Man*
Barry Goldensohn — *The Listener Aspires to the Condition of Music*
R. L. Green — *When You Remember Deir Yassin*
Gail Holst-Warhaft — *Lucky Country*
Raymond Luczak — *A Babble of Objects*
Kate Magill — *Roadworthy Creature, Roadworthy Craft*
Tony Magistrale — *Entanglements*
Gary Mesick — *General Discharge*
Andreas Nolte — *Mascha: The Poems of Mascha Kaléko*
Sherry Olson — *Four-Way Stop*
Brett Ortler — *Lessons of the Dead*
Aristea Papalexandrou/Philip Ramp — *Μας προσπερνά/It's Overtaking Us*
Janice Miller Potter — *Meanwell*
Janice Miller Potter — *Thoreau's Umbrella*
Philip Ramp — *The Melancholy of a Life as the Joy of Living It Slowly Chills*
Joseph D. Reich — *A Case Study of Werewolves*
Joseph D. Reich — *Connecting the Dots to Shangrila*
Joseph D. Reich — *The Derivation of Cowboys and Indians*
Joseph D. Reich — *The Hole That Runs Through Utopia*
Joseph D. Reich — *The Housing Market*
Kenneth Rosen and Richard Wilson — *Gomorrah*
Fred Rosenblum — *Vietnumb*
Fred Rosenblum — *Playing Chicken with an Iron Horse*
David Schein — *My Murder and Other Local News*
Harold Schweizer — *Miriam's Book*
Scott T. Starbuck — *Carbonfish Blues*
Scott T. Starbuck — *Hawk on Wire*
Scott T. Starbuck — *Industrial Oz*
Seth Steinzor — *Among the Lost*
Seth Steinzor — *To Join the Lost*
Susan Thomas — *In the Sadness Museum*
Susan Thomas — *The Empty Notebook Interrogates Itself*
Paolo Valesio/Todd Portnowitz — *La Mezzanotte di Spoleto/Midnight in Spoleto*
Sharon Webster — *Everyone Lives Here*
Tony Whedon — *The Tres Riches Heures*
Tony Whedon — *The Falkland Quartet*

Fomite

Fomite

Roger Lebovitz — *Twenty-two Instructions for Near Survival*
dug Nap— *Artsy Fartsy*
Delia Bell Robinson — *A Shirtwaist Story*
Peter Schumann — *Belligerent & Not So Belligerent Slogans from the
    Possibilitarian Arsenal*
Peter Schumann — *Bread & Sentences*
Peter Schumann — *A Child's Deprimer*
Peter Schumann — *Charlotte Salomon*
Peter Schumann — *Diagonal Man Theory + Praxis, Volumes One and Two*
Peter Schumann — *Faust 3*
Peter Schumann — *Planet Kasper, Volumes One and Two*
Peter Schumann — *We*

Plays
Stephen Goldberg — *Screwed and Other Plays*
Michele Markarian — *Unborn Children of America*

Essays
Robert Sommer — *Losing Francis: Essays on the Wars at Home*

CPSIA information can be obtained
at www.ICGtesting.com
Printed in the USA
FSHW011514310819
61601FS